Penguin Books

GW01464386

Sere

Melanie La'Brooy is the author of the bestselling novels *Love Struck* and *The Wish List*, both of which she highly recommends. Melanie is a regular contributor to *The Age* and also reviews classic books on Triple J's *Sunday Night Safran*.

When she's not writing or being walked by her dog, Melanie can be found supporting the International Women's Development Agency, whose website you can visit at www.iwda.org.au

Praise for *Love Struck* and *The Wish List*

'Take your basic chick-lit novel, double the wit and quirkiness, add a splash of vulnerability, a sprinkling of slapstick and loads of spicy dialogue and you have *Love Struck*.'
AUSTRALIAN BOOKSELLER & PUBLISHER

'A hilarious ride on a very fast train of urban courtship that manages to be as street-wise and sassy as *Sex and the City*, while somehow retaining a wholesome Kaz Cooke-ish, girl-next-door quality.'
THE AGE

'You'll meet some fabulous people, enjoy some Sydney silliness and laughable pretensions, and get some strange looks from fellow commuters if you insist on laughing out loud.'
WOMAN'S DAY

'This light-hearted look at love, flatmates and friendship is so absorbing that I could imagine myself hanging out with these gals. Bit sad to realise I can't. Must get life of my own.'
SUN HERALD

Serendipity

Melanie La'Brooy

Penguin Books

VIKING

Published by the Penguin Group
Penguin Group (Australia)
250 Camberwell Road, Camberwell, Victoria 3124, Australia
(a division of Pearson Australia Group Pty Ltd)
Penguin Group (USA) Inc.
375 Hudson Street, New York, New York 10014, USA
Penguin Group (Canada)
90 Eglinton Avenue East, Suite 700, Toronto, Canada ON M4P 2Y3
(a division of Pearson Penguin Canada Inc.)
Penguin Books Ltd
80 Strand, London WC2R 0RL England
Penguin Ireland
25 St Stephen's Green, Dublin 2, Ireland
(a division of Penguin Books Ltd)
Penguin Books India Pvt Ltd
11 Community Centre, Panchsheel Park, New Delhi – 110 017, India
Penguin Group (NZ)
67 Apollo Drive, Mairangi Bay, Auckland 1310, New Zealand
(a division of Pearson New Zealand Ltd)
Penguin Books (South Africa) (Pty) Ltd
24 Sturdee Avenue, Rosebank, Johannesburg 2196, South Africa

Penguin Books Ltd, Registered Offices: 80 Strand, London, WC2R 0RL, England

First published by Penguin Group Australia Ltd, 2007
This edition published by Penguin Group (Australia)

13 5 7 9 10 8 6 4 2

Text copyright © Melanie La'Brooy 2007

The moral right of the author has been asserted

Cover design by Elizabeth Dias and Claire Wilson © Penguin Group (Australia)
Cover illustration by Alli Arnold
Author photograph by Peter Mack
Typeset in Stempel Schneidler by Post Pre-press Group, Brisbane, Queensland
Printed in Australia by McPherson's Printing Group, Maryborough, Victoria

National Library of Australia
Cataloguing-in-Publication data:

La'Brooy, Melanie.
Serendipity.

2nd ed.
ISBN 978 0 1 43 00779 1 (pbk.).

I. Title.

A823.4

for my parents
Marie & Keith

for always saying yes when I asked for a book

Prologue
New York

Hero always said it was Sunday's fault that she ever met Oscar in the first place. Although it was true that Sunday couldn't possibly have foreseen that Hero donning a wig would lead to the gorilla-gram, the life-size cardboard cut-out of George W. Bush or the incident in the sex shop.

Whenever the subject arose, Sunday denied all responsibility. For her part, Hero firmly maintained that it all came back to the moment in Greenwich Village when Sunday had triumphantly lifted something red and hairy out of a plastic carrier bag.

'What's that?' Hero asked, startled.

'It's a wig. Sit down. I want to arrange it on you.'

Hero submitted to the wig being placed on her head, and when Sunday brought her a hand-mirror she admired the sleek, deep-red bob and agreed that it was completely unlike her own long brown curls.

'That's the whole point,' Sunday said, pulling a blonde wig out of the bag and starting to tuck her own hair up. 'We're wearing these when we go out tonight. We're going to be different people.'

'I don't know, Sun,' Hero said unwillingly.

Sunday turned and regarded her with hands on hips. 'Why not? We're on holiday in New York, for god's sake! No one knows us here, and you're always moaning about how boring you think you are. Tonight's our last night so we're going to go out and be whoever we want to be. So choose a name.'

Hero looked at herself in the mirror. She did look quite different with red hair. And the blunt, angular cut made her look more edgy, more daring somehow. 'If I have to change my name, then I'm going to be Anne,' she decided.

'*Anne?*'

Hero defended her choice. 'When your real name is Hero, Anne seems exotic.'

'Not a chance. I was christened Sunday but you don't see me picking Jane.'

'Well, who are you going to be, then?'

'Wednesday,' Sunday said decidedly. 'And you can be Octavia. She was the second wife of Mark Antony, you know.' Sunday was a classical historian and was finishing her PhD at Sydney University, on the representation of women in classical literature. Since she'd started her degree six years ago, she'd spent all her time buried in the past and in libraries, meaning that her grasp of popular culture and the mores of contemporary life was tenuous, to say the least. In the two weeks they'd spent in America, she had been constantly amazed by things like the Shopping Channel and Cheese in a Can.

'I don't want to be Octavia. If I have to be someone else and I can't be Anne, then I'm going to be . . .' Hero paused and considered her reflection. The girl in the mirror with the dark-red hair stared back at her, daring her. 'Lola,' Hero decided.

2

Sunday nodded approvingly. 'Okay, now take the wig off.'

'Why?'

'Because I'm going to fix it properly so that it stays on all night.'

'What's that?' Hero asked apprehensively, as Sunday took a small tube out of another bag.

'It's a kind of adhesive.'

'Oh no, you don't.' Hero clutched her own hair protectively. 'I don't want to have to wear a wig for real because you've Super-glued my hair and I've had to shave it off.'

'Don't be ridiculous. The glue doesn't go on your hair – it goes on these showercap sort of things that we wear under the wigs. You'll look even sillier if you start dancing tonight and your wig flies off.'

After reading the instructions on the tube, Hero consented to this plan but asked, in amazement, 'When did you get all this stuff?'

Sunday smiled fondly. 'While you were spending another three hours in front of that Picasso painting in the Met. Have you worked out how to steal it yet?'

'Not yet. Maybe we could do it tonight while we're in disguise,' Hero said wistfully, as she put on a final layer of lip-gloss.

'I think it's kind of . . . *interesting*. But I really don't understand what you see in it,' Sunday admitted.

'I'm not sure that I know myself, but it makes me think of a perfect summer's day. Of blue skies and flowers and daydreaming and being in love and . . .'

Sunday hastened to avert the sudden sadness in Hero's eyes. 'So what does Lola do for a living? Any ideas?'

Hero shook off her pensive mood. 'We have to have jobs?'

'We have to have stories. And they have to be as different from our real lives as possible.'

'Okay, I'm going to make up yours. For a start, do we need surnames?'

Sunday settled her wig firmly into place on her head. 'No, surnames are too serious for us tonight. Now sit still. I'm going to put your wig on.'

Hero sat obediently still while Sunday carefully transformed her into a redhead. 'I think Wednesday should be a publicist for an underground record label.'

Sunday grinned appreciatively. 'What exactly do I say if someone asks what my job involves?'

'Just make up a whole lot of band names and talk about how they're kind of like a cross between Ben Lee and Decoder Ring.'

'Who?'

'Never mind. What's Lola's story?'

'She's a trapeze artist,' Sunday announced.

'Oh, come on. It has to be something within the realm of possibility.'

'Why? We won't know the people we're talking to. I think we're both going to be trapeze artists, actually. We're with Circus Oz.' She swung around. 'How do I look?'

In her long blonde wig, Sunday was forcibly reminding Hero of Dougal from *The Magic Roundabout*, but she thought it best to give two thumbs up.

Sunday beamed. 'Ready, Lola? It's our last night in New York. Let's make sure we never forget it.'

* ✳ *

An hour later, as they sat at a crowded bar in the Meatpacking District and finished their third round of drinks, Hero was still uneasy.

'What are Lola and Wednesday doing in New York?' she bawled over the noise into Sunday's ear.

'You think trapeze artists don't get holidays?' Sunday yelled back. She thought for a moment and then shouted, 'We're on a girls' holiday. You're recovering from a broken heart. The sword-swallower left you for the strong man. With hindsight you realise you should have seen it coming.'

The teasing note vanished from Sunday's voice as she suddenly realised what she'd said. 'Hero, I'm so sorry . . . I wasn't thinking.'

Hero mustered a smile. 'Don't be silly. Anyway, knowing Elliott, he probably has run away to join the circus by now.' She raised her glass. 'Here's hoping the lions are hungry and Elliott smells like dinner.'

They clinked glasses and Sunday stood up. 'I'm going to the bathroom. I'll be right back.' She looked doubtfully at the crowd blocking her path to the bathroom, which was over the far side. 'On second thoughts, I might be a while.' Taking a deep breath, she disappeared into the melee.

Hero sat a little straighter, determined not to be mistaken for a friendless, sad loser who drank alone. It was hard to sustain this image without resorting to taking out her mobile phone, so she was immeasurably relieved when one of the bartenders caught her eye.

'What would you like to drink?'

'Gin and tonic, please.'

He nodded and disappeared down the other end of the bar, returning a few minutes later with an elaborate, frothy confection in a balloon glass, which he set down in front of her.

Hero looked from the drink to the bartender with bemusement. 'What's this?'

'It's a chocolate milkshake.'

'I asked for a gin and tonic!'

'I know, but you're on holiday. I can tell. No native New Yorker would order a basic spirit when someone else is paying.'

'I'm paying for my own drink, and I don't want a milkshake.'

'Trust me on this, you have to try it. And it's on the house.' He watched as she took a sip and grinned at her expression as she realised that it wasn't a milkshake at all but an elaborate and potent cocktail. 'Good, aren't they?'

'Mmm,' she said non-committally, wondering how soon she could order another one. 'Thank you. But I really would prefer to pay for it myself.'

He waved away her objection. 'Forget it. I've always had a thing for redheads.'

'Jessica Rabbit or Ginger Spice?' Hero enquired.

He screwed up his face. 'That's so unfair. If I say Ginger Spice, you'll think I have terrible taste in both music and women.'

'Probably,' Hero agreed. 'But if you admit to Jessica Rabbit, I'll think that your formative sexual thoughts were about a cartoon character, which just makes you weird.'

'Rubbish. That would make me completely normal. *Everyone*'s first sexual thoughts were about a cartoon character.'

'Oh really? Who did you have a thing for?'

'Josie and the Pussycats.'

'Which one?'

'All of them,' he admitted shamefacedly.

Hero laughed.

'So,' he said, recovering, 'which cartoon character did you secretly pine for?'

'I really don't think I did,' Hero said, in between sips of her milkshake. 'Have you tested this theory on anyone else?'

He shook his head. 'Nope. Just came up with it. So what cartoons did you like?'

Hero thought hard. 'I can't remember. No, wait a minute, I remember liking *The Wacky Races*. Muttley was my favourite. I liked his wheezy laugh.'

'Muttley? Dick Dastardly's dog?' He looked at her doubtfully. 'You know, it's still just a theory at this stage. We'll test it out on some more people before you book in for therapy.' He wiped his hand on a cloth and held it out. 'I'm Oscar, by the way.'

'H—' She gulped. 'Lola.'

'Lola? Like the song?' He instantly looked contrite. 'Sorry, you must get that all the time.'

'All the time,' Hero agreed firmly. 'You're Australian.' She said it as a statement of fact rather than a question.

'Is it that obvious?'

'Well, you haven't commented on my accent yet, or told me how much you love Aussies.' Hero pronounced the double 's' in the American way, with a sibilant rather than a 'z'. 'That usually happens straight after "hello". How long have you been in New York?'

'Ten months. What about you?'

'Two weeks,' Hero said. 'I'm on holiday with a friend.' She paused and added wistfully, 'You're very lucky. I wish I could run away and live in New York.'

'You can. We just need to find you a job. Unless, of course, you're independently wealthy, in which case I'd like to propose to you right now.'

'I'm not rich,' Hero said witheringly.

'Oh. It's probably best if we get to know each other a bit better anyway.'

'Hey, buddy, how about some service?' an irate voice next to Hero demanded.

Oscar grinned apologetically and got back to work, but managed to stay close enough to Hero that they could continue their conversation. 'So what do you do, Lola?'

Hero cursed her altered appearance and substitute personality. For a moment she was tempted to abandon the pretence but then she caught sight of Sunday making her way back across the room. Her resolve firmed. 'I'm a . . . um, a performer.' Unwilling to elaborate on the lie, she hastily changed the subject. 'Where do you live?'

'Soho.'

'We're staying in Greenwich Village.'

'Lucky you, it's one of the best parts of Manhattan.'

Sunday joined Hero and looked curiously at Oscar, who was leaning over the bar. 'Sorry I took so long,' she apologised to Hero. 'Do you know they have attendants in the loo who give you soap and a towel to wipe your hands? You have to tip them. I can't believe you have to pay every time you go to the toilet. No wonder they don't drink that much beer over here. You know what they say —'

'You don't buy beer, you rent it,' Oscar finished cheerfully. 'Hello. I'm Oscar.'

'Sunday,' Sunday immediately answered, holding out her hand.

Hero could have kicked her. She had stuck with the Lola story but Sunday appeared to have completely forgotten that she was meant to be Wednesday. And her blonde wig was slightly askew.

Sunday eyed Hero's drink. 'What are you drinking?'

'Chocolate milkshake. It's really good. You should have one.'

'I'll make you one,' Oscar offered. 'Just to prove that New Yorkers aren't all heartless.'

'We don't think they're heartless at all,' Sunday said. 'Everyone's been really nice to us. And anyway, you're Aussie.'

'Well, yes, but I have started to eat bagels for breakfast. Hey Sunday, what was your favourite cartoon when you were a kid?'

'*Scooby-Doo*.'

'What is it with you two and cartoon dogs?'

'Oh, Scooby wasn't my favourite character,' Sunday said innocently. 'I liked Shaggy the best.'

Oscar gave Hero an irrepressibly mischievous look. 'I think my theory's recovered. I'll just go make your drink.'

Sunday looked bewildered as Hero chuckled. 'I'll explain later, *Sunday*,' she said, with heavy emphasis.

Sunday looked guilt-stricken. 'I forgot,' she whispered, as soon as Oscar was a safe distance away.

'Well, he thinks my name is Lola, so don't go calling me Hero.'

Sunday nodded. 'He seems very nice.'

'For a complete stranger working behind a bar, he seems fine,' Hero said flatly, refusing to adopt Sunday's conspiratorial tone. 'And we're leaving tomorrow, remember?'

'Stop being so defensive. I'm not suggesting that you fall in love with him.'

'You're suggesting something with that tone of voice, not to mention the look on your face.'

Sunday scowled at Hero's determination to stomp on her attempt to kindle a romance. 'Suit yourself, *Lola*. You know, you remind me of a very boring friend of mine called Hero.'

Hero stuck out her tongue at Sunday and then quickly composed her features as Oscar headed back and with a flourish handed Sunday her drink.

'So what kind of performer are you?' he asked Hero.

'She's a trapeze artist,' Sunday said firmly, refusing to meet Hero's gaze.

'Really?' Oscar's gaze lingered on Hero's red hair. 'I've heard you can go on a trapeze over the Hudson River. It's meant to be amazing.'

'We're leaving tomorrow,' Hero said hastily.

'Oh. That's a shame. But I guess it would be a bit like a busman's holiday anyway, wouldn't it? Too much like work?'

'Exactly,' Hero agreed, relieved that he wasn't going to launch an interrogation into her circus vocation.

Sunday, who had finished her drink in about three seconds, now announced, 'I want to dance. Do you want to stay here, Lola?'

Hero, who had no desire to immerse herself further in a quagmire of fibs, grabbed this opportunity to thank Oscar politely for the drink and walk away.

He watched her go, her bright-red hair making her stand out in the crowded room, before he regretfully turned away to serve another customer.

$\star \;\; {}^{\displaystyle \star} \;\; \star$

'I think I'm drunk,' Hero announced several hours later, in the tone of one who had made a very important discovery. She had addressed the remark to no one in particular, but Oscar paused in the act of putting away a tray of glasses, taking in her bleary expression as she slouched at the bar.

A moment later, a huge glass of iced water was placed in front of Hero. She looked at it with distaste and shook her head. 'I want another one of those milkshake things.'

'You can't have one,' he said. 'We only serve those before two in the morning. But you're in luck. Happy hour for iced water has just started.'

She looked at him sulkily, then took a grateful gulp.

'Where's your friend, Sunday?'

Hero squinted and looked around the bar. 'Dunno. Wait a minute.' She listened intently as fragments of song drifted in from the back bar, led by one very plastered Australian.

'*Start spreading the blues, I'm heaving the hay!*'

Hero jerked her thumb towards the back. 'That's her. She always gets the words to new songs mixed up.'

'New? That song's about thirty years old!'

Hero took another swig of her water. 'For Sun, that's new. She'll probably be teaching them monastic chants soon.'

'*I want some make-up, like a lippy that never see-eeps . . .*'

'People are funny, aren't they,' said Oscar philosophically.

'Funny ha-ha or funny peculiar?'

'Both.'

'Which am I?'

He considered her. 'I don't think you're funny.'

'Thanks a lot,' Hero said, humiliated that he thought she had no sense of humour.

He shook his head impatiently. 'I didn't mean it like that. I just mean —'

His next words were drowned by the rising crescendo from the back bar.

'*It's up to you, Jude Law! Juuuude Laaaawww!*'

'Sunday's very good at getting lyrics wrong, isn't she?' Oscar commented appreciatively.

Hero nodded. 'I'm actually more impressed that she knows who Jude Law is. She's an historian. Specialises in classical literature. She's not really very up with the twenty-first century in general. What's the word for getting song lyrics wrong?'

'Mondegreen,' Oscar supplied.

'That's it. Well, Sunday is a champion mondegreenarian,' Hero continued, wishing that she'd quit trying to be impressive while she was ahead.

The crowd had thinned out considerably and Oscar took advantage of the lull to lean over the bar to talk. 'So what's your favourite thing about New York?' he asked.

'The Met,' Hero said, without hesitation. 'It made me cry. What's yours?'

He smiled wryly. 'The corner of Sixth Avenue and West Forty-fourth street.'

'What's there?'

'It's midtown, a couple of blocks up from Times Square. A few weeks ago I was walking back home from the Upper East Side, all the way along Sixth Avenue. I was homesick and miserable and to top it all off I got caught in a massive thunderstorm and was completely drenched. The streets emptied in about a minute, there were no cabs, and it was coming down so hard I couldn't even make it to the nearest subway.' He dried glasses as he spoke. 'Anyway, I took shelter under an awning and started talking to the couple next to me. They were from the midwest and there was another guy there from England and a woman from Japan. And that's when I realised that pretty much no one in New York is actually *from* New York. New York is where you come if you want to be lonely and homesick with other people.' He laughed off his solemnity. 'So there you go. My favourite part of one of the most culturally rich and impressive cities in the world is a street corner with anonymous office buildings on it. Philistine, aren't I?'

'Are you still lonely?' Hero asked in a small voice, feeling ashamed that this stranger was pouring out his heart when she had lied to him.

He shrugged. 'Sometimes. But I know that I can go home anytime to Sydney. And I never wanted to spend my whole life in one place.'

'I envy you,' Hero blurted out. 'Living in New York, living an adventure.'

Oscar looked at her curiously. 'Well, it's not as though you lead a normal nine-to-five life.'

Hero reddened. 'No. I don't.' She hastily changed the subject. 'But don't you miss your friends and family?'

A shadow passed over his face. 'Of course I do. But when you move to a big city, you kind of get used to going out by yourself and slowly you meet people.'

'I don't think I could ever do that,' Hero said, remembering how uncomfortable she had felt for the few minutes when Sunday had left her alone to go to the bathroom.

'Sure you could.'

'I suppose I'd just have to not care what other people think,' Hero said wisely.

Oscar shook his head. 'No. That's not it at all. You have to make up an imaginary friend.'

'Pardon?'

He clapped a hand to his forehead. 'I can't believe I haven't introduced you to Brad yet.' He turned to the empty space beside him. 'Brad, this is Lola. Lola, this is Brad Pitt.'

'Your imaginary friend is Brad Pitt?'

He nodded. 'If you're going to have an imaginary friend, it may as well be someone who'd be cool to know. What would be the point of hanging out with a made-up guy called Bruno? Where's the fun in that?'

'I have no idea,' Hero murmured, edging away from Oscar slightly.

'And it's so much more work,' he added thoughtfully. 'You'd have to create their whole identity. At least with Brad, we can talk about mutual interests, like architecture and Angelina Jolie.'

'Is Angelina Jolie one of your imaginary friends too?' Hero asked cautiously.

'Don't be ridiculous. You can't confuse fantasies with imaginary friends. They're completely separate categories.'

'Oscar?'

'Yes?'

'You're one of the weirdest people I've ever met.'

He remained unperturbed. 'I'm not really. Lots of normal people like architecture. So who would you choose as your imaginary friend?'

She considered for a moment as he refilled her water glass. 'George W. Bush,' she finally announced.

He looked at her doubtfully. 'You'd choose George Bush?'

'Yep. I'd much rather that he wasn't real and was completely under my control.'

'Now I feel shallow for choosing Brad Pitt,' he said, wiping down the counter.

Hero tried to look humble. 'Some of us use our imaginary friends for the greater good, others for personal gain. Then there are the universal imaginary friends, like Santa Claus and the Easter Bunny, who we all benefit from. And —'

'Lola?'

'Huh? What?' She blinked, belatedly remembering that *she* was Lola.

'You're babbling. Now, what time do you leave tomorrow?'

'Nine o'clock at night.'

He came out from behind the bar to join her. 'Excellent. Why don't you meet me at the Met tomorrow? Say . . .' He consulted his watch and winced at the time. 'Midday?'

For a long moment Hero held his gaze. It was her last night in New York. All she had to do was lean in and kiss him. But she didn't do things like that. She looked down into her glass of water.

'Lola?' The tone of his voice had changed.

The name hung in the air, asking a question that she suddenly knew also provided the answer. Because tonight she wasn't Hero. She was Lola. And red-headed Lola was someone quite different to sensible, responsible Hero. Taking a deep breath, she looked up into Oscar's eyes, the sounds of the bar fading away. As she met his steady gaze, she felt as though she was falling, but to her wonder, the tumbling rush into the unknown somehow wasn't frightening at all.

A wild exhilaration filled her heart. Leaning in, Lola closed her eyes, made a wish and then, without further ado, she kissed him.

* ✳ *

Oscar's apartment wasn't at all what Hero had expected. It was small, of course, but by Manhattan standards it was positively luxurious for only one person, particularly when that person was employed as a bartender. Oscar led the way and Hero tried not to gawk at the framed snapshots lining the narrow hallway.

'Sorry it's so stuffy,' he said over his shoulder. 'I'll turn on the air-conditioner and we'll be fine in ten minutes.'

'I didn't realise New York would be so muggy in the summer,'

Hero said. Dear god, she thought. I'm about to have my first one-night stand and I'm talking about the weather. She searched frantically for the sort of topic that Lola would no doubt be well versed in (the latest off-Broadway hit? the impossibly cool Brazilian club that had just opened in the Meatpacking District?). But all thought fled as she entered the small but neat living room.

With its polished floorboards, white-shuttered windows and a comfortable couch scattered with patchwork cushions, it was tidy and welcoming but in no way remarkable enough to account for Hero stopping dead and staring, mouth half open.

Except that there, on the wall above the couch, hung a framed reproduction of Hero's favourite painting from the Met.

She swallowed and then managed, in a hoarse voice, 'Did you rent this apartment furnished?'

Thankfully, Oscar was too busy turning on the air-conditioner and putting on music to notice her odd reaction. 'No, everything in the flat is mine,' he said cheerfully. 'It would have made far more sense to rent a furnished apartment, but as soon as I saw this place, I loved it. You haven't seen the best bit yet – there's a rooftop garden with a great view over Manhattan. I'll get us some drinks and take you up there.' He looked up, noticing that her gaze was fastened on the picture. 'Do you like it?'

Hero cleared her throat and tried to sound nonchalant. 'Yes. It's a Picasso, isn't it?'

He nodded. 'You might have seen the original at the Met.'

'I think I did.' Unable to restrain herself, she asked, 'Why do you like it?'

Oscar looked surprised by her interest. 'I'm not sure,' he said slowly. He looked at Hero closely and realised that her question was not an idle one. Turning back to the girl in the picture, his gaze softened. 'I guess it makes me feel comforted somehow.'

'Comforted?'

'She looks so peaceful, surrounded by the blue sky and flowers.' He gazed at the picture for another long moment and then added, softly, 'I hope she's happy there.'

Hero said nothing but she had the oddest feeling that she was intruding on something intensely private, and that Oscar wasn't alluding to the girl in the picture at all.

Oscar gave her a sudden bright smile, snapping out of his introspective mood. He held out his hand and, shyly, she took it. 'Are you still feeling drunk?' he asked.

She shook her head.

'Good. But just to be on the safe side, I'll make us two virgin Bloody Marys to take upstairs.' He paused and said wickedly, 'I don't want to be accused of taking unfair advantage of you.'

A slight shiver of anticipation passed over Hero as she fervently wished that he would take advantage of her, preferably in the very near future.

$*$ $*$ $*$

Several hours later, in the pre-dawn stillness, when Hero's wish had been granted, she lay sleeping in Oscar's bed. Oscar lay wide awake, holding her close, wanting to kiss the warm skin where her neck and shoulder met, but unwilling to wake her. Unable to sleep, he gently disentangled himself and made his way into the kitchen to get a glass of water.

He had left a small lamp on in the living room, in case Hero needed to get up during the night. By its light he saw that her bag, which she had thrown carelessly onto a chair, had spilled out its contents. On the floor lay a guidebook and scattered postcards, one of which made him stop and look closer. The very same Picasso image that hung on his wall was replicated on the small rectangle of cardboard.

Feeling guilty, but unable to resist, he turned the postcard over and read the words Hero had written.

I want to remember always how I felt the first time that I stood in front of this painting. Alive and overcome with the beauty and possibility of the world. Certain that fate had brought me to this moment for a reason.

And I want to believe in true love again. I want to be in love like I was before.

I'm so frightened that I'll settle for less.

Oscar stood there for a long moment, re-reading the words. When he made his way back into the bedroom, he took Hero into his arms, this time not caring that he had woken her. All he was conscious of was the need to kiss her and hold her, wanting to never let her go.

* ✶ *

The heavy front door to the apartment slammed and Sunday rolled over. Without opening her eyes she emitted a groan that sounded like 'urrrrrggggggghhhhhhhh'.

Hero danced into the room and flung her handbag into one corner. 'Morning, Sun!' she said cheerfully.

Sunday groped for the bottle of water on the bedside table and somehow managed to get the lid unscrewed without opening her eyes or lifting her face from the mattress. She took a long drink, then rolled over and opened one eye.

Hero beamed at her, causing Sunday to howl with revulsion and close her eye again.

'I knew you were drunk, but I didn't know you were *that* drunk,' Hero said, observing her friend with concern and fascination.

'Fuck off,' Sunday said with unexpected spirit, her usual Pollyanna instinct subsumed by a throbbing head and a mouth that tasted like a sandpaper rat had died in it. 'You look . . .' She considered Hero closely. 'You're *glowing*,' she said accusingly. There was another brief silence and then Sunday sat bolt upright in bed, her hair completely crazed. 'Oh my god!' she shrieked. 'You just got home, didn't you! You shagged him!'

Hero said nothing, but her eyes sparkled.

'Ow, that hurt,' Sunday admitted, sinking back down. 'I can't scream any more, but I'm very happy for you. Tell me everything.' Before Hero could reply, however, Sunday suddenly sat up again and hurled a pillow at her.

Hero dodged it easily but looked indignant. 'What did you do that for?'

'For scaring me out of my senses! I can't believe you went back to some strange guy's place in New York. You could have been killed! What the hell were you thinking, Hero?'

'It wasn't me, it was Lola,' Hero retorted. She replaced the pillow and sat on the bed next to Sunday. 'And for your information, I wasn't quite as reckless as you think. You dropped us off in a cab, remember? And I made you write down the address and his name and number.'

Sunday wrinkled her brow. 'Do you know I have absolutely no recollection of how I got home?'

'Well, it's comforting to know that if he had turned out to be a murderer, you would have been of no help whatsoever,' Hero said scathingly.

'Never mind, you look fine to me. Better than fine, in fact. I can't believe you kept your wig on all night.'

'I didn't have much of a choice, did I?' Hero replied. 'He would have completely freaked if I suddenly peeled off my hair. I'm just glad that I took your advice about the glue.'

'Are you going to see Oscar again before you leave?'

'Yep. As long as you don't mind, I'm meeting him at the Met at twelve for an hour or so, and then you and I can spend the afternoon together before our flight leaves.' She began to hunt through her suitcase for something to wear.

'I don't mind, but are you going to keep the wig on?'

Hero shook her head. 'No, I'm sure I only got away with it last night because it was dark. I snuck away before he woke up, so I'm going to have to tell him my real name, too.'

'That must mean you want to keep in touch with him,' Sunday said shrewdly.

Hero flushed. 'Not necessarily.'

'Of course it does. If it was only a one-night stand, you wouldn't be seeing him today and you wouldn't need to tell him the truth.' Sunday yawned and stretched. 'So what time is it, anyway?'

'It's ten o'clock and it's our last day in New York, so it's definitely time that you woke up.'

Sunday took another deep swig of water and then propped herself up on one elbow. 'It's weird. I remember Oscar,' she said cautiously, 'but everything else is kind of hazy.'

'You were singing "New York, New York" in the back bar,' Hero informed her.

'I was?' Sunday asked, much struck by this revelation. 'I don't remember that. I do remember that I got stuck talking to some dweeby-looking guy for most of the night.'

Hero inhaled deeply before venturing, 'Sun?'

'Mmm?'

'You might want to race me for the shower, because you're meant to be meeting someone at twelve, too.'

'Really? Who?' Sunday said, starting to get excited at the thought of an unremembered love interest.

'The dweeby-looking guy. Whose name, by the way, is Eugene. He's a Canadian backpacker and you're taking him shoe shopping.'

Sunday choked. 'You're making that up,' she accused Hero, when she had recovered.

'I am not. You told him you were excellent at shopping and you promised to take him to Century 21 to buy a new pair of sandals. His old pair broke in Washington.'

Sunday opened her mouth to contest the veracity of this unlikely story and then closed it abruptly as a memory flashed back. 'Does . . . what did you say his name was?'

'Eugene. He's Canadian.'

'Does Eugene have sandy-coloured hair?'

'Yep.'

'And was he wearing an orange shirt?'

'That's him.'

'And he has a recurring corn on the fourth toe of his left foot?'

'I didn't get that far, Sun. I didn't want to move in on your territory.'

There was a moment's reflection during which the only sound was Hero scrabbling around in her toiletries bag and then Sunday burst out: 'I've seen his naked *feet*!'

'He's probably very nice,' Hero soothed, throwing two skirts on the bed to compare.

'It's fine for you,' Sunday grumbled. 'You're going to the Met with Don Juan while I'll be taking Eugene-with-the-recurring-corn shoe shopping.'

'Race you to the shower?' Hero said cheekily.

Sunday groaned again and pulled the pillow over her head. 'Oh god,' she said, revolted. 'You're in *love*.'

* ✱ *

Swinging her bag down beside her, Hero settled onto a bench in Central Park and gazed dreamily at the fountain playing in the centre of the square. The squeals coming from a carriage full of tourists snapped her out of her reverie and she checked her watch – she still had at least twenty-five minutes before she was due to meet Oscar at the Met.

Pulling a clutch of postcards out of her bag, she noticed with a twinge of annoyance that she wasn't wearing the ring she'd picked up at the Greenwich Village markets. It wasn't valuable but she'd only bought it last week, after instantly falling in love with it.

Making a mental note to check the apartment before they left for the airport, Hero settled down to writing, guiltily aware that she had forgotten to send any postcards until now. Selecting one of her favourites, a reproduction of Andrew Wyeth's painting *Christina's World*, she re-read the two words she'd written on its back the day before.

Dear Elliott

Just as she had yesterday, she stopped and chewed her pen. She looked around the square again. For heaven's sake, it wasn't that hard.

She just had to write three clichéd sentences to fill the card up. Only she couldn't. The vengeful desire that she'd felt yesterday, to prove to Elliott that she was fine and having a fabulous time in New York, seemed to have dissipated overnight.

Dear Elliott, last night I went to a bar wearing a red wig and pretended that I was a trapeze artist called Lola. And then I went home with someone who I think I've fallen in love with, just a little.

Hero wondered what Elliott would be doing back in Sydney. Sleeping probably, given the time difference. But then again he was just as likely to be taking a midnight salsa dance class. Or to have gone fruit picking. Or to have embarked on a new career as a life-drawing model.

She didn't want to admit it, but she was filled with a sudden, burning regret that Elliott hadn't seen her as Lola, someone as unconventional and carefree as him. Perhaps, however, it was best that he hadn't been privy to everything she'd got up to last night, she conceded with a naughty grin. A shiver of delight passed over her skin as she remembered Oscar's caresses.

Dear Elliott, she suddenly thought. *Fuck you.*

She ripped up the postcard. The very least she could do was to tell him in person.

$$\star \quad \overset{\displaystyle \star}{} \quad \star$$

The stone stairs leading up to the entrance of the Metropolitan Museum of Art were swirling with people as Hero made her way along Fifth Avenue. Her heart sank as she wondered how on earth she was going to spot Oscar in the crowd, but she needn't have worried. He was holding a balloon.

Biting back a giggle, Hero made her way through the summer

throng towards him. And then he glanced up and looked straight at her – and his gaze passed over her.

Hero took another tentative step forward, but Oscar was no longer looking in her direction. He was searching for someone else. He was searching for Lola.

Hero stood rooted to the spot as people surged around her. She wasn't red-haired Lola, the trapeze artist with kohl-rimmed eyes and a sense of adventure. She was brown-haired Hero, a magazine subeditor, and she was going home tonight.

She could feel her heart thudding as she turned and slipped away, making her way along the hot New York streets, away from the beauty and passion within the Met, and away from whatever it was that might have been. If only she had been someone different.

If only she could have been anyone but herself.

1

Girl dreaming

'How long are you going to be?' Pelham checked his watch as they stood on the stairs outside the Art Gallery of New South Wales, a stream of people coming and going around them.

'I'm not sure.' Hero tried to keep a note of irritation out of her voice. 'Does it matter? You don't have to wait for me. I can catch a bus home.'

'Don't be ridiculous.'

Hero sighed inwardly. Only Pelham would think that taking the bus was ridiculous. 'Fine. I'll catch a cab.'

'How many pictures are there in this exhibition? Eighty? One hundred? So if you see them all, you'll be approximately an hour and a half, right?'

'Pelham, I don't time myself when I go to an exhibition. I don't allocate a specific amount of time to each painting. I'm not a lawyer accounting for billable hours. I'm going to take my time and I would really prefer it if you didn't wait for me.' Her tone softened as she took in his slightly hurt expression. She stood on tiptoe and kissed him swiftly. 'I'll call you when I'm done, okay? Why don't you go and play golf or something?'

Pelham's expression lightened. 'If you're sure . . .'

'Of course I'm sure. I'll speak to you later.' She waited as he walked briskly down the stone steps towards the parked car. Breathing a small sigh of relief, she turned and made her way into the gallery.

It was the final day of a touring exhibition of selected modern masterpieces from the Metropolitan Museum of Art in New York, and the gallery was blissfully cool and calm after the heat and bustle of the outside world. Hero bought a ticket, declining the offer of a headset. She had tried to see the exhibition weeks ago but had left in despair at the crowd, eight-deep around the more famous works. It had been impossible to see the paintings properly, let alone enjoy them.

Entering the quiet rooms, she was thrilled to recognise paintings by Matisse, Kandinsky and Hassam.

And there it was.

She sat down on the leather banquette in front of the Picasso and smiled, the painting's beauty giving her an actual physical sensation of pleasure. 'Hello,' she whispered.

The girl lay on her side on a carpet of flowers, her head up-tilted towards the blue sky. The correct title of the painting was *Nu couché aux fleurs*, 'Reclining Nude With Flowers', but Hero preferred its alternative, less formal title, *Le rêve*. 'The Dream'.

Lost in a dream of her own, Hero didn't look up when someone sat down next to her. When she finally turned, she almost toppled off her seat in shock as she looked straight into green eyes that were instantly familiar, despite the two years that had elapsed since she'd last seen them.

'Hello, Lola,' Oscar said softly.

Hero was feeling about ten things at once. The predominant emotion was pure joy at seeing him again. Vying for second place was shame, both for the lies that she had told him and the way that she had stood him up. Coming a close third was pleasure that she had chosen to wear her new sundress that day. Fourth was the guilty feeling that it shouldn't matter what she was wearing, while emotions five through to ten were too confused to name but variously involved anxiety, lust and the urgent desire for a hairbrush.

When Hero finally spoke, her voice croaked. 'You recognised me?'

'It took me a few minutes to work out where I knew you from.' He shrugged casually. 'Maybe it was the New York context that helped. Do you need help getting in to your wheelchair?'

'What?'

'You had a terrible accident the day you stood me up and you've been confined to a wheelchair ever since, right?'

'Very funny.'

'Then why did you stand me up?'

'Because I don't have red hair,' Hero said flatly. 'And my name's not Lola. It's Hero.'

'Hero?' Oscar said, startled. 'That's not exactly run-of-the-mill. I don't know why you bothered to change it.'

'I wanted to be Anne,' Hero admitted. 'But my friend Sunday wouldn't let me.'

'No, Anne wouldn't have worked,' Oscar agreed. 'You don't look anything like an Anne.' He thought for a moment and then said, 'So you're not —'

'A trapeze artist?' Hero shook her head. 'I thought you would have seen straight through that one.'

'I wondered. But males have a tendency to live in hope. So what do you do?'

'I'm a subeditor for a women's fashion magazine called *Angel*.'

'I know that magazine. My company advertises in it.'

'You're not bartending any more?'

'No, I just did that till I found my feet in New York. I moved back home about a year and a half ago. I work for a company called Serendipity.'

'I know them,' Hero said, surprised. 'They're the ones that organise romantic events, like a sunrise balloon ride if you want to propose or a dozen red roses delivered hourly to someone's office.'

'That's us.'

'What do you do there?'

'Oh, this and that,' he said vaguely. 'De-thorn roses. Feed the cherubs. Remove the Turkish delights from boxes of assorted soft-centred chocolates. That kind of thing.'

'Oh.' Hero was silent for a moment. 'Well, it was lovely to see you. Goodbye.'

'Hey, wait a moment, I just found you again. Where are you going?'

'Home.' She took a deep breath. 'My boyfriend's picking me up.'

He didn't say anything and only by a supreme effort of will did Hero control herself as she walked away.

She was trying to hail a cab outside the gallery when she heard a voice at her side.

'You know, I'm beginning to think that either you're a pathological liar or you have a very odd way of picking up potential boyfriends.'

Hero gasped. 'Will you please stop *appearing* next to me like that!'

Oscar looked wounded. 'I've only done it twice in two years. Admittedly both times have been in the last ten minutes but I still think you're being a bit over-sensitive. So where do you live?'

'Glamarama,' Hero said, giving the local nickname for the beach-side suburb of Tamarama.

'Lucky you. Do you live with your boyfriend?'

'He lives on the North Shore. I share a house with my friend Sunday, the one who was with me in New York. Do you remember her?'

'I have vague memories of a blonde so I'm guessing she really has black hair,' he teased, grinning when Hero winced as his shot hit home. 'Well, I live in Bronte and my car's parked over near St Mary's. Come on, I'll give you a lift home.'

Hero looked at him, unsure as to whether she should trust him – or herself.

'I haven't the faintest idea why you're staring at me like that,' he said, amused. 'I'm not planning on ravishing you in broad daylight. Besides which, I've already had my evil way with you, remember? With your consent, I might add.'

Hero blushed scarlet as she remembered the night they had spent together. Deciding that it probably was a bit stupid to start acting coy now, she followed him through the Domain.

'It's odd that we've never bumped into each other before, given that we virtually live right next to each other,' Oscar remarked chattily.

'We probably have. You just didn't recognise me.'

'But that doesn't explain why you wouldn't have recognised *me*,' Oscar pointed out.

'I obviously never noticed you,' Hero replied, enjoying a small moment of vengeance for Oscar failing to notice her that day at the Met.

Oscar sank into what she presumed was a subdued silence, until she stole a glance at him. He was looking preoccupied but far from subdued. They reached his car and she gave him her address before wondering whether it was wise to have told him where she lived. It was too late now, however. Besides which, he didn't appear to have paid undue attention to the information.

'This boyfriend of yours,' Oscar began, as he swung left into William Street.

'Pelham Grenville-Walters.'

'Good lord. Yes. Him. How long have you been going out?'

'Just over a year.'

'Oh. Well, it's not going to work. You'll have to break up with him.'

'What on earth are you talking about?'

'You can't go out with Pelham if we're seeing each other,' Oscar explained, as they stopped at a traffic light. 'It just won't work.'

'Er, Oscar? *We're* not in a relationship.'

'Not yet, obviously. That's my point – you have to break up with Pelham first.'

'I'm not going to break up my long-term relationship for someone that I met once two years ago! We had a one-night stand!' Hero's voice had risen in indignation and to her embarrassment she saw the driver in the next car give her an interested look. She dropped her voice as she hastily wound her window up. 'What is wrong with you?'

'Nothing,' Oscar said. 'So what's he like?'

'Who? Pelham?'

'Of course. Who else?'

'He's in private equity. We've known each other for years. We had an on-off sort of relationship to begin with and then things sorted themselves out. We're very happy.'

'Sounds it,' Oscar murmured. 'You still haven't told me what he's like.'

'He's . . .' Hero stopped as she wondered how to describe Pelham, suddenly aware that the words she'd normally use would sound incredibly dull to Oscar. Squaring her shoulders, she reminded herself that it didn't matter a bit what he thought. 'He's a private equity player. A venture capitalist.'

'You've already told me that.'

'Yes, well, he has a very senior position with his firm. He's very ambitious and capable. And clever. And hard working,' Hero added, conscious that she was repeating the word 'and'. 'And responsible. Unlike you.'

'How do you know I'm irresponsible?'

'For a start, Pelham wouldn't take off to live in New York on a whim.'

'Is that what I did?' Oscar said, his face inscrutable. 'Even if I did, I have a very definite memory of you admiring me for that and wishing that you could do exactly the same thing.'

'I'm sorry,' she said stiffly. 'But you do give the impression of being a bit – unstable. Like now, for instance. Pelham would never insist on someone dating him three minutes after they'd met.'

'He sounds very dull, Hero. But anyway, I didn't meet you three minutes ago and I didn't ask for your boyfriend's professional resumé. I want to know what he's like with you.'

Hero was tempted to tell him that it was none of his business but it occurred to her that it might be a good thing to talk Pelham up. 'He's very —' She paused. She had been going to say 'caring'. Or 'fond of me'. Until she realised how incredibly tepid these phrases sounded.

Oscar took his eyes off the road to survey her knowingly. 'Thought so.'

'You thought so what?' Hero demanded.

'You're not really in love with each other, are you?'

'Of course we are. Just because I don't particularly want to discuss my boyfriend with you, it doesn't mean anything.'

'Okay, then answer me a few questions. What's your song?'

'My song?' Hero repeated, puzzled.

'Not *your* song – yours and Pelham's. You know, the one on the car radio when you were on the way to the beach on a perfect summer's day. The one that was playing when you had your best-ever shag. The song that reminds you of each other.'

Hero looked blank. 'We don't have a song.'

'No song. Just as I thought,' Oscar muttered, sounding like some sort of demented love doctor.

'Wait just one moment —'

Oscar spoke over the top of her. 'What nicknames do you have for each other?'

'We don't,' Hero answered shortly. 'My name is too short to warrant a nickname and Pelham happens to be very proud of his name. It's a tradition for the first-born son in his family to be called Pelham. Now, can you please —'

'No song and no nicknames.' Hero would have been unsurprised if he added 'A-ha!' and twirled an imaginary moustache. 'Final question.'

'I'm not answering any more questions about Pelham!'

'Which way do I turn?'

'Oh.' All of the wind left Hero's sails. 'Left. And then my street's the first on the right.'

'Thanks. But that wasn't my final question. Just tell me whether you remember the best kiss of your life.'

Hero felt a hot flush sweep over her at the thought of the kisses they had shared in New York. 'No,' she lied.

'I've had two best-ever kisses,' Oscar reminisced fondly. 'One was with you.'

Hero choked. '*One* was with me?'

He nodded.

'I suppose I'm meant to be flattered?'

He shook his head. 'Not necessarily. I'd be happy with touched.'

'I think you're touched in the head,' Hero said hotly. 'You can't go around telling people to call off their relationships five seconds after meeting them again.'

'I don't go around telling *people* to do that. I'm telling you to do that, which is a completely different thing. Did I mention that you're beautiful when you're passionate?' He pulled into her street. 'What number?'

Hero gritted her teeth. 'Fifteen. Oscar, I am in a relationship. Nothing meaningful happened between us and —' She broke off as he gazed at her with a mutely wounded expression. She groaned. 'Stop looking at me like that!'

'How am I meant to look?' he protested. 'I'm overjoyed at seeing you again and you're saying that what happened between us means nothing to you. Do you have any idea how vulnerable the male sense of sexual esteem is?'

'I was going to say that it was meaningless from an emotional point of view rather than a physical one,' she said, trying to be diplomatic.

He looked at her hopefully. 'So you didn't, you know, fake it?'

'No, I didn't. But that's beside the point.'

'Would you say that it was the best sex of your life?' he pushed.

'Unlike you, I don't make vulgar comparisons.'

'You do, too,' he said, unperturbed. 'You compared me with Pelham before.'

'I did no such thing.'

'Yes, you did. You said that he was boring and safe and I was reckless and charming. Or words to that effect.'

'But that wasn't a sexual comparison.'

'So you do think I'm charming?' He pulled up in front of her house but left the engine idling.

'I think you're certifiable,' she retorted. Taking a deep breath, she decided to reason with him. 'Look, Oscar, there's no point in us having this conversation. You can be charming, I'll admit, in a weird way, and I'm sure there are hundreds of girls out there who would love to date you. I'm just not one of them, for the simple reason that I'm not available.'

She looked to see if this had sunk in. His head was bowed and he appeared to be thinking deeply. Finally he looked up.

'Just do one thing for me.'

'What?' she asked warily.

He moved in closer to her. She tried to back away but there was nowhere for her to go. Lifting her chin with one finger, he forced her to meet his gaze directly.

'I want you to look into my eyes and remember the night that we spent together,' he said softly.

He held her gaze for a full minute and then, as though satisfied with what he had seen, he dropped a light kiss on her lips and moved away.

She sagged, feeling suddenly weak, but rallied enough to say, 'So that's it, then? We're agreed that we'll just be friends. Nothing more.'

Oscar grinned. 'Not a chance.'

And as he drove off, he honked his horn in cheerful promise.

2

Nice is for cupcakes

'*You met New York boy?*' Sunday shrieked.

Despite herself, Hero grinned. It was kind of fun to re-hash it, she had to admit. 'Yep. He was at the Met exhibition.'

'That's fate, don't you think?'

'No. But it was nice to see him again.'

'Nice?' Sunday snorted. 'Nice is for cupcakes. Are you still in love with him?'

'In love with him? Are you out of your mind? I don't even know him!'

'Fine. Are you still in lust with him, then?'

There was a pause while Hero fought down the memory of Oscar's irritatingly memorable smile. 'He's looking well.'

'Well. That's *nice*,' Sunday said in a deeply sarcastic tone. 'Don't go getting too emotional there, Hero, it's embarrassing.'

'What do you expect me to say? I met him two years ago in New York, we had a one-night stand and I ran into him again today. End of story.'

There was a pause and then Sunday asked, 'Is he seeing anyone?'

'I don't know. No. I don't think so. What does that have to do with anything? I'm seeing Pelham.'

Sunday appeared not to hear this last sentence. 'Did you get his number?'

'No, I did not! Sunday, I have a *boyfriend*, remember?'

Sunday shrugged. 'Have it your way. But I bet you anything this isn't the last we hear of Oscar.'

'I'll probably run into him now and again, given that he lives in Bronte,' Hero conceded. 'But anything else is out of the question. He was interested in Lola, not me. And I have a boyfriend. Why are you looking like that?'

Sunday stood up. 'No reason. I'm going out.'

'Where?'

Sunday smiled cheekily. 'I've got a sudden urge for cupcakes.'

* ✱ *

'We've got a new special project,' Oscar announced as he strode into the Serendipity office the following morning.

'Again?' Beth asked wearily, regarding him from over the top of her glasses.

Oscar looked at his beloved receptionist, affronted. 'What do you mean, again? We haven't had a special project for ages!'

'What about the Calder wedding?' Oscar's business partner, Jake, protested. 'That was only two months ago.'

There was a shudder as they recalled the Calder wedding, which had involved an opera diva bride, an octogenarian groom and eight stepchildren exhibiting varying degrees of animosity towards their new parent and anyone attempting to smooth the path to their nuptials. Cake had been flung.

'Beth, get someone to look after reception for twenty minutes. I need you in this meeting. And the Calder wedding doesn't count,' Oscar said firmly, leading the way into the meeting room. 'That was horrible. This project will be pure bliss from start to finish. We're going to pull out all the stops.'

'What's it about?' Jake asked, professional curiosity aroused. 'Is it a wedding?'

'Not yet,' Oscar said, a small smile playing on his lips. 'The subject's name is Hero. And at this stage it's a courtship. An *intensive* courtship,' he added.

'Special obstacles?' Beth asked, taking notes.

Oscar hesitated. 'She has a boyfriend.'

'She has a boyfriend?' Jake shook his head vigorously. 'Uh-uh. No way. Forget it. You'd be breaking your own company's policy. We don't do mistresses and we don't knowingly assist adultery. And a boyfriend is commitment enough, as far as I'm concerned.'

'This is different. I found her, Jake. I found New York girl.'

There was silence for a moment and Jake looked confused. 'Wait a minute, I thought you said her name was Hero. New York girl was called Lola.'

'She just told me that her name was Lola. It's really Hero. She's not a trapeze artist, either. She works for a fashion magazine.'

'She lied to you about her name and job and yet you still want her?'

Oscar nodded. 'And she's not a redhead. She was just wearing a wig that night.'

'I'm starting to think that she is your perfect match,' Beth interjected. 'She sounds just about weird enough even for you.'

'Look, I know it sounds crazy but I can't walk away without even trying. I know there's something there. We've just never had a proper chance. And now she's with the wrong guy. It's not her fault – sometimes it happens,' he acknowledged fairly. 'But it will be on the conscience of both of you if they end up together forever.'

They regarded him, unmoved.

'She has a boyfriend,' Jake repeated stubbornly.

'He's a venture capitalist,' Oscar tried, hoping they would see this as evidence of just how unsuitable Pelham was for Hero. Unfortunately, they didn't. Beth was looking faintly impressed, while Jake clearly wasn't quite sure what a venture capitalist did for a living.

'A venture capitalist is sometimes called a private equity player,' Beth explained, observing Jake's blank expression. 'They buy and sell companies or parts of companies.' Seeing that Jake was still bemused, she elaborated. 'Like Richard Gere's character in *Pretty Woman*.'

'Oh. Wow.'

'We were talking about Hero being in the wrong relationship,' Oscar said, annoyed that Pelham's career had impressed them. 'And how you're going to help me make her realise that.'

'It's against company policy,' Jake said. 'No.'

'They don't have a song,' Oscar tried.

Beth looked uncomfortable.

'They call each other by their full names,' he said desperately.

Jake fidgeted but shook his head in answer to Oscar's pleading expression.

Oscar took a deep breath and loosed his final shot. '*He lives on the North Shore.*'

There was a silence.

'Mosman or Kirribilli?' Jake ventured.

Beth rounded on him. 'What does it matter?' she said passionately. 'Oscar's right. We have to help the poor girl.'

Jake held both hands up in acquiescence. 'Okay, okay, we'll help. But don't say we didn't warn you.'

Oscar beamed.

'I assume we're going to do a Grade A assault?' Jake said, snapping into planning mode. 'So we're talking a sunrise balloon ride over the eastern beaches, then a champagne breakfast followed by . . .' He trailed off as Oscar shook his head. 'What?'

Oscar leant back in his chair and put his feet up on the table. 'Not going to work.'

'Why not?'

'Doubt that I could get her up in the balloon with me.'

'Is she afraid of heights? We could switch to a sunset cruise on the harbour in that case. Now what?' he said wearily, as Oscar shook his head once more. 'She's not afraid of boats, too?'

'She's not afraid of either, as far as I know. But I think it's best if we start off with smaller gestures and move gradually towards an actual date with, er, me.'

Beth and Jake were both watching him closely. 'She doesn't want anything to do with you, does she,' Beth said suddenly, an unholy gleam of amusement in her eye. When Oscar said nothing, she started to chuckle and was soon joined by Jake.

'I'm sorry,' Beth choked. 'It's just so *funny*.'

'Hilarious. For years I've been looking for this girl and when I find her, she's apparently going out with the human equivalent of a Liberal Party politician. And for some reason she seemed furious instead of happy to see me again,' Oscar said, his bitterness tinged with disbelief.

'I think *I* love her,' Jake said reverently. Catching Oscar's outraged look, he added, 'Oh, come on, mate, it'll do you good. Women always fall for you. I've said a million times that I wanted to meet the woman who wasn't impressed by good looks, charm and romance.'

'Yes, but why isn't she?' Beth asked, a puzzled frown between her eyes. 'Oscar, maybe she's really in love with her boyfriend. What did you say his name is?'

'Pelham. And I know she doesn't love him.'

'You don't want to believe that she does. How do you know, anyway?'

'When she talks about him, she sounds *businesslike*.'

Jake nodded. 'Fair enough. Shame he doesn't have an "i" in his name. If she dotted it instead of drawing a heart, we'd have a watertight case.'

'Why won't you believe me?'

'Because you're off your rocker,' Beth said frankly. 'You met her once, years ago. You didn't even know anything real about her until yesterday. She's going out with someone else, and she doesn't like you. That's not a romantic challenge – it's the love story equivalent of resolving the Middle East crisis.'

Oscar stood up. 'Fine. If you two won't help me, then I'll do it alone.'

'Ooh, I love it when he gets all dignified,' Jake whispered loudly to Beth.

Oscar made it to the door before Beth's voice stopped him. 'All right, we'll help you, but on one condition.'

He swung around to face them and raised an eyebrow, waiting.

'If you fail, you give up gracefully. You do not grow progressively more maniacal and determined to win. Nor do you treat love like an extreme sport, as is your wont.'

A smile lit up Oscar's face. 'Agreed.' Buoyed by their support, he enthusiastically paced the room. 'Now, I have a question for you two. Why have we never gone in for singing telegrams?'

'Because they're daggy,' Beth said without hesitation.

'"If music be the food of love, play on",' Oscar quoted by way of objection.

'Shakespeare was talking about music,' Beth replied. 'Not some guy in a gorilla suit torturing "Brown Eyed Girl" to a bad backing tape.'

'But it's so romantic,' Oscar persisted. 'What about all those old musicals? Bing Crosby singing to Grace Kelly in the rowboat in *High Society*, Fred serenading Ginger in *Top Hat*?'

'Did you ever look closely at the woman being serenaded? A woman getting a Brazilian wax would look more comfortable. What in the hell are you meant to *do* while someone's singing at you?'

'Look into the singer's eyes. Sigh. Listen. Look dreamy.'

Beth sighed in exasperation and Jake patted her hand. 'There's nothing you can do about him,' he said kindly. 'As a very young child he was dropped on his head onto the telly while it was on the Hallmark channel. The brain damage is irreversible.'

Oscar looked obstinate. 'I'm going to check out the competition. I think it's a service we ought to offer and I want to try something new for Hero. In the meantime I'll send her some flowers or something.'

'Do you want me to organise that?' Beth offered.

'No. I'll do it myself.' He added, nobly, 'It's your *moral* support that I need.'

He closed the door behind him, leaving Beth and Jake looking at each other.

'Do you think he has any chance of succeeding?' Beth asked.

Jake shrugged. 'Who knows. But I don't think we need to worry too much at this stage. He'll send her some flowers and try to soften her up a bit. It can't do much harm.'

'You don't think he's going to get his heart broken?' Beth said, in a troubled tone.

'I doubt it. To have his heart broken, it'd take a bit more than a memory from two years ago. And from the sound of it, this girl isn't going to let him get too close.' Jake looked rueful. 'Personally, I feel sorrier for Hero right now. The poor girl has absolutely no idea what she's in for.'

3

Geoffrey and George

Hero squinted at her computer, trying to make sense of an article on black being the new black. It wasn't the concept that was causing confusion – after five years of editing a women's magazine, nothing surprised her – it was the writer's inability to conjugate verbs. It had taken Hero less than six months in her first editing job to realise that most writers couldn't actually write. Grammar was a foreign concept, punctuation unheard of. What the feature writers of *Angel* did have, however, was style. And Hero desperately wanted to become one of them.

Chewing her lip, she minimised the article and opened up the document she'd prepared for her meeting with Sasha, *Angel*'s formidable editor-in-chief. She repeated each point under her breath, rehearsing her argument as to why she should be given the chance to submit articles of her own. She looked up, startled, at the sound of somebody clearing their throat.

'Er, Hero?'

Hero's assistant, Geoffrey, was standing in the doorway. One of the perks of her promotion to chief subeditor a year ago had been the acquisition of her own office and assistant. While she'd had initial reservations when Geoffrey turned up for the interview wearing a beautiful Jackie Onassis suit, complete with pillbox hat and gloves, his qualifications had been faultless.

Always a snappy dresser, today Geoffrey was looking particularly resplendent in an electric-blue tiered and frilled taffeta dress circa 1985, which looked like something Molly Ringwald might have worn to the prom. Geoffrey was a competent personal assistant but Hero knew that he had taken the job in order to get a foot in the door at *Angel*. His true love was fashion and it was his dream to work his way up to the position of stylist, a vocation for which he had a reverence bordering on the fanatical. Consequently, he turned up to work every day looking like an escapee from an haute couture show, in the hope of catching Sasha's eye and being catapulted into fashionista heaven. It was, Hero had often reflected, quite like working with Klinger from *M*A*S*H*.

'Yes?'

'There's a delivery for you.'

'Well, sign for it and bring it in,' Hero said patiently.

'I, um, think you might want to come out and see for yourself.'

The vaguest thread of suspicion started to weave its way through Hero's mind. 'What *exactly* is it, Geoffrey?'

Geoffrey looked helpless. 'It's a . . . a guy. With flowers.'

Hero groaned. It had to be Oscar. Not once had Pelham ever felt the need to publicly humiliate her by bringing her flowers at work.

She strode out of her office, gearing herself up to deliver a kind but firm rebuttal to Oscar, only to be brought up short by the sight of a delivery woman standing next to a life-size cardboard cut-out of George W. Bush.

'What the hell is that?' Hero demanded.

The delivery woman consulted her clipboard. 'You're Hero Hathaway?'

'Yes.' Hero was unable to drag her gaze away from the beaming visage of the forty-third president of the United States.

'Sign here.'

Dazed, Hero signed for the delivery. The woman looked at her kindly. 'I've delivered weirder things than this in my time, love.'

'You couldn't possibly have,' Hero retorted, wondering how on earth she was going to put the wretched thing through the shredder.

'No, really, I have. I blame eBay. Before they came along, it was all standard deliveries, flowers and nicely wrapped parcels. But nowadays it could be anything. Once I had to deliver a heart-shaped cushion,' she went on conspiratorially. 'Stuffed with the bloke's *hair*.'

'I have no doubt that it was sent by the same lunatic who sent me this,' Hero said, refusing to be moved by someone else's dilemma when she had an imaginary friend to deal with.

After the delivery woman had left, Hero, Geoffrey and George stood for a moment in silence.

'Geoffrey, this isn't a *guy*,' Hero attacked, knowing that it was a manifestly inadequate response but wanting to take her frustration out on someone.

'But he has got flowers,' Geoffrey pointed out. And indeed George was holding a bouquet of mixed wildflowers, courtesy of some holes in the region of his hands and a nifty arrangement of florist's wire. 'Who's it from?'

'An insane person that I met in New York who now lives in Sydney,' Hero said briefly. 'If you get rid of that thing, you can keep the flowers.'

'Don't you want them?' Geoffrey asked in surprise.

'No.'

'Oh. Well, thanks. They're beautiful.'

'You're welcome. I've got a meeting with Sasha now,' Hero said. 'When I come back, I want that thing gone. Understood?'

'Absolutely.'

✳

'Geoffrey, I thought I told you to get rid of that thing!'

'I tried, but George won't fit into the shredder until I've chopped him up a bit, and my scissors are useless. He's made of incredibly tough cardboard and I think he's laminated, too. I'll have to get a Stanley knife from somewhere.'

Sasha joined them and walked around George with a look of interest. 'Where did you buy it?'

'I didn't,' Hero said shortly.

'A guy sent it to her with flowers,' Geoffrey informed Sasha, clearly of the opinion that Hero wasn't fully alive to the romance of the situation.

Sasha's impeccably shaped eyebrows shot up even further. '*Pelham* sent you flowers?'

'No,' Hero replied, unaccountably annoyed that Sasha was more surprised by the idea of Pelham sending her flowers than she was by the idea of Pelham sending her a life-size cut-out of George W. Bush. 'A guy I met years ago in New York sent it to me.'

'Is he a Republican?'

'He's more of a lunatic.'

'But why would he send you George?'

'No idea,' Hero said hastily, unwilling to be sidetracked into a conversation about imaginary friends. 'Look, Sasha, you'll think about my proposal?'

'Sure. Just start writing. If the pieces are any good, of course I'll run them. I'd hate to lose my chief subeditor, but it's a long way from publishing an article now and again to becoming a full-time feature writer so we'll worry about that when and if it happens.'

Sasha departed and Hero grinned, filled with excitement now that she had her boss's go-ahead to submit articles.

'I found this stuck to the back of George,' Geoffrey said, in a casual tone that failed to conceal his excitement at the intrigue. 'I assume it's for you?' He handed Hero a sealed envelope and watched her curiously.

Hero groaned when she saw the name 'Lola' scrawled on the outside. 'Thank you, Geoffrey.' To his immense disappointment she didn't rip the envelope open, which is certainly what he would have done. 'See what you can do about the Stanley knife, would you?'

'Okay. But it's not like sedition, is it? Cutting up George isn't the same as burning the flag?'

'If the federal police knock on the door, I'll take the blame,' Hero promised. She went into her office and shut the door firmly behind her.

Twenty minutes later Geoffrey had another excuse to go into Hero's office. When he opened the door, he saw to his disbelief that the envelope was lying unopened on her desk.

Hero was frowning at her computer screen, apparently oblivious to her assistant's excitement. 'Thank you, Geoffrey. You can leave the proofs on the table.'

'It's not the proofs. It's your order from the café downstairs.'

'I didn't order anything from the café,' Hero said, as Geoffrey carefully placed a tall, frothy milkshake on her desk.

Geoffrey looked at her in surprise. 'But if you didn't order it, then who —'

'Yes,' Hero said quickly, wanting to forestall gossip. 'That is, I did order a milkshake. I forgot. Thank you, Geoffrey.'

'I don't think I've ever seen you order a milkshake before,' he said suspiciously.

'It's a health drink,' Hero said, improvising madly. 'New calcium-based diet. We're putting it in a forthcoming issue so I'm trialling it now.'

Geoffrey eyed the heart-shaped blob of cream floating in a sea of powdered chocolate with disbelief.

Hero adopted a kindly schoolmarm tone. 'If you're thinking that the same person who sent me flowers has now sent me a milkshake, you're mistaken. Anyway, it's one thing to buy someone a drink in a bar, it's quite another to send a drink to their office. What kind of lunatic does that?'

Geoffrey shrugged. 'I've seen the movies. There are lots of weirdos in New York, you know.'

'Yes, but I only met him in New York. He's Aussie.'

Geoffrey didn't hesitate to defend his nation's reputation. 'We have weirdos, too.' Then, unable to contain himself any longer, he burst out, 'Aren't you going to open the envelope?'

'Not right now. I have a lot of work to get through.'

With such a pointed hint, Geoffrey had no option but to leave, which he did reluctantly. Hero shook herself and refocused on her computer screen. A few minutes later, she absentmindedly took a sip of the chocolate milkshake.

It tasted like New York and a flood of memories from that night came rushing back. Against her will, Hero's gaze was drawn to the envelope. She took another sip of milkshake and decided that by leaving the envelope unopened, she was lending it too much importance. Wiping a trace of froth from her upper lip, she picked it up and tore it open.

Inside were two tickets to Circus Oz. On the back of one ticket was a mobile number, while the other had a sentence scrawled on it. 'Want to run away to the circus with me, Lo?'

Hero's lips twitched, but as she dialled the mobile number, she gathered herself to assume a stern tone. 'Oscar? It's Hero. Hero Hathaway.'

'Oh my god, you scared the hell out of me. For a moment I thought you were my high school principal. Did you like the flowers?'

'My assistant sends his thanks. He said that they're lovely.'

'Your assistant can get his own damn flowers. They're meant for you.'

'Yes, I know. But I can't keep them, as you very well know. Pelham wouldn't approve of me accepting flowers from someone else.'

'Oh really? So why doesn't he buy you flowers himself?'

'How do you know he doesn't?' Hero shot back, trying to remember if Pelham had ever bought her flowers.

'What kind of flowers did he last buy you?'

'This conversation is utterly beside the point,' Hero said icily. 'I am not discussing my relationship with you.'

'You know, you've gotten very prim and proper since we first met, Hero.'

'If that means I don't do outrageous things, that's fine by me.'

'I suppose that means you didn't like George?'

'Not particularly, no. Where on earth did you get him?'

'On eBay of course. I'm sorry he was secondhand but I didn't have the faintest idea how to get a new one.'

'That is a shame,' she agreed. 'I can't help feeling it shows a lack of commitment that you don't know how to get a brand-new cardboard cut-out of the American president.'

Oscar chuckled. 'If only you'd chosen Brad Pitt as your imaginary friend, I could have given you a life-size inflatable doll. Brand new.'

'What a truly disturbing idea.' Realising that she had been diverted into banter, Hero resumed her stern tone of voice. 'Oscar, I want to make myself perfectly clear. I'm in a relationship. I'm committed to someone else. I don't want you sending me any more flowers, imaginary friends, milkshakes or tickets to the circus. I don't want any more gifts. I know you mean well but it's inappropriate. Okay?'

'Does that mean you're not coming to the circus with me?'

'I don't think that's a good idea. Now, what's your address?'

'Why Miss Hathaway, you surprise me.'

'I want to post the tickets back to you,' Hero said repressively.

'Keep them. Take a friend. Just make sure you think of me when the trapeze artist is performing.'

'I don't want to keep them!' Hero's frustration was growing. 'I'm going to send them back.'

'There's no point. The tickets are for tonight.'

'Then I won't put them in the mail, I'll drop them off myself. Just give me your address and I can shove them in your letterbox.'

'What did you say? I didn't catch the last bit.'

Hero raised her voice. 'I said I'll leave them in your letterbox myself.'

'I don't have a letterbox. I have a mail slot in my front door.'

'Fine,' Hero said, growing more and more exasperated by what should have been a simple exercise. 'Give me your address and I'll shove them through your front door.'

'Sorry, I'm about to drive through the harbour tunnel and you keep dropping out. You know how bad the reception can be – I'm only catching every second word. What did you say?'

'ADDRESS!' Hero bawled. 'I'LL SHOVE THROUGH!'

There was a small, surprised silence before Oscar took a deep breath and held the phone closer to his mouth. 'I love you too, dearest,' he said. And on that tender note, he snapped his phone shut.

The sound of Geoffrey trying to chop George into manageable pieces filtered into Hero's office as she sat there stunned, the phone dangling from one hand, her mouth open in disbelief.

4

The song

The office of Maestro Brundalf, who ambitiously claimed to be the Purveyor of the World's Most Entertaining Singing Telegrams, was located in a narrow inner-city laneway, up a dingy flight of stairs.

The office itself wasn't much of an improvement on the entrance and Oscar looked around the cramped, ill-lit space with a sense of foreboding.

'Most of our business is done via the telephone,' the receptionist said sourly, noting his wary expression. 'We don't encourage clients to visit the office.'

'Oh. Well, I'm sure your premises aren't a reflection on the talent of your singers.'

'I wouldn't bet on it.'

Oscar gave her his most charming smile. 'I want to send someone a singing telegram.'

'No kidding,' the receptionist drawled, the charming smile entirely wasted on her. She waved a hand in the direction of a thick file sitting on the coffee table. 'The song directory is over there. When you've chosen something I'll need you to fill in some forms.'

Oscar had just started to leaf through the bewildering selection of alphabetically listed song titles when the door was flung open and an extremely distressed man entered, panting and wiping sweat from his reddened face. He was wearing a gorilla suit and a tuxedo, with his gorilla head clamped firmly under one arm. Slamming the door behind him with the air of one shutting out barbarian hordes, he sank into the chair next to Oscar. The receptionist seemed to think this a perfectly natural entrance, paying the gorilla absolutely no attention and only by the merest sniff betraying that she had noticed him at all.

Oscar gazed at him sympathetically. 'Tough day?'

The gorilla drew a deep, shuddering breath and then exhaled. In a tone of deepest horror, he said, '*Hens' party.*'

Oscar passed him a cup of water from the cooler. The gorilla accepted it gratefully and calmed down as he sipped it slowly.

'What did they do to you?' Oscar asked.

'Thought I was a stripper-gram,' the gorilla said morosely. 'Happens all the time. I turned up and they were already half-pissed on pink champagne. I sang "Lovin' You", quite well if I do say so myself, and followed it with an upbeat version of "I Am Woman". They were all clapping along, loving it. But do you think they're capable of appreciating music purely for its own sake?'

'No?' guessed Oscar.

'No!' the gorilla said bitterly. 'Before the final notes had died away they started whistling and chanting for me to get my fur off. They were brandishing bananas at me and then suddenly I was *surrounded*. One of them tore my waistcoat – look.' He displayed a vicious tear in his tuxedo. 'I'm telling you, I was lucky to escape with my head.' He broke off and stared into space for a long moment.

'Well, you're okay now,' Oscar said, trying to cheer him up. 'And both of your heads look fine to me.'

'I'm studying at the conservatorium. I'm an *opera singer*. This is so demeaning,' the gorilla moaned.

'Can't you get singing work somewhere else? My company handles lots of weddings. Maybe we could recommend you,' Oscar said kindly.

The gorilla looked shamefaced, but before he could answer, the receptionist cackled. 'Not too many people want a gorilla at their wedding. And he can't sing without the costume. Not a note.'

'Is that true?'

The gorilla seemed to be on the verge of tears. He nodded. 'Stage fright,' he whispered.

The gorilla continued to sit silently, occasionally twitching, until he roused himself and peered over Oscar's shoulder at the song directory. He couldn't restrain a derisive snort. 'Let me guess, you want "Brown Eyed Girl" by Van Morrison. You and every other musically uneducated ignoramus,' he added, just under his breath.

'No. I was thinking of sending her "Lola" by the Kinks. It's her name.'

The gorilla shook his head. 'I wouldn't, if I were you. The lyrics are a bit ambiguous. Maybe you could choose something that uses her middle name instead?'

'Lola's not her real name,' Oscar explained. 'It's just the name she gave me when we first met. Her real name's Hero.'

The gorilla brightened and stroked his chin. 'Hero? That's a different one. It'd make a nice change from singing bloody "Sweet Caroline", I can tell you. Let me think . . . Hero . . . Hero . . .' The gorilla paced the room, beating his chest occasionally for inspiration. Then his expression cleared and he looked up triumphantly. 'Got it! What about Bonnie Tyler's big number from the *Footloose* soundtrack?'

'I don't think I know that one.'

'Sure you do. It's the one where she sings about needing a hero who's strong and fast and fresh from a fight and – oh bugger. Maybe not.'

'Hero's kind of – terse – already. I don't want to encourage her aggression.'

'What about "Wind Beneath My Wings"?' offered the receptionist. She started to sing in a truly horrible voice, and Oscar quickly interrupted.

'Wasn't that the theme song from a movie about terminal illness?'

The receptionist sniffed. 'Well, if you're going to be *picky*.'

'She applied for a job as a singing telegram,' the gorilla whispered to Oscar. 'She's never recovered from the disappointment of being offered the receptionist job instead. She *hates* all of us singers.'

Oscar continued to flick through the pages. Finally a song caught his eye and he pointed. 'That's it!'

'Hmph,' the gorilla said, impressed. 'That's a good choice.'

'Thanks. Okay, can I go ahead and book the telegram now?'

'Where do you want it delivered?'

'To her office. She works for a magazine.'

The gorilla shook his head. 'I've seen too many telegrams go horribly wrong in workplaces. And she could get into trouble. I'd send it to her at home.'

'Which character do you want?' the receptionist asked, keen to get rid of Oscar so that she could return to her copy of *Who*.

The gorilla cleared his throat and looked hopeful.

Oscar tried to ignore him, feeling guilty. 'What do you have?'

She reeled the list off in a bored voice. 'Animals, including chickens and gorillas, or for that special Aussie touch, koalas or kangaroos. Sexy, including naughty nurses, French maids, schoolgirls —'

'Eew. Her nickname's Lola, not Lolita.'

'Suit yourself. Male stripper-gram or "humorous", incorporating "overweight" and "little people", or there's celebrity look-alikes. Our Paris Hilton's booked solid for the next three weeks but I could do you a cut-price rate on Daryl Somers. No refund if you think he looks more like Larry Emdur,' she added, her warning tone hinting at past battles bitterly fought and won.

'I don't think Hero would like any of those,' Oscar said, crestfallen. 'Don't you have something a bit more, you know, romantic?'

She checked her list. 'Gorilla wearing a tux is the best that I can do. We have a knight of the round table but he did a hens' night a few weeks back and he's still recovering from what they did to his sword.'

The gorilla cleared his throat again and looked imploringly at Oscar with puppy dog eyes, which was confusing given he already belonged to two species.

'All right then,' Oscar sighed. 'I'll hire the gorilla in the tux. This exact gorilla, if it can be arranged.'

'Of course it can. They're like prostitutes. They're all out for hire for the right price.'

The gorilla cleared his throat again.

'Now what?' Oscar demanded.

'I was just wondering, do you have your heart set on the tuxedo?'

'Why? What possible difference can it make?'

'You try wearing a gorilla suit in the middle of summer *and* putting a tux over it. It's bloody hot,' the gorilla said indignantly.

'Look, I want this to be special. So if you don't mind, I'd rather you were formally dressed. I don't want to send Hero a naked ape. She might get the wrong idea.'

The receptionist and the gorilla both looked at him blankly. 'So what would be the right idea?' the gorilla asked.

'Shut up. I'm paying for it. You're wearing the tux.'

'If you want the telegram recorded on a DVD, it's an extra eighty dollars,' the receptionist droned, with all the enthusiasm of an insurance salesperson reading out an obligatory disclaimer. 'That includes the cameraman's hire and the presentation of the recording in a giftbox to ensure you preserve that special memory for life.' She pointed to some very limp-looking cardboard boxes with scrolled gold lettering that proclaimed: 'My Telegramemory'.

Oscar was about to reject this over-priced piece of tat when it occurred to him that a DVD would be his only record of Hero's reaction to his gift. 'Fine,' he said, handing over his credit card.

The gorilla beamed at him. 'She's going to love it,' he promised.

5

The gorilla-gram

Hero had had a very trying week. Although the gifts had ceased to arrive hourly at her office, they had, unfortunately, continued to arrive daily. She had also had to put up with Geoffrey's pointed disapproval of what he quite obviously considered to be Hero's callous treatment of a creative and romantic suitor. Hero suspected that this was the reason that the George Bush cut-out was still standing, relatively unharmed, next to his desk, while the guidebook to the Metropolitan Museum of Art (Wednesday) and the DVD of *The Wacky Races* (Thursday) were prominently displayed on the coffee table in reception.

On Friday afternoon, on sighting a delivery van from her window, Hero had cravenly fled the office. She just *knew* that Geoffrey had enjoyed leaving the message on her voicemail that politely informed her that the second set of proofs were ready, that Mr Fenessy had called back about the obesity statistics and that a dear, sweet little flowering shrub in the shape of a puppy, à la Jeff Koons' *Puppy* sculpture, was now sitting on her desk. Furthermore, despite Hero's protestations of innocence and the fact that she had concealed the extent of the gifts,

Pelham was finding it hard to believe that she had done nothing to encourage such ardent devotion in one who was clearly a lunatic.

Hero was therefore in an extremely cranky mood as she staggered to the front door early on Saturday morning in response to an authoritative knock.

Sunday, her hair all on end, and wearing her favourite toga-style nightdress, bumped into her in the hallway. 'Who is it?' she yawned.

'Dunno,' Hero mumbled. She flung the door open and they stood side by side, mouths agape, as a cameraman started filming and a gorilla wearing a tuxedo pressed 'play' on a portable stereo and launched into the Stevie Wonder song, 'For Once In My Life'.

'Hero? Why have you got the stereo up so loud?' Pelham demanded irritably from down the hall.

It was at this point that Hero gathered her wits and promptly slammed the door. 'What? Sorry. I'll turn it down,' she yelled. 'Stay in bed.'

Sunday, who had been enjoying the gorilla's performance, peered through the window. 'Oh no, Mrs Davidson from across the street has come over for a look,' she said in a worried tone. 'I hope she hasn't come to complain. She complained about Mr Andrews' dog barking once. She hates animals.'

'Sun, it's not an animal!' Hero hissed. 'It's a man in a gorilla suit singing a Stevie Wonder song. How am I going to explain this to Pelham?'

Sunday's eyes widened. 'You think it's Oscar?'

'I think it's definitely *from* Oscar, even if he's not inside the suit,' Hero retorted grimly. 'Oh god, Pelham's getting out of bed, I can hear him. Is the gorilla almost finished?'

Sunday peered through the window once again. 'I think he's trying to breakdance.' She eyed the gorilla's contortions with interest. 'And Mr Andrews and his chihuahua have turned up, too.'

'Hero, what in the blazes is going on out there?' Pelham barked, tying his monogrammed dressing gown over his sensible blue and white striped pyjamas as he joined them.

'Nothing. Christmas carol singers.' Hero tried to stand between Pelham and the closed door.

'Christmas carol singers?' said Pelham incredulously. '*In February?*' Moving Hero out of the way, he threw the door open and, to his complete horror, found himself standing in front of a serenading gorilla, a rolling camera, a smattering of interested neighbours and one overexcited chihuahua.

The gorilla had reached the third verse and was really starting to cut loose, in an attempt to make his song penetrate Hero's heart.

Whatever the effect on Hero, he was failing to reach at least one member of his audience. Pelham was too distracted by the shrill barking of the chihuahua to pay any attention to the winsome lyrics, which were claiming that Oscar now had someone special in his life, someone he knew would never desert him again.

'Can you please shut that dog up!' Pelham snapped at Mr Andrews, who clutched his yapping chihuahua defensively and cast Pelham a baleful glare.

'It must seem very odd to the chihuahua that the gorilla is singing,' Sunday said, in the dog's defence.

For Pelham, who found the entire situation beyond odd, this comment was manifestly inadequate. However, any further comment was checked by the gorilla, who had reached the emotional climax of the song and was singing his little primate heart out.

Throwing his all into the final note, the gorilla collapsed onto one knee and the neighbours and Sunday burst into spontaneous applause. Hero, who was clutching the door in a white-knuckled grip, anxiously looked over to gauge Pelham's reaction. It wasn't good.

'Hero,' Pelham began, in a deadly tone of voice, 'what the hell is going on?'

Hero was thinking quickly. 'It's a gorilla-gram,' she said brightly. 'For Sunday.' She elbowed Sunday hard before she could blurt out the truth.

'Ow!' Sunday said aggrievedly, rubbing her ribs.

'Who's it from?' Pelham asked, eyeing the gorilla closely, as though assessing whether the police or the RSPCA would be the most appropriate authority to call.

There was silence as Hero and Sunday madly racked their brains for a likely candidate. Their salvation came from an unexpected source.

'Me,' said the gorilla, still breathing heavily after his exertion.

'*You?*' Hero, Sunday and Pelham chorused in unison, with varying degrees of surprise.

'Me.' The gorilla nodded firmly.

Hero and Sunday both opened their mouths to steer the conversation out of dangerous waters, but Pelham got in first. 'Why?'

'Why what?' asked the gorilla, a trifle defensively.

'Why did you dress up in a gorilla suit to sing to Sunday?'

'It's not Sunday,' the gorilla said, puzzled. 'It's Saturday.'

'Sunday,' hissed Hero. 'It's her name.'

'Your name is Sunday? Wow. That's really pretty.'

Sunday blushed and murmured something incomprehensible.

Pelham looked the gorilla up and down sternly. 'Look, I think it's time you went.'

Sunday fired up in the gorilla's defence. 'This has absolutely nothing to do with you, Pelham. I'll deal with it.'

'Are you sure?' Hero whispered gratefully.

Sunday squeezed her hand. 'Absolutely.'

'Can I stop filming now?' the cameraman asked, in a bored tone of voice.

Hero had a sudden change of mind and smiled sweetly at him. 'Not just yet.' She turned to Pelham. 'Pelham, darling, go back to bed. I'll be right with you,' she purred, for the benefit of the rolling camera. After one final, hard look at the gorilla, Pelham went back inside and Hero pointed at the cameraman. 'You. Is that still recording?'

'Yes.'

'Right. I want you to zoom in on me. And make sure you get this, loud and clear.'

The cameraman complied, but backed away nervously when he focused on Hero's enraged face as she addressed the camera.

'*Mr Martin*. I believe you work for a very successful company so obviously there is a highly deluded audience out there for this kind of sentimental swill.'

'Oi!' the gorilla protested, insulted.

Hero ignored him and swept on with her tirade. 'However, you have utterly misjudged me if you think I would be impressed by such a vulgar public display. As I have repeatedly told you, I have a boyfriend. You have constantly disturbed me at work and now you're molesting me at home. If you don't refrain from making me the object of your entirely unwanted attentions, then I will be forced to take out a restraining order against you. Consider this your first warning.' She gave one last, Gorgon-like glare into the camera and then turned on her heel with a flourish.

The cameraman cleared his throat. 'Excuse me, miss, you haven't said "I love you".'

'What?' Hero spun around and pinned the unfortunate man with a piercing look. 'Why on earth would I say that? Didn't you hear a word that I said?'

'Nah,' the cameraman said laconically. 'I've been doing this so long, I never listen any more. I just tune back in to make sure I've got the "I love you". Never missed one since my first day, when I got ripped apart by the boss. That's the only bit anyone cares about, you see.'

Lost for words, Hero marched back inside, slamming the door behind her.

Muttering dark imprecations against Hero, the cameraman packed up his equipment and left. Sensing that the show was over, the neighbours dispersed, Mr Andrews hastily picking up his chihuahua before anyone noticed that it had weed on the gorilla's leg.

'Would you like a glass of water?' Sunday asked the gorilla. 'You must be very hot.'

'Thank you,' the gorilla said gratefully.

He followed her in to the kitchen and removed his head while Sunday poured him a glass of iced water. 'You have a lovely voice. You sounded exactly like the Stevie Wonder version.'

The gorilla smiled shyly. 'Are you sure the telegram wasn't meant for you?'

Sunday looked surprised. 'Of course it wasn't. Oscar's obsessed with Hero.'

'Well, if it were me sending a telegram, I'd send it to you, not your friend. You're a lot nicer than she is.'

Sunday blushed. 'Hero's lovely, really. I'm sorry if she was a bit rude to you but I think she was a little upset about getting a singing telegram in front of her boyfriend.'

'A little upset? I'd hate to see her when she really gets going.'

'Let's introduce ourselves properly. I'm Sunday,' Sunday said, diplomatically changing the subject.

The gorilla's face brightened. He held out his hand. 'I'm Toby.'

Sunday smiled back. And a curious feeling shot through her as she placed her hand in Toby's paw.

* ✶ *

'Toby said that he'd call me!' Sunday's cheeks were flushed as she came running back into the living room after seeing Toby out.

Hero was sitting on the couch, trying to brainstorm ideas for feature articles for the magazine in a futile attempt to calm her agitated spirit. 'Who's Toby?'

'The gorilla.'

'My gorilla?' Hero asked, startled.

Sunday bristled. 'He's not *your* gorilla. You didn't even want the gorilla!'

'Please, Sun, I am not fighting with you over the gorilla.'

'Good. Because when he said goodbye, he said that he'd call *me*. What do you think he meant?'

Hero gave it her serious consideration. 'Well, I think it probably means that he's going to telephone you. But I might be reading too much into it,' she added.

Sunday threw a cushion at her. 'Come on, I'm serious. What do you think I should do if he calls?'

'I don't know. Go out with him, if you feel like it.'

'What did you think of him?'

'The guy turned up on our doorstep in a gorilla suit and serenaded me. He has a lovely voice. He seemed well groomed and didn't search himself for ticks. That's about as much as I know.'

'It's just so risky going out with a complete stranger,' Sunday mused in a worried tone. 'I mean, what if he turns out to be a psychopath?'

'You already know that he has two heads,' Hero pointed out. 'I find it hard to believe it could get worse. Besides, what are the odds of both of us attracting psychopaths at the same time?'

'Speaking of which, what are you going to do about Oscar?'

'I won't have to do anything once he gets that tape,' Hero said grimly. 'I threatened him with a restraining order, for heaven's sake. Even Oscar can't ignore legal action.'

'You don't think you're overreacting a bit?'

'This isn't a game, Sun. He's actively trying to break up my relationship and he's using the sorts of tricks that Elliott would approve of. For guys like them, it's all about the chase. I need to put a stop to this once and for all.'

Hero returned her attention to the notepad, and Sunday decided, all things considered, that it was best to keep her opinions to herself.

6

The order of things

'Strategy meeting in my office now,' Oscar said as he entered the Serendipity office on Monday morning.

Beth sighed and Jake caught her eye, as if to say, 'Do you know what this is about?' They followed Oscar into his office and he closed the door behind them, pacing as they took their seats.

'We need a list of the successive stages of wooing. I can't believe we haven't thought of this before.'

'Me either,' said Jake, shaking his head sorrowfully. 'Oh, that's right. It's because the word "wooing" hasn't been in common usage for about two hundred years.'

Oscar ignored him and continued to pace. 'I've figured it out. The reason that Hero didn't like my singing telegram is because it was out of order.'

'So it didn't go well?' Beth asked, interested.

In silence Oscar inserted a DVD into the machine and darkened the room. For the next five excruciating minutes they all silently watched the poor gorilla sing his heart out, followed by Hero's tirade to camera, culminating in her slamming her front door.

Oscar switched the lights back on. 'Yes, I thought you'd find it funny,' he said, surveying faces red with suppressed laughter.

Jake erupted. 'She . . . she *hates* you!'

Beth mopped her eyes. 'What do you want to do?' she asked, her voice unsteady with laughter.

'I've already told you. I want to compile a list of all the stages that people go through when they fall in love. That way I can do this properly.'

'You're going to fall in love by ticking off points on a list?' Beth said more soberly. 'That sounds horrible.'

'Don't be ridiculous,' Oscar said impatiently. 'I'm already in love with Hero. Have been for years. But she's got a few – issues – we need to sort out, so I want to make sure I do this properly.'

'She hasn't got issues. She has a boyfriend!'

Oscar waved his hand to dismiss this. 'He's just a symptom. It's obvious Hero thinks she should be with Pelham because he's safe and secure. You saw him. He's the sort of guy who has a stable corporate job and mows the lawns once a week and makes sure the rubbish bins are put out.'

'You got all that from his dressing gown?'

'Most of it. And if that's what Hero wants, I'll show her that I can be just as traditional as the next bloke.'

'And you're going to do that by following a list?' Jake asked, clearly dubious.

'Exactly. But I'm usually a hot-air balloon kind of guy, only the usual Serendipity methods aren't going to work this time. So come on, what happens from beginning to end if you don't rush into things? From dating to falling in love to getting married? Jake, give me the male point of view first.'

Jake sighed. 'I dunno. You go out, see a pretty girl, but she's dancing with her friends and you can't dance and you don't want to risk a humiliating knockback in front of a group of strangers so you end up drinking eight beers until you have enough courage to talk to her. Of course, by that time you think that you *can* dance so you go on to the dance floor and although you think you're moving like Patrick Swayze in *Dirty Dancing*, you're actually dancing like David Brent in *The Office*.'

'Uh-huh. Go on,' said Oscar, not looking up as he wrote all this down. Beth, however, was gazing at Jake with compassion. He caught her gaze, cleared his throat and looked away.

'Well, then she knocks you back so you drink another eight beers and end up kissing some girl who you probably wouldn't have noticed if you hadn't gone into the women's toilets by mistake. You end up going home together and when you wake up the next morning, neither of you can remember who the other one is and you have to surreptitiously go through their wallet while they're in the bathroom. The one who does the licence peek first wins a huge advantage over the loser, who will forever carry the guilt of not remembering the other's name after the first shag.'

'So you end up in a relationship?'

Jake shrugged. 'Sometimes. You might end up spending the day together and realising that she's a really nice girl, and before you know it you're living together and you've bought a dog and then it's only a matter of time before the trip to the gift registry.'

'Right. Let's see if I've got it all.' Oscar read aloud from his notes. '"Get drunk, embarrass self on dance floor, public rejection by dream girl, get drunker, first kiss in toilets with unknown girl, *not* original dream girl, have sex straightaway, clarify identity of sex partner, move in, buy dog, get married".'

'Yep. That's pretty much how it goes.'

Oscar looked deflated. 'It's not very romantic.'

'What did you expect? Mate, we have a successful business because no one has a clue any more how to do this stuff for themselves!'

'Beth, what about from a woman's point of view?'

'It's pretty much the same, but generally we're the first to get to the wallet. It would be very unusual for a female to let the potential of such a tremendous guilt advantage go to the other side.'

Oscar looked at the image of Hero's face on the monitor, frozen in contorted rage. He seemed to gain heart from the sight of his beloved's wrathful visage, for he drew a deep breath and decisively turned over a new page in his notebook. 'Well, that's not how it happens in my world,' he declared.

'What are you talking about? That's *exactly* how it happened! You met Hero on her last night in New York. She gave you a fake name and you two had a drunken shag and didn't even bother to exchange phone numbers.'

'But we didn't have our first kiss in a toilet,' Oscar said stubbornly. 'So come on, help me with my list. Okay, let's say our couple has met. He'd ask her out to dinner, wouldn't he?'

Jake shook his head. 'Too intense. Three hours of talking to someone you hardly know? No way. He'd invite her to a movie, the old standby. That way you know you're going to have at least one thing in common to talk about afterwards.'

'Fine. Movie date,' said Oscar, writing this down. 'Assuming that goes well, what next?'

'I think you could progress to dinner. But nothing too candle-lit or intimate. Just a nice restaurant where you'd feel comfortable.'

'Excellent. What's next?'

'Beach picnic?' offered Jake.

Beth disagreed. 'You've skipped over "impressive cultural activities".'

'Oh bugger, I always forget about them. Beth's right. After the dinner date, the next one would have to be the ballet or a classical music concert in the park, or an art gallery. You know, the kind of thing you'll never go to again for the rest of your life but you have to in this instance to show her you've got depth. Jazz at the zoo is a good one.'

Beth nodded sagely. 'Cute furry animals combined with an esoteric music form that no one ever listens to voluntarily is a winner. You come across as vulnerable *and* sophisticated.'

'Ballet, depth, furry esoteric animals,' murmured Oscar, taking notes. 'This is perfect, exactly what I need. Although strictly speaking we did find each other again at an art exhibition so we've already covered that one. But keep going.'

'I suppose then you could go away for a romantic weekend,' Beth contributed. 'That's always a milestone, spending consecutive days and nights together, having wild sex *and* discovering how the other person approaches the toothpaste tube. It's nakedness in many forms,' she added mysteriously.

'I squeeze the tube in the middle,' Jake said. 'Is that good?'

Beth smiled. 'So do I. It's the anal ones who roll the tube up from the bottom that you have to watch out for. Mark my words, there's never been a serial killer who hasn't rolled their toothpaste tube up tightly.'

'I gargle with mouthwash too,' Jake confessed, deciding to make a clean breast of it.

Oscar looked up in surprise. 'Why on earth are you babbling on about your dental hygiene routine?' he asked sternly. 'Stick to the topic. Now, our hypothetical perfect match has just had their weekend away. What happens next?'

'You'd have to meet each other's parents and get the family's tick of approval,' Beth supplied, before Jake could retaliate.

Oscar's list had filled nearly the entire page; in tiny, cramped letters, he scribbled 'meet parents' beneath 'dinner date'. He finished writing and looked up at them expectantly.

'A proper fight and a temporary break-up is essential in lots of ways,' Beth said thoughtfully. 'Making up after your first fight is always significant.'

'Excellent. Then what?'

'Then, my friend,' Jake said with a grin, 'why then you're officially a couple and it's time to start choosing names for your dog. But if I were you, I'd stop dreaming.'

'What do you mean?'

'Oscar, the girl threatened to take out a restraining order against you. The very least you should do is apologise.'

'I was being romantic!'

'That's what all the stalkers say,' Beth pointed out dryly. She sighed as she took in Oscar's chastened expression. 'Darling, *we* know that you're not a dangerous lunatic —'

'You're just a lunatic,' Jake interposed.

'But look at it from Hero's point of view,' Beth continued, with unruffled calm. 'If you keep bombarding her with unwanted romantic gestures, she really is well within her rights to take action against you.'

'Which could hurt Serendipity if it went public,' Jake said, all traces of laughter vanishing as he realised the full implications of Oscar's behaviour.

Oscar flinched as he met their serious gazes. 'All right! Stop looking at me like I've just shot Bambi's mother. I'll go and see her now. But I bet you anything she's calmed down and changed her mind about the gorilla. With a bit of luck, I won't even need this list.' He leapt to his feet, his natural optimism returning. 'You're right, we probably just need to have a talk to straighten things out.' He shot Beth and Jake a look that was brimful of mischief. 'I've always liked the name Rufus for a dog.'

As the door banged shut behind him, Jake groaned.

7

The truce

'Hero?' Geoffrey's voice was bursting with suppressed excitement.

Hero didn't even bother to look up. 'If it's a heart-shaped wreath of roses or a field of waving daffodils, I don't want to know, Geoffrey. If it's anything to do with the business of running a magazine, you may have my undivided attention.'

'I wish I'd thought of a field of daffodils.' Oscar's voice sounded regretful. 'That's quite good.'

Hero's head snapped up as Geoffrey stepped aside and Oscar strolled into her office.

'This is nice.' Oscar's gesture took in her spacious office. 'Pretty impressive for an editor.'

'I'm the chief subeditor,' Hero replied. 'You can close the door, Geoffrey,' she said pointedly.

'Sure.' Geoffrey couldn't take his besotted eyes off Oscar. 'It's just that I've been wanting to thank you for the tickets to the circus.'

'You're very welcome. I'm glad someone was able to use them. How was the trapeze artist? They're my favourite.'

'They're my favourite, too,' Geoffrey said eagerly, glad to have found something in common with Oscar. 'They were wonderful. Lovely strong thighs and calf muscles and snug shiny tights . . .' He trailed off in a pleasurable reverie before Hero's glare made him recall where he was. 'Can I get you anything to drink?'

'Mr Martin won't be staying that long.'

Oscar shrugged and shot Geoffrey a conspiratorial glance, which caused a blush to rise on Geoffrey's cheeks.

'I made sure they had water, you know,' he said in a rush. 'The flowers and the sweet little puppy plant.'

'Did you? Thank you. Was that before or after Hero tried to throw them out?'

Geoffrey giggled. 'She didn't tell me to throw the flowers out. Although she did try to make me cut up George, but he's too tough so you can have him back if you want,' he added, obviously trying to prolong the conversation.

Oscar shook his head. 'It would be unconstitutional to not let him serve his full term.'

'*Thank you*, Geoffrey,' Hero interjected, glowering at her recalcitrant assistant.

With a final, lingering look at Oscar, Geoffrey reluctantly closed the door.

Hero indicated that Oscar should take a seat on the couch. To her annoyance he sprawled on it, looking very much at home. He patted the seat next to him invitingly, but she folded her arms and glared at him.

'What do you want?' she demanded, not mincing words.

He looked at her guiltily. 'I've come to apologise. For the gifts and the singing telegram. I didn't realise they would upset you so much. Most women would love that sort of thing.'

'No, they bloody well would not! "That sort of thing", as you call it, was a completely arrogant dismissal of my relationship and my stated wishes, and showed a lack of respect for my professional status.'

He looked horrified. 'I never meant to cause you trouble at work.'

'Well, you didn't, luckily,' Hero said, relenting slightly. 'But you did disrupt my working environment and, more to the point, you didn't take a single bit of notice of anything that I said to you on the phone the other day. What's so romantic about being ignored?'

Oscar ran a hand through his hair. 'Look, Hero, I don't know what's happened to us. We got off to an amazing start in New York and when I saw you again, I just thought it must be fate. I don't understand how you can't see that, too.'

'It's not fate! What's so unlikely about two people who met in New York both attending an exhibition of paintings from a New York museum? People want to believe in fate because they want to believe that their love stories are preordained, a matter of destiny. In actual fact,' Hero said, warming to her theme, 'the only thing that is certain is that everyone wants to fall in love and be loved. In my opinion, *who* you happen to fall in love with is a matter of chance, not fate. And the probability that we're capable of falling in love with a whole range of people is something that most people refuse to acknowledge.'

Oscar was silent for a moment as he digested this. 'Wow. Did you just make all that up?'

'Not exactly. I read it in Alain de Botton's *Essays in Love*. But it makes a lot of sense.'

'You really believe it?' he asked, crestfallen.

'I really believe it,' Hero said firmly. 'The literal definition of romance is "fiction". As in something not real.'

Oscar contemplated her as though confronted with an intriguing but hitherto unknown species. 'So you don't believe in *love*?'

Hero heaved an exasperated sigh. 'See, that's the problem. Like most people, you're confusing romance with love. It is possible to have love without romance, you know.'

'Does that mean you don't like anything romantic at all?'

'No, I don't. Not really.'

'Why not?'

'Because romantic gestures are what you get when people act out of character. They're not what real relationships are made of.'

'So what are real relationships made of, in your opinion?'

'Trust. Reliability. Honesty.'

'Oh. Well, if you value those things so highly, how come you lied to me about your name and job and didn't show up to our meeting at the Met?'

Hero flushed as she remembered the excitement that had turned to humiliation that day in Manhattan. But she held his gaze steadily. 'Because we weren't in a relationship. We had a one-night stand. It was the opposite of romance.'

'So that night in New York was really just about sex for you?'

Hero tried to meet his gaze confidently but she couldn't quite do it. Oscar let the silence hang between them, and when he suddenly smiled, Hero had the uncomfortable feeling that he'd decided her silence was the answer he wanted.

'Anyway, I guess it really doesn't matter how twisted your ideas on romance and relationships are,' he said. 'Because I came here today to ask if we could just try to be friends.'

'Friends?' she repeated suspiciously. 'You mean no more pestering me to break up with Pelham and go out with you? No more gifts or singing telegrams? You'd really be happy just being friends?'

He crossed his heart, spat on his palm and held it out.

'Eew.' She looked with distaste at the proffered hand. 'That's disgusting.'

'You have to spit on your palm and then we shake on it.'

'Does it have to be spit?'

'Yep. Unless you want us to cut our thumbs and mix the blood together.'

'What are you, eight?'

He grinned but stood there stubbornly. With a sigh, she gingerly spat on her palm and shook hands.

Oscar gave her a bright smile. 'To friendship.'

'To friendship.'

'Okay, gotta go.'

Hero stared at him, bemused. 'Where are you rushing off to?'

'Well, for starters I want to wash my hand. It's got your spit on it. It's gross.' He winked and walked away.

Hero wiped her palm down the side of her skirt. She was irritatingly aware that it was going to be much harder to wipe the smile from her face.

$$\star \; \textbf{\textasteriskcentered} \; \star$$

'*Friends?*' Sunday said disbelievingly. 'After all this, he's happy just being friends?'

'That's what he said. And we shook on it.' Hero pulled a bottle of wine from the fridge and opened a cupboard in search of two glasses.

'I don't believe it,' Sunday said.

'Well, it's true. So my life can go back to normal. No flowers, no singing telegrams, *definitely* no more life-size cardboard cut-outs, thank god. And best of all, no Oscar!'

'Oh, really?'

'What do you mean, "oh really"?' Hero paused in the act of pouring the wine.

'I mean, is the deal that he disappears from your life completely? Or is it – let me guess, now you're friends, he can actually call you and see you without you blowing a gasket?'

Hero looked at Sunday, deflated. 'You think it's all just a sneaky manoeuvre?'

'I think it's very odd that someone as determined and unconventional as Oscar would all of a sudden roll over and give in. It's far more likely that he's playing hard to get.'

'*Playing hard to get?* What would be the point? I don't *want* to get him. It'd be like playing hide-and-seek by himself.'

Sunday shrugged. 'I bet you anything he's just switching tactics. I think this is all a plot to make you lower your defences.'

Hero mulled this over and then her brow cleared. 'It doesn't really matter if it is a plot. Because either way, I get breathing space and don't have to put up with him for a while. And maybe he'll come to his senses when he realises that I'm really not interested.'

'Are you quite sure about that?'

'Of course I'm sure,' Hero said sharply. 'I admit I had a bit of a crush on him when we first met —'

'A bit of a crush?' Sunday snorted. 'You were practically singing the morning after, like someone who'd just got out of bed in a mattress commercial.' She looked more closely at her friend. 'You know, you never did tell me why you didn't meet up with him that day. Or why you said no when I offered to give you his address.'

'Sun, he was thirty years old and he'd run away to New York to work as a bartender. He was there for a good time. He probably picked up a different girl every shift he worked.'

'You don't know that,' Sunday argued. 'And I know you. If you really believed it, you never would have gone near him, tipsy or not.'

Hero ignored her entirely valid point. 'Anyway, that was years ago and I'm very happy with Pelham. I'm certainly not going to throw away a solid relationship for someone who thinks that *Wuthering Heights* is a bit understated.'

Sunday regarded her thoughtfully. 'Solid? That's how you describe your relationship with Pelham?'

Hero flushed. 'Yes. I happen to think that's a desirable thing. Solid means dependable, reliable, someone who can be counted on. And quite frankly I'd rather have a foreseeable future with Pelham than be forever subjected to Oscar's passing whims and crazes.'

'Hero, if you're thinking of Elliott . . .' Sunday began tentatively.

'This has nothing to do with Elliott,' Hero retorted, adding illogically, 'even if Elliott and Oscar are both career Casanovas.'

'You don't know that,' Sunday said. 'Just because Elliott —'

'I don't want to talk about it, Sun,' Hero interrupted flatly.

Sunday was of the firm conviction that lifting the taboo on the topic of Elliott would do Hero a world of good, but she knew from experience that there was no point in pushing. Instead, she raised her wine glass. 'To new friendships.'

Hero clinked her glass against Sunday's and raised an eyebrow. 'Speaking of which, have you heard from Toby?'

Sunday beamed. 'As a matter of fact, I have a date with him on Friday night.'

'Let me guess, you're going to see *King Kong* and then go out for banana splits?' Hero teased.

'Very funny. He's taking me out for dinner. But the date's kind of significant, don't you think?'

'You mean the fact that he's taking you out for dinner?' Hero said, puzzled. 'I suppose.'

'Not the dinner date, the *calendar* date.' Hero still looked bewildered and Sunday gently explained, 'It's Valentine's Day on Friday. We'll be having our first date on Valentine's Day.'

Hero nodded, as if to say that of course she knew Friday was Valentine's Day. But as Sunday launched into a detailed discussion on the pitfalls of dressing suitably for a first date, her mind was elsewhere.

She was wondering why, all of a sudden, Oscar's offer of a truce seemed sinister in the extreme.

8

Valentine's Day

Hero awoke on Friday with a feeling of deepest dread. It took her some time to realise what was bothering her, but then she groaned and rolled over, pulling the pillow over her head.

When she finally got out of bed and dressed, she sat at the kitchen table and stared glumly into her coffee.

'What on earth is the matter with you?' Sunday demanded, looking askance at Hero's long face.

'It's *Valentine's Day*,' Hero replied, in tones of deepest horror. 'I'll have to call in sick and stay barricaded in the house all day. God only knows what Oscar's planned.'

'Oh, poor you. You're probably going to be bombarded with bouquets in the most imaginative way possible. My heart's bleeding. Anyway, I thought you were just friends?'

'I did think that, until you freaked me out and made me suspicious all over again,' Hero retorted.

Sunday shrugged and sipped her coffee. 'I've been known to be wrong before. Specifically when I wrote a paper on how *Ben-Hur* marked the final commercial success of Roman history in cinema, about two months after *Gladiator* was released.'

Hero tried to shake off her misgivings. 'I hope you are wrong. After all, we're both mature adults . . .' She faltered as she remembered the George Bush cut-out, but managed to continue. 'And I've made it completely clear that I don't want his attentions.'

'Mmm.' Sunday drained her coffee. 'Let me know what happens, won't you?' She gave a cheeky grin. 'I must say I'd miss Oscar if he wasn't around. Life is certainly more exciting.'

'You can call it that. I prefer to call it annoying,' Hero replied tartly, gathering up her bag and keys and preparing to head to work, determined to treat this day like any other.

* ✱ *

Hero let out a relieved sigh when she switched her office lights on. Everything appeared to be normal.

By midday, however, her nerves were stretched to breaking point. Every time the phone rang or Geoffrey buzzed her, she braced herself for news of outrageous behaviour on Oscar's part. Finally, she decided that she didn't have to be at his mercy. She could take matters into her own hands. She dialled his number.

'Hello?'

'Oscar, it's Hero.'

'Hey, how are you?' He sounded completely normal and friendly. 'What's up?'

Hero cursed herself. She had been so sure that she would catch him out in some act of romantic mischief-making, she hadn't bothered to think of an excuse for her call. 'Um, not much. How's work?'

'Frantic. Today's the busiest day of the year for us, apart from the twenty-third of November.'

'What happens on the twenty-third of November?'

'God only knows. But I can tell you that a *lot* of people get engaged on that day.'

There was a small silence.

'So Hero, what can I do for you?'

'I, um, just rang to say hi, really.' Hero held the phone away while she banged her head against her computer monitor.

However, Oscar hadn't seemed to notice anything out of the ordinary in her calling. 'I'd love to chat, and I'm sorry to cut this short but it's crazy around here. A client organised a hay-ride for her fiancé and we've just discovered that he gets hayfever. We're going mad trying to find a histamine-free substitute for hay. At this point it looks like we'll have to paint AstroTurf yellow.'

'Oh. Well then. Good luck. 'Bye.'

'Hero?'

'Yes?' she asked suspiciously. She could hear the laughter in his voice.

'Happy Valentine's Day.' He hung up.

$\star$ $\ast$ $\star$

'So how are things going?' Sunday had called Hero on the mobile.

'Everything's fine. I think he's got the message. I rang him to make sure and he was almost – abrupt.' Hero tried not to sound hurt.

'You haven't received a single flower?'

'Nope.'

'Huh. Maybe he isn't as thick-skinned as we thought.'

'Do you know where Toby's taking you for dinner tonight?' Hero asked, deciding to change the subject.

'We're going to Longrain,' Sunday practically purred, naming one of the best Thai restaurants in Sydney.

'Wow. Being a singing gorilla must be more lucrative than I thought.'

'What about you and Pelham? Are you doing anything?'

'No. He has to work. And anyway, he thinks Valentine's Day is a commercial rip-off.'

'Killjoy.'

'No, I sort of think he has a point. I mean, look how much money the company Oscar works for is making out of today.'

'I still think it's nicer to make money from doing something that makes people happy and promotes love than to make money by making rich people more money.'

Hero sighed. 'Okay, Sun. I don't want to argue about this right now. If I don't see you before you leave tonight, have a great time and make sure you order those yummy betel leaf thingies. Just thinking about them makes me drool.'

'I will,' Sunday promised. 'What are you going to do tonight?'

'Watch telly. Maybe try to write an article, or have a bath. It really doesn't matter what I do. It's just a regular weeknight.'

* ✱ *

By seven o'clock that night, Hero was going crazy. After seeing Sunday off on her romantic date, she now had a choice of three romantic comedies on the commercial television stations, a documentary about love on SBS, or a period drama involving women in bonnets falling in love on the ABC. Given she was halfway through a Georgette Heyer novel, there was no respite to be had from the theme of romance in reading, either. It was one thing not to feel the need to celebrate Valentine's Day, she thought bitterly, but it was quite another to have the entire forces of cultural production aligned against you.

Half an hour later, after abandoning a draft of an article for *Angel*, tentatively titled 'Stupid Cupid', she dialled her parents' number out of sheer desperation.

'Mum?'

'Darling! How lovely to hear from you. How are you?'

'Fine. How's everything there?'

'Oh, same as always. Your father's decided to build a pagoda —'

A shouted correction from the background interrupted her.

'Hold on, your father's yelling something. What is it, dear? Oh.' She returned to her conversation with Hero, her calm undisturbed. 'Dad says it's not a pagoda, it's a gazebo. Or a pergola. Or something like that. You know, I'm sure retirement isn't meant to be this stressful. How's Sunday?'

'She's fine, too. She's out on a date.'

'With that man from the Russian department?' Coralie thrived on the gossip from Sunday's university.

'No, this is someone new. He's a primate,' Hero added.

Her mother sounded startled. 'Sunday's dating an archbishop?'

'No, I mean a real primate. The endangered *Gorillas in the Mist* kind.'

'Well, that seems very peculiar of Sunday. If she wants to save the gorillas, can't she just send a cheque to that nice Sigourney Weaver?'

'Mum, forget Sunday and the gorilla. I need to ask you something.'

'Of course, darling, what is it?'

Hero took a deep breath. 'How did you know that you were in love with Dad?'

There was a short silence. When her mother spoke, her tone had sharpened. 'Has something happened with Pelham? Have you had a fight?'

'No! Mum, can you just answer the question? Please? It's for an article we're running in the magazine,' she invented.

Coralie sighed. 'I don't know what to tell you, Hero. You just *know*. You want to be with that person and you envisage a future with them and you forgive them their flaws and foibles and they forgive yours.'

'So true love involves compromise?'

'Of course it does.'

'Crown Princess Mary didn't compromise,' Hero argued stubbornly.

'Darling, she married a man named Frederik Glücksborg whose family think it's desirable to dine on pickled herrings. Trust me, she compromised. Now what's happened? Are you sure you're not fighting with Pelham?'

'No,' Hero said quickly. For a moment she contemplated telling her mother about Oscar and New York and the flowers and the singing gorilla-gram, but decided against it. Her mother wasn't overly fond of Pelham, and Hero didn't want to give her any reason to think their relationship was troubled.

'Hero darling, I'd love to keep chatting but your father's taking me out for dinner to the new Bollywood-themed restaurant that's opened up around the corner.'

'Good lord, the suburbs just keep getting more and more frightening.'

'Don't be cheeky. I suppose you're off to somewhere extremely fashionable tonight, Miss Glamarama?'

For one horrible moment, Hero actually felt a sharp stabbing pain in her heart. 'Naturally,' she replied weakly. 'Have fun. Don't let Dad try to sing. Or belly dance.'

'I can't promise anything. Between the pagodas and Bollywood-themed restaurants, life was much calmer when he was working, I'll tell you that much.'

She rang off and Hero desolately flicked through the TV channels before wandering into the kitchen in search of dinner, but the cupboards were bare and she wasn't in the mood for toast. She dialled the number of her favourite Thai takeaway place, only to be put on hold for ten minutes and then actively discouraged from ordering as the wait would be over two hours. Apparently there were lots of couples too busy having outrageous Valentine's Day sex to get dressed and leave the house in search of food, or perhaps Hero's neighbourhood was populated by lonely people too ashamed to leave the house by themselves. Either way it was depressing.

She hung up and sat there gnawing on her bottom lip for several minutes. Then she lifted her head defiantly. Goddammit, why shouldn't she go out? She was hungry. She was going to get takeaway. She was in a relationship, even though she was alone on Valentine's Day. There was no reason for her not to be out in public.

Twenty minutes later, Hero was perched uncomfortably on a high stool in a horrible noodle shop and bitterly regretting her decision. On the plus side, the restaurant boasted only three counter stools and was thus mercifully bereft of loved-up couples. The downside was the only other customer in the shop, an overweight middle-aged bloke in a stained T-shirt, who alternated between leering at Hero and slurping his noodle soup in a manner that he apparently believed to be sexually suggestive but in fact forcibly reminded her of the time her toilet had been blocked.

Hero averted her gaze from noodle-soup man's coriander-flecked teeth to the street outside. At that exact moment a beautiful couple passed by, the type who wouldn't look out of place in an advertisement for Glamorous Couples Whom Others Want To Be Like. Holding hands, they glanced briefly into the noodle shop. And then, with a flex of the biceps from him and a flick of shiny hair from her, they were gone. For perhaps the first time in her life Hero truly empathised with Cupid, filled as she was with the burning desire to shoot all happy couples with a bow and arrow.

Feeling truly pathetic, Hero tried to project an air of 'I have a boy-friend who is working at his very busy and important job and we don't believe in the commercialisation of love', which was an excessively hard thing to carry off without the aid of a customised T-shirt.

Resorting to the desperate defence of insecure-in-public people everywhere, Hero pulled out her mobile phone. She rang Pelham's work number and to her relief went straight through to his voicemail; he hated being disturbed when he was staying late at work, which she could completely understand.

'Hello darling, it's me,' she said, in a tone a trifle louder than normal. She tried to ignore the fact that both the counter attendant and the fat guy were looking at her with vague interest. 'I'm just picking up some dinner and then I'll be home. Okay, love you. 'Bye.' She snapped her phone shut with a sense of Mobile Phone Euphoria, that strange satisfaction born of having proved to complete strangers that you have an active social life. Her euphoria was short-lived, however, as the counter guy was now looking at her with a narrowed, suspicious gaze.

'You only ordered one prawn pad Thai,' he said accusingly. 'That's not enough for two.'

'Yes. I mean, I know. We're not that hungry. That is, I'm not that hungry. Pelham, my boyfriend, will probably eat most of it. He loves Thai food. How much do I owe you?'

'It's not enough for two,' the counter guy repeated. 'You want some rice? Maybe a curry?'

'No, really, this will be fine.' Hero thrust a twenty-dollar bill at him. As he continued to withhold her order, she added in exasperation, 'We're getting pizza, too.'

'You're eating noodles *and* pizza?' he asked, clearly disgusted. Even the fat guy paused in his chewing long enough to look repulsed by Hero's gluttony.

'Yes,' Hero said desperately, snatching the bag from his grasp. 'May I *please* just have my change?'

The counter guy drew the coins slowly from the till. 'But you're not getting a Hawaiian pizza, are you?' he asked. Hero saw the cook poke his head out from the kitchen to listen in. The counter guy's tone changed to pleading. 'You wouldn't combine prawn pad Thai with *pineapple* pizza?'

The cook was making his way out of the kitchen now and Hero grasped her takeaway bag more firmly, terrified that it would be taken away by an enraged cook who considered her a culinary barbarian.

'You know what? Keep the change.' She edged her way towards the door and was startled when the fat guy grabbed her elbow.

He looked deeply into her eyes, his gaze filled with compassionate sorrow. 'Binge eating,' he whispered hoarsely. 'Trust me, darlin', it's no way to fill the emotional gaps in your personal life. *I've been there. I know.*'

Realising that she had somehow managed to convince the fat guy, the counter guy and possibly the cook that she was both pathetically lonely and had an eating disorder, Hero gave up and fled to the relative sanctuary of the DVD store.

9

The movie date

All of the new releases had already been snapped up by people who were either lonelier or more organised than Hero. She browsed amongst the shelves and had just selected a movie when she heard a voice that had become all too familiar. Peering tentatively around the corner, she stared right into the eyes of Oscar, who was looking highly amused to see her acting so secretively.

'Hello, Hero.'

'Did you follow me here?' Hero demanded.

'How could I follow you here when I was here first?' he asked, reasonably.

Hero looked at him suspiciously.

Oscar sighed and turned to the movie-store owner. 'Quentin, how long have I been coming here?'

'About eighteen months,' Quentin answered, without taking his eyes off the television bracketed to the wall. 'Most annoying customer I've ever had.'

'He means that affectionately,' Oscar explained to Hero. 'We have a taunt-based relationship.'

Quentin harrumphed but didn't look up.

'Which DVD are you getting?' Hero asked, slightly mollified.

'I'm getting three. I'm just having trouble deciding on the third.' Seeing her curious look, he said, 'I like to rent DVDs with a theme.'

'Like romantic comedies or action movies?'

Quentin snorted. 'Amateur.'

Hero did a double-take at Quentin's dismissal, and Oscar grinned as he stepped in to explain.

'Kind of. But it's slightly more sophisticated than that. For example, this week's theme is the worst-ever movies of John Travolta. See, I've got *Battlefield Earth* and *Two of a Kind*. They're easy. But the artistry comes in the final selection. Should I go for *Be Cool* or *Look Who's Talking Now*?'

'But that still doesn't explain why,' Hero said.

'Why what?'

'Why would you sit through one terrible movie featuring John Travolta, let alone three?'

Quentin and Oscar stared at her. 'Because it's this week's theme,' Oscar explained patiently.

'Yes, I realise that, but *you* choose the theme. Why can't you choose something you'd actually enjoy?'

'Because that's not the *point*,' Quentin said, in a despairing tone that quite clearly meant '*Girls!*' 'Anyone can watch a movie they *enjoy* or that's *popular*. But you have to be a *connoisseur* to draw up categories like ours and appreciate the really hard stuff.'

'You mean like the *Three Colours* trilogy or the films of Jim Jarmusch?'

'The films of Jim Jarmusch?' Quentin said contemptuously. 'Any first-year pothead film student can sit through *those* and make unintelligible comments guaranteed to impress someone who knows even less. But give them half an hour of something *really* difficult to sit through – something like the mid-nineties oeuvre of Jennifer Lopez, for example – and all of a sudden you're Stephen Hawking trying to explain string theory to the current crop of *Big Brother* housemates.'

Practically purple from this outburst, Quentin turned his back on Hero, leaving Oscar to intervene diplomatically. 'Sorry. It's something Quentin feels very passionate about. I guess what he's trying to say is that watching these moves is like being one of those people who read nineteenth-century Russian novels or William Faulkner. They're not actually enjoying difficult prose, they're enjoying the sensation of having to slog through something not many people really understand.'

'You're comparing *Battlefield Earth* to *War and Peace?*'

'Oh sure. You're all friggin' postmodernists in *theory*,' Quentin erupted. 'But put a genuine crossover genre film in the DVD player, something like *Santa with Muscles* —'

'Hulk Hogan plays an evil millionaire with amnesia who thinks he's Santa Claus,' Oscar interjected, for Hero's benefit.

'— and suddenly *everyone*'s running back to the classics, wanting to watch friggin' *Citizen Kane*.' In high dudgeon, Quentin slammed the till and practically threw the DVD of *The Cook, The Thief, His Wife & Her Lover* across the counter at a frightened customer. 'That's yours until next Sunday,' he yelled as they scurried away. 'And I don't want it returned a minute before!'

Hero had been coming to this DVD store for years, and while she had never exchanged more than minimal conversation with Quentin, she had once witnessed his scathing attack on a hapless customer who had enquired after the availability of *Coffee and Cigarettes*. She couldn't remember Quentin's entire tirade but it had definitely involved the allegation that Steve Buscemi's presence in a movie didn't automatically guarantee friggin' credibility, and had culminated in Quentin wondering why the customer was in Quentin's DVD store when clearly they should be at friggin' Sundance attempting to insert their head up Harvey Keitel's fundament.

'What other categories have you had?' Hero asked, once Quentin had more or less returned to his normal colour.

'Films featuring a former celebrity couple that are almost as crap as *Gigli*.'

'Gratuitous use of Chloe Sevigny,' Quentin contributed.

'Canadian ice-skating films.'

'Nineteen seventy-five to eighty-three,' Quentin reminded him.

'And thinly veiled fictional musical bio-pics featuring pop stars. Like *Glitter* with Mariah Carey, and Britney Spears in *Crossroads*. So you can see, Hero, there's a high level of skill involved in choosing both the theme and the movies that will represent that theme. Hence my dilemma,' Oscar finished.

Hero regained her power of speech following the revelation that anyone had voluntarily sat through *Glitter* and *Crossroads*. 'I still don't see your problem. Why wouldn't you choose *Michael*?' There was dead silence as Quentin and Oscar looked at each other with chagrin, and then at Hero with growing respect. 'It's not only one of John Travolta's worst movies,' Hero continued, 'it's one of the biggest stinkers of all time.'

'She's right,' Quentin admitted. '*Michael* is much, much worse than *Be Cool*.'

With this sorted out, Hero placed the DVD of the horror flick *Saw* on the counter and opened her wallet.

'Cheerful choice for Valentine's Day,' Oscar commented, glancing at the gruesome cover image of a rotting severed leg.

'I can't believe you're not at home flicking between channels,' Hero said, by way of response. 'There's a choice of *Love Actually*, *Amélie* and the entire back catalogue of Tom Hanks and Meg Ryan movies. It's like Barbara Cartland wrote the television guide.'

'Is it just Valentine's Day you're against or do you spend Easter shooting bunny rabbits?' Oscar enquired politely, as Quentin, having finished Hero's transaction, picked up a pile of DVDs for re-shelving and disappeared.

Hero smiled sweetly. 'Oh, I think it's just Valentine's Day. There's something about the commercialisation of love and romance that's just so repugnant, don't you think?'

He acknowledged her barb with a glint in his eye but refused to take the bait. 'So what are you doing now?'

'What does it look like I'm doing? I'm going home to watch a movie.'

'By yourself?' he asked, glancing at the lone noodle box in her bag.

'Yes. Pelham's working.'

To Hero's immense relief, Oscar didn't comment on the fact that she wasn't celebrating Valentine's Day with Pelham. Instead he said, 'Why don't you watch my movies with me? That way you can understand for yourself the joy of something so bad, it's good.'

'I'm not going back to your place,' Hero said firmly.

'Fine. We can go back to yours.'

'No, we can't. Sunday has a date, and if they come back to our place, I want to disappear into my room and give them some space and privacy.'

'I could always leave straightaway,' Oscar offered.

Hero shook her head. 'Not the point. He might be embarrassed to see you at all.'

'Why would Sunday's date be embarrassed to see me?'

'Because Sunday's date is your gorilla-gram.'

'Your friend Sunday is dating my gorilla?' Oscar seemed nonplussed that he had been outmanoeuvred by a singing telegram.

'Yep.'

'But – but I can't even get you to accept flowers or watch a movie with me and *he*'s already out for dinner with her and is probably going to end up back at your place?'

'Yep.'

'Huh.' Oscar reflected on this for a moment and then concluded, in a tone of deepest respect, 'The sneaky little chimp.'

'Well, it was nice seeing you,' Hero said, picking up her horror movie.

'Wait a sec. Just give me one minute, okay?'

'But why – oh, for heaven's sake.' Hero exhaled exasperatedly as Oscar raced down the end of the store, where he had a vigorous exchange with Quentin. He was beaming with triumph when he returned.

'Okay. It's all sorted. We can watch the movies here.'

'Where, here?'

'Here, here,' Oscar said, indicating the large plasma screen at the back of the store. 'Quentin's got some beanbags out the back that we can use.'

'You want me to watch bad John Travolta movies in a *DVD store* with you?'

'Why not? You got something better to do?' Oscar asked. He disappeared out the back, presumably in search of beanbags.

With a sigh, Hero realised that she didn't.

Oscar hauled out two beanbags, looking pleased to find her still waiting. 'Excellent. You don't have a spare pair of chopsticks, do you? The smell of those noodles is driving me crazy.'

* ✱ *

Oscar heaved a contented sigh as *Two of a Kind* came to an end.

'It's a good thing the future of the Earth doesn't depend on *us* falling in love,' he remarked, helping himself to another handful of popcorn. 'Or you'd be responsible for the destruction of the entire planet.'

'Why would it be my fault?'

'Because I'm already in love with you,' he pointed out. 'The loss of life as we know it wouldn't be *my* fault.'

Hero sat up as straight as it was possible to sit in a beanbag. 'You can't be in love with me! You don't know anything about me.'

'You think if I find out your favourite colour is purple, I won't love you?'

'Don't be so simplistic. I mean that you don't know what my values are, what I want from the future, how I behave when I'm sad or angry.'

'Are you kidding? "Angry" is about the only mode I ever see you in.'

'Exactly! So why would you find that attractive?'

Oscar shrugged. 'I like the way you get angry. I like that you blow up. I can't stand people who go quiet and simmer away resentfully but never tell you what they're really feeling.'

Hero took a deep breath, determined not to explode again, since that would apparently only deepen his affection. 'Can't you see that what you feel for me is a kind of . . . infatuation?' She blushed as she articulated the final word, feeling deeply arrogant at saying it aloud. She pushed on. 'It's not based on anything *real*.'

'I know what both of us felt in New York,' he said stubbornly.

Hero seized on the flaw in his argument. 'But that was two years ago, and that night I wasn't being me. I was acting completely out of character. I never do crazy things like that, and you do them all the time, so that's why you think we're suitable when really we're completely incompatible.'

'It was definitely you that night, so obviously you do act crazy sometimes. Now do me a favour and just answer yes or no to the following questions. Have you ever wanted to get married?'

'Yes. No. I don't know. It depends on whether I meet the right person or not. It's not a lifestyle choice, like saying that one day I'm going to learn how to scuba dive. I don't think it's something you can plan, because it's completely contingent on meeting your soul mate.'

'Fair enough. Do you want kids?'

'Same answer. I don't understand women who say they're going to be mothers some day. I don't see how you can know, when for me it's dependent upon meeting the person that I want to have kids *with*.'

'Okay. And finally, what's your favourite colour?'

'Purple.'

'Liar.'

'Green,' she admitted.

'What kind of green? Olive? Emerald? Moss?'

'Sea green. Is the inquisition over now?'

'Yep.' He sat back, looking satisfied.

'I don't know why you're looking so smug. You haven't learnt anything remotely insightful about me.'

'Ah, but that's where you're wrong. Now I know quite a bit about you, and I'm even more convinced that we're alike.'

'Your favourite colour is sea green?' Hero asked, in a deeply sarcastic tone.

Oscar shook his head. 'Nope. But we're both hopeful romantics.'

'Romantic? *Me?* You must be out of your mind.'

'Of course you're a romantic. You don't want either marriage or children unless it's with your soul mate. If that's not romantic idealism, I don't know what is.'

'There are a lot of women who don't want marriage or children,' Hero said crossly.

'Yes, but that's not what you said. You said that you only want them as a natural consequence of finding The One.'

'So what?'

'So, Hero, not everyone is like that. We all know lots of people who are certain that they're going to get married and have children one day. They see it as part of life's natural progression, a certainty. And while I'm not saying those marriages are all loveless, I do know that not everyone sees true love as a rarity. Whereas we do. So in that respect, at least, I think we're well suited.'

Hero was silent as he pressed 'play' on the remote control again.

'And by the way, my favourite colour is blue.' Oscar grinned. 'Sea blue.'

10

Like de-hairing the bath plughole

'So how did your date with Toby end up?' Hero asked Sunday over a leisurely breakfast the next morning.

A besotted smile crept across Sunday's face. 'Lovely,' she sighed. 'He sang for me at the end of the night.'

'In the restaurant?' Hero asked, startled.

'Nope. In the dark. When we got home.' She hesitated, and added confidentially, 'He has a stage-fright problem.'

Hero wasn't quite sure how to respond to this confidence. It seemed like far too much intimate information regarding a person she had last seen wearing a gorilla suit and singing her a love song. 'Does he know what causes his, er, stage-fright problem?' she ventured, not really wanting to pursue the conversation but feeling that it was her duty to be supportive of Sunday. 'Does it happen when he drinks alcohol?'

Sunday shook her head vigorously. 'Oh no. Alcohol actually helps him overcome it. I think it's just excessive shyness.'

'Oh. Well, you probably just need to get to know each other better. When he's more relaxed, I'm sure he'll be able to . . . perform.'

'That's what I told him. Just relax and let it come naturally.'

To Hero's great relief, Sunday changed the topic, which was just as well considering she wasn't quite sure how much more detail she could handle on the topic of Toby's impotency.

'So what did you end up doing?'

Hero fidgeted uncomfortably. 'I, er, watched some movies.' She cleared her throat. 'With Oscar.'

Sunday's head snapped up. '*You spent Valentine's Day with Oscar?*'

'It was Valentine's Night. Not the same,' Hero mumbled.

'Don't quibble. God, he is *really* good, isn't he?' Sunday said admiringly. 'I mean, I know he's a professional and all, but still, you've got to hand it to him.'

'You make it sound as though he's some sort of puppet master pulling my strings,' Hero snapped. 'I was bored. I watched some movies with him. With a chaperone. It was about as romantic as de-hairing the bath plughole.'

'Did he see you home?'

'Yes,' Hero replied unwillingly. 'But that's just good manners.'

'Did he kiss you goodnight at the door?'

'He kissed me on the cheek. My aunts kiss me on the cheek.'

'Your aunts don't look like Oscar. Did he try to talk you into a relationship?'

'Yes,' Hero admitted. 'But it was a good thing, because I was able to make my points clearly and concisely. The whole night was completely platonic and I really think he finally got the message.'

'Uh-huh. Correct me if I'm wrong but you celebrated Valentine's Day with Oscar, *not* Pelham, he's still intent on having a relationship with you and he walked you home and kissed you goodnight.'

'It wasn't like that,' Hero said irritably. 'You make it sound far worse than it is.'

'It doesn't sound bad to me. It sounds lovely, actually. But all I am saying is that you're kidding yourself if you think Oscar's given up. This isn't over by a long shot.'

✳

On Monday morning Oscar strolled into reception at Serendipity to find Jake draped over the desk, sharing an early morning coffee and muffin with Beth. 'Stop chatting up my receptionist,' he said sternly.

'She's my receptionist, too,' Jake protested.

'Oh. So she is. Well, in that case, stop chatting up our receptionist.'

'I like being chatted up by him,' Beth objected.

'You do?' Jake asked, a little too quickly.

Beth looked startled at being taken seriously but recovered her composure immediately. 'Of course I do.'

Oscar, whistling as he rifled through his mail, was listening with only half an ear. 'That's not fair,' he said. 'When I suggested to Beth that we should marry one another if we're both still single by the time I'm forty —'

'I reminded you that when you turned forty, I'd be fifty-three,' Beth said kindly. 'And by that time you'd be too far past your prime for me. If I'm still single when I'm fifty, I want a toyboy. Preferably Jake Gyllenhaal.'

'Why is it that our Jake gets away with murder and I'm always on the receiving end of your Mary Poppins act?' Oscar complained.

Beth laughed. 'Because, my darling, I have known you for far too long, and Jake is a proper grown-up. Now stop sulking and tell us how your weekend was.'

Oscar promptly brightened. 'I spent Valentine's Day night with Hero.'

Jake spluttered into his coffee. 'You did *what*?'

Oscar nodded, beaming. 'We went to the movies. Kind of.'

Jake was eyeing him with undisguised envy. 'How the hell do you go from having a woman threaten you with a restraining order to manipulating her into spending Valentine's Day with you?'

'I didn't *manipulate* her. She spent time with me of her own free will.'

Seeing that Jake had lost all power of speech, Beth stepped in. 'So how did it go?'

'We saw three movies,' he related eagerly. '*Michael, Battlefield Earth* and *Two of a Kind*.'

'Sweet Jesus and Mary, the Holy Mother of God, you made her sit through one of your insane DVD nights? Is she still talking to you?'

'I think so. And Quentin thought she liked me second best after him, so that's a positive sign.'

'Who's Quentin?' asked Beth, puzzled.

'The DVD store owner. We watched the movies in his store.'

'Let me get this straight. Instead of taking Hero to a cinema to see the latest-release romantic comedy, plying her with popcorn and trying to slip your arm around her shoulders in time-honoured fashion, you convinced her to watch bad John Travolta movies *in a DVD store*?'

'Yep,' Oscar said proudly. 'It's progress, don't you think?'

Beth and Jake stared at him in disbelief.

'I think Hero felt rushed at the start when I sent her flowers and came on too strong,' Oscar said reflectively. 'Now I'm trying to back off a bit and get to know her again, as a friend. But the best bit is, even though we're just friends, I can still tick the movie date off my list. So I really feel like it's all working out to plan.' He leant over the desk, grabbed a muffin, smiled at them and departed for his office.

They watched him go in silence.

'Do you think we should try to stop him?' Jake asked finally.

'Probably. Any idea how?'

'Nope. I need a drink.'

'It's eight thirty in the morning!'

'That doesn't change the fact that I need a drink.'

'Oh, fine. There's a bottle of whiskey in the kitchen cupboard. We can turn these into Irish coffees.'

11

The dinner date

'Sunday, we're going to have a dinner party,' Hero announced on Wednesday morning, entering the living room with a pile of cookbooks in her arms.

Sunday put down the illustrated copy of *The Kama Sutra*, which had mysteriously appeared on her bedside table, and looked curiously at Hero, who was flicking through the topmost recipe book. 'Sure, but what's brought this on?'

'Well, partly it's for Pelham. We're forever going to his work functions and out for dinner with his friends. It's about time he made more of an effort with my friends.' She paused, and then added, casually, 'And I'm inviting Oscar.'

Sunday sat bolt upright. 'You're inviting *Oscar*?'

'Yep.'

'Oh. Okay then. When is this dinner?'

'I thought maybe this Saturday night, if everyone's free at such short notice. But aren't you going to ask me why I'm inviting Oscar?' Hero asked, nettled.

'I assumed you'd given in to him.'

'What does that mean? If I'd given in to him, I'd be dating him, and I can't date Oscar, because I'm in a relationship with Pelham!'

'No, I suppose you can't,' Sunday said regretfully.

'You sound like you want me to date him.'

'Well, he can be very charming.'

'*Charming*? He's practically a stalker.'

'You're the one inviting him to a dinner party,' Sunday pointed out. 'Stalkers don't usually receive invitations, as far as I'm aware.' Her brow furrowed as she thought this through. 'Hero, why *are* you inviting him?'

Hero smirked. 'I thought it might be nice if he met Pelham. Don't you see? At the moment Pelham isn't a real person to Oscar. As soon as they meet and he realises that my relationship with Pelham is real, he'll back off.'

'And he'll probably be intimidated by Pelham,' Sunday said shrewdly.

Hero shrugged. 'That's his problem. So do you want to come with me to the fish market on Saturday morning? I'll do the cooking.'

Sunday sighed. There was trouble ahead, not the least of which would involve Hero trying to cook. She just knew it.

* ✱ *

Hero was somewhat taken aback when she rang Oscar to invite him to the dinner party. She had rung during her lunchbreak, expecting at least ten minutes of barbed comments, but instead Oscar said calmly that it sounded very pleasant and asked whether she would prefer him to bring red or white wine.

'Er, either is fine. Look, you do realise that Pelham will be there, don't you?'

'Naturally. I'm looking forward to meeting him. Would it be rude if I brought someone, too?'

'You want to bring a *date*?' Hero asked, incredulous.

'Yes. Why? Do you mind?' Oscar sounded amused.

'Of course I don't mind,' Hero scrambled out. 'I'm just – surprised, I guess.'

'Oh well, life goes on,' Oscar said cheerily. 'You can't always get what you want, as the Stones said. See you at seven on Saturday, then.'

Hero hung up, slightly dazed. She sat thinking for a moment and then dialled Sunday's number.

'He's bringing a date?' Sunday repeated in amazement, exactly as Hero had done moments before.

Hero nodded, quite forgetting that Sunday couldn't see her.

'I wonder what she'll be like,' Sunday said thoughtfully.

Hero had been wondering exactly the same thing but she held her tongue, waiting to hear Sunday's views.

'I mean, he's so bizarre. He's likely to bring anyone from a professional pole dancer to an Amish milkmaid.'

Although Hero privately agreed with this sentiment, she couldn't help feeling a little insulted. 'He's had a crush on me,' she said pointedly, 'and I'm not a pole dancer or a milkmaid.'

'Sorry, Hero. But you know what I mean. I'm just worried that with Pelham there, well, it could get nasty.'

'What on earth do you mean by that? Pelham is never rude to anyone. He has impeccable manners!'

'Yes, I know, it's just . . .' Sunday bit her lip, wondering how to extricate herself from the conversational mire. 'He's just not very good with people who aren't from his own social circle. You know that he's not.'

Hero's innate honesty made it impossible for her to refute this comment. She decided to change the subject. 'Is Toby coming?'

'Of course. He said he'd make dessert, if we wanted.'

'He's too good to be true.'

'I know,' Sunday said happily.

✷

Strolling around the Sydney Fish Market early on Saturday morning, Sunday, Toby and Hero did their best to knowledgeably assess the freshness of the tuna fillets.

'It's just so different seeing tuna out of a can,' Hero observed.

'Did you remember to check whether Oscar or his date are vegetarian or allergic to anything?' Sunday asked, as the fishmonger handed over a parcel of succulent oysters.

Hero looked immensely proud of herself. 'Would you believe that I did? There's not a single vegetarian, vegan or vegaquarian amongst us. Oscar is allergic to mussels, but apart from that we could serve up chilli con carne made with horse meat and apparently everyone would tuck in.'

'Please tell me you're not making chilli con carne with horse meat,' Sunday begged.

'Of course I'm not. We're going to have oysters to begin and then —' Hero stopped. She was planning on serving oysters, lobster and then strawberries, in a kind-hearted attempt to stimulate what she believed to be Toby's depressed libido. But she didn't want to embarrass either Toby or Sunday by making it obvious. 'It's a surprise,' she finished lamely. 'But I'm making lots of Pelham's favourites.'

'This will be the first time I've met Pelham properly,' Toby mused, as Hero moved off to examine some lobsters.

'Lucky you,' muttered Sunday.

'What's wrong with him?'

'You mean apart from the fact that he's a venture capitalist and lives on the North Shore and drives one of those hideous tank-like four-wheel drives and voted for One Nation?'

Seeing that Toby was still looking confused, Sunday checked to make sure Hero was out of earshot and then elaborated. 'He can be a bit, well, not rude exactly. He's just . . . he's like a poison dart. He somehow manages to deflate you and leave toxic little doubts in your mind.'

'But if he's so horrible, what does Hero see in him?' Toby asked, perplexed.

Sunday peered at a display of crayfish and made an unimpressive attempt to assess qualities of crayfish-desirability. 'Oh, he's not that bad all the time, I suppose. It's more that he's the sort of guy Hero thinks she *should* be with.'

'What does that mean?'

'Just that Hero always plays by the rules. You haven't met her family yet, but when you do, it'll make sense. Her parents are great but they were the only hippies in our suburb when we were growing up. Hero rebelled against them by dressing conservatively and taking a corporate job. And then she met Elliott.'

Toby shrank back as an octopus eyeballed him from its tank. 'Who's Elliott?'

'Hero's ex-boyfriend. They were together for two years. He was great. Funny and romantic and crazy. Hero's parents *loved* him.

Everyone loved him. He was always whisking her away on surprise trips and writing lovely messages on our bathroom mirror in lipstick for her to find.' Sunday sighed wistfully at the memories. 'Actually, now I think of it, the lipstick was bloody hard to get off. We used to spend a fortune on Windex. And Hero almost got sacked once after Elliott baked chocolate-chip cookies for her to take into *Angel* for morning-tea. Chocolate-chip *hash* cookies. Apparently the entire office spent the rest of the day staring at their screen savers. Luckily Sasha, Hero's boss, had some sort of brilliant brainwave for the next edition while she was stoned off her head so Hero got off lightly. But apart from things like that, it was a lot of fun having Elliott around.'

'So what happened to him?' asked Toby, wondering where he could buy a washable crayon to leave a message on Sunday's bathroom mirror.

Sunday made a face. 'Hero found out that he was having a lot of fun all around the place. In the most dramatic way possible.'

'That's horrible.' Toby looked compassionately over at Hero, who was making her way back through the crowd, clutching a parcel.

Sunday nodded. 'It was. She was a mess. I had to drag her away for a holiday in New York just to make her smile again. And then about a year later she started going out with Pelham. He's definitely not perfect, but after Elliott I can see why Hero would think he's the sort of guy she should be with. And I think that makes her happier than stopping to think about what sort of a person he really is.'

'Where do you get the time to figure things like this out?' Toby asked in awe.

Sunday laughed and kissed him lightly on the nose. 'It's all perfectly obvious if you love someone enough to take the time to look. And I'll tell you something else that's obvious to me, Tobes. I don't think I'm the only one who understands Hero. He might not know about Elliott, but I have the feeling that Oscar has her figured out as well.'

Hero entered the dining room in response to Sunday's increasingly loud groans. 'What's the matter?'

Toby was stacking beers in the fridge, while the rest of their guests were expected at any second.

Sunday was staring at the dining table in despair. 'It's the seating arrangements. They're impossible.'

'Why? Just do boy, girl and don't seat couples next to each other.'

Sunday shook her head. 'It's not going to work, Hero. No matter which way you look at it, it's a disaster. I keep ending up with Oscar next to Pelham, or you next to Oscar's date. And then I switch places around but you end up across the table from Oscar and you'll have to look straight at him and that's probably worse.' She threw herself face down on the couch, her muffled voice resolute. 'There's nothing for it. We're going to have to get new friends.'

Hero took control. 'I'll do the seating. You sit there and fold the napkins into swans or something.'

Sunday grimaced but consented to fiddle with the napkins while Hero calmly sorted through the seating arrangements.

The doorbell rang and Hero went to open it. She felt a jolt in the region of her stomach as Oscar smiled and kissed her cheek.

'Hero, I'd like you to meet someone.'

Oscar's date stepped forward. Hero braced herself and then blinked. She was looking into the pleasant face of a woman in her early sixties.

The woman held out her hand and shook Hero's. 'I'm Jean. Oscar's mum.'

It was at this point that Hero began to have the distinct feeling that her dinner party was not going to go according to plan. At least, not according to *her* plan.

Oscar beamed at her, as though bringing one's mother to a dinner party was perfectly normal practice.

Hero politely ushered them inside and introduced Jean to Sunday, enabling her to promptly round on Oscar and have a fierce but short argument in undertones.

'I know what you're up to!'

He tried to look innocent. 'I wanted you to meet my mum. It's worked out perfectly really, because I wasn't sure how to get you over to her house.'

'You took advantage of my invitation to manipulate me into meeting your parents.'

'Just Mum,' he pointed out. 'My dad passed away several years ago.'

'Oh,' she said, thrown off course by this disclosure. 'I'm very sorry.'

'Me too. He would have liked you a lot.'

'Whether he would have liked me or vice versa is beside the point. Now listen —' At that moment the doorbell rang again. Unwilling to end the discussion, Hero beckoned for Sunday to answer the door.

Greeting Pelham, Sunday was dismayed, as always, to feel a slight chill in the air. Intending to kiss his cheek, she instead held out her hand, and then wished she hadn't as she instantly felt formal and awkward. *Why* couldn't she behave like herself around Hero's boyfriend?

'Sunday.' Pelham nodded, proffering a bottle of expensive wine.

'Nice to see you again. It's always a pleasure to visit this part of the world.'

Sunday felt the familiar stiffening of her smile that always happened around Pelham. 'You live in Mosman. It's only over the bridge from Tamarama. This is your part of the world,' Sunday said, as politely as she was able.

'You know what I mean. As far as I'm concerned they should pull up the drawbridge and never let it down again.' He winked to show he was joking and Sunday wondered why it was that people who were offensive and then made out it was a joke were even more offensive than those who were just blatantly rude.

'So how are things in the pre-Christian era?'

'Fine, thank you,' Sunday answered politely. 'How's work?'

Pelham smiled. 'Oh, you know. Puttering along. Managed to make several million for my elders and betters last week in a nice little lever-aged buy-out, so things could be worse. You know, I envy you scholarly types. Us poor drones in business have to deal with the real world. I often think it would be nice to avoid it the way you do.'

He moved up the hall, leaving Sunday practically choking. Avoid the real world? Try having to pay your rent and bills every month on an academic salary *and* trying to conduct research and teach with virtually no funding but sacrificing everything anyway, simply to do something you truly love, you insufferable, sanctimonious —

Realising that she was clutching the bottle of wine so tightly she was in danger of breaking it, she breathed deeply and tried to concentrate on how much she loved Hero.

'Sun?' Toby poked his head in to the hall. He was looking rather pale. 'Are you okay?'

Sunday gave a feeble smile. 'I'm fine. You?'

'Fine. Except that Pelham just *wondered* why I was still studying *at my age*,' Toby said hollowly.

They both sighed. It was going to be a long night.

$$*\;\overset{\displaystyle *}{}\;*$$

'Pelham! Darling!' Hero flung herself at her beloved, kissing him passionately on the lips. That Pelham was utterly startled by this effusive greeting was not lost on Oscar, who grinned appreciatively and folded his arms as he leant against the mantelpiece.

'Pelham, this is Oscar Martin, a . . . friend of mine from a long time ago. Oscar, this is my boyfriend, Pelham Grenville-Walters.'

'Pleasure to meet you, Pelham,' Oscar said, pumping away at Pelham's hand. 'Any friend of Hero's is welcome in our home.'

'In whose home?' Pelham asked, puzzled by this unorthodox greeting, while Hero seethed at Oscar's making it sound as though he was the host.

'My home. My mother's home. Anyone remotely acquainted with me, really.'

'Oh. Well, thank you. Have we met before?'

'I don't think so.'

'It's odd. I can't place your face but your name sounds very familiar.'

Before Oscar could answer, Hero intervened. 'Would you like a drink, Pelham?' She adopted her best hostess manner. 'A scotch on the rocks? Or maybe a gin martini?'

Oscar, who had been handed a beer without ceremony, grinned at Hero's attempt to offer suitably businessman-like drinks.

'Just a Perrier for me, thanks.'

'We don't have any Perrier,' Sunday said blankly.

'Well, Evian is fine.'

Sunday sorrowfully shook her head. 'You know we only have tap water. But if I get it from the bathroom tap, it does have a lovely sparkly quality. It might be the result of pollution but that's the kind of thing you have to put up with when you come out to this part of the world.'

Hero hastily dragged Sunday to a corner. 'Stop it,' she scolded. 'You're deliberately trying to stir him up.'

Sunday scowled. 'All right, but I swear if he so much as mentions his "shack" at Whale Beach, I'm going to talk very loudly about female underarm hair.'

Meanwhile, Pelham was staring very hard at Oscar, trying to mentally place him. 'I know who you are,' he said slowly. 'You're the one who sent Hero flowers.'

Oscar grinned at this description of his floral effort, correctly discerning that Hero had told Pelham rather less than the entire truth. 'I didn't realise at the time that she was in a relationship,' he said, utterly untruthfully. 'Of course now I know the situation, I've abandoned the playing field.'

'Well, that's very big of you,' Pelham said, surprised by this show of sporting behaviour. 'Unlucky, eh? But that's the way it goes. I won the toss, you could say.'

'Absolutely. I stepped up to the crease and made a good innings but you were already first past the post,' Oscar said solemnly, mixing his sporting metaphors with glorious abandon.

Pelham shrugged. 'Luckily it never went to a tie-break because I think I had the advantage.'

'No, no, there was never any question of a tie-break. It was always going to be a love match.'

'That's really very good,' Pelham said admiringly, while Oscar tried to look modest.

Neither of them had noticed that Hero was having an apoplectic fit at being discussed in terms of sporting metaphors. A minor tussle ensued, in which they both tried to shake the other's hand in as masculine a manner as possible, while maintaining eye contact and smiling.

'Oysters, Toby?' Hero asked loudly, holding out the plate. 'No, take more than one. Take as many as you like. Here, let me.' To Toby's bemusement she piled a stack of oysters onto a plate and pushed him firmly into a chair. 'Eat them all,' she instructed sternly, leaving him clutching his small fork in terror.

'So you're a Waratahs man, Plum?' Oscar asked casually, much as one Freemason might grip another's hand, testing for a secret handshake. 'You don't mind if I call you Plum, do you?'

Pelham minded very much but he'd already brightened at the mention of his favourite rugby team. After they had discussed the team's chance of winning the cup now that someone or other had a crippling groin injury, Pelham was led to reminisce about his own similar injury, sustained during his playing days at the King's School.

They were getting along famously and Pelham was well on the way to considering Oscar a very decent bloke, an impression that was unfortunately derailed by the next topic.

'So Plum, how's work?' asked Oscar, in his heartiest, most blokey voice, noting with satisfaction that Hero, engaged in distracted conversation with Jean, was trying her hardest to eavesdrop.

Pelham tried to look modest and failed utterly. 'Busy. Crucial. Stimulating. All the things you'd expect when you handle tens of millions of dollars a day and help to keep the capitalist system afloat. What do you do, Martin?'

'I play Cupid,' Oscar said soulfully.

'What?' Pelham looked startled and then regained his composure. 'Oh, that's right. You're a friend of Toby's, aren't you? He came around here in a gorilla suit once. Horrible sight. Not the sort of thing one wants to see first thing on a Saturday morning before breakfast.' Pelham mused distractedly on the memory of Toby in his gorilla suit and then roused himself with a small shake. 'So he's a gorilla and you're – Cupid, did you say?'

'Yes. Or Eros, if you prefer the classical Greek name.'

'So you, er, dress up as a sort of winged cherub?' Pelham was making a valiant attempt to sound casual, but the incredulity and disdain in his voice were apparent.

'No, no, no,' Oscar chided. 'The childlike Cupid is a later invention. Eros was somewhere between a god and a man, you know.'

'Ah. I see. If you'll excuse me, I have to —' Pelham looked around the room wildly. Hero was still talking to Jean, and he realised that there wasn't anyone else he wanted to talk to.

'Go to the bathroom?' Oscar supplied helpfully.

'Exactly,' Pelham said, seizing the chance to make his escape.

12

The recalcitrance of donkeys

Midway through the main course, Pelham suddenly put down his cutlery and gazed at Oscar with a look of pure delight. '*That*'s why your name sounded familiar!' he announced, startling everyone into silence. 'Instead of carrying on with all that Cupid stuff, why didn't you tell me that you're Oscar Martin, the owner of Serendipity?' Pelham was hale and hearty once again, confident now that he was with a peer.

Hero stared at Oscar, her fork suspended. 'You *own* Serendipity?'

'I co-own the company, with my partner Jake,' Oscar admitted.

'Started it up with Jake only eighteen months ago,' Jean said proudly. 'They've been a huge success right from the word go.'

'But I thought —' Hero bit back her words, furious with Oscar for letting her believe that he was the odd-job boy.

'I read an article about you two in the *Financial Review*.' Pelham smiled warmly at Oscar. 'You're doing very well for yourselves, I understand. Ve-ry well indeed.'

Hero cringed. There was no way around it – Pelham was *fawning*. To Hero's great relief, Oscar made no response other than a polite nod.

Pelham's new-found toadiness was bad enough; she didn't think she could survive the humiliation of Oscar rebuffing him as well.

'More wine, Pelham?' Hero interjected, anxious to change the subject.

He looked at her quizzically. 'My glass is full. So Martin, any plans to open up interstate branches? How much moolah is in this romance caper anyway?'

'Moolah?' Oscar enquired, one brow rising fractionally.

Pelham nodded. 'Yes. Does it have legs? Is it a marathon or a sprint?'

'I haven't the faintest idea what you're talking about.'

Pelham looked crestfallen at Oscar's inability to understand his business slang, and Hero seized the moment to again divert the conversation. When everyone was safely occupied with a different topic, she said, in an undertone, 'Pelham? Could you please not talk about business tonight?'

'Don't be ridiculous. That company's worth a fortune. He ought to have it valued properly. I could set him up with a partner and in a couple of years Serendipity would list at ten times its current value. He ought to be grateful for my advice.'

'It's rude to enquire into the financial affairs of anyone, let alone someone you hardly know,' Hero whispered, in agony.

Pelham, who prided himself on his manners and breeding, patted her arm. 'Hero, it's *business*. Trust me, your friend understands. And if he knows what's good for him, he'll listen to me. Being a glorified flower-seller won't last forever.'

Appalled, Hero realised that everyone had heard what Pelham had said. Oscar opened his mouth to shoot back a reply, but Hero cast him such a mute look of pleading that he stayed silent.

Slightly discomfited from having been overheard, Pelham emitted a forced laugh. A strained silence fell over the table.

'That's a lovely photo of you two girls over there,' Jean said diplomatically, nodding at a framed photograph of Hero and Sunday that sat on the bookshelf.

Hero sent her a grateful look. 'That was taken years ago, in Greece. We must have been . . . nineteen? Twenty?'

Sunday glanced at the photo and laughed. 'We backpacked around Europe together for six months. I still have no idea how we came out of it alive.'

'I've never understood why backpacking overseas is an Australian rite of passage,' Pelham said irritably, pouring himself more wine. 'Scrimping your way around foreign countries and staying in flea-infested hostels with strangers. It sounds revolting.'

Oscar nodded in solemn agreement. 'And backpacking can be *so* pretentious.'

'Pretentious?' Hero echoed, feeling more secure now that the conversation had shifted away from Oscar's business. 'How on earth is backpacking pretentious?'

Oscar snorted. 'Staying at a five-star hotel is less pretentious than backpacking. Whenever I've backpacked, I've never met so many people who are so concerned with image and trying to outdo each other. Every conversation revolves around how long you've been travelling, the most obscure place you've been, how little you've managed to spend and the scams you've managed to pull in order to save half a euro. They don't even let you into some hostels unless you've been thrown off a train for faking something on your Eurail pass.'

Pelham had been listening in horrified fascination. 'You must be kidding.'

'I wish I was, but it's like reverse evolution. The filthier and more primitive you are, the more everyone looks up to you. At the top of the food chain is some guy who's been backpacking for eight years, bathes once a year and only eats uncooked two-minute noodles. Even though I knew I couldn't compete with the professionals, I was just starting to feel tough when the eighty-year-old nun who'd been sleeping in the top bunk bid me farewell because she was catching a ride on the roof of the overnight train to Kazakhstan, by herself. Backpacking is very bad for the self-esteem, I've decided.'

Sunday started to giggle.

'But there are compensations, of course,' Oscar continued. He paused and then said, very deliberately, 'I met the most incredible girl when I was in New York.'

Hero's fork clattered to the floor and she dived under the table. Deciding that a crisis situation called for crude measures, she jabbed the fork sharply into Oscar's calf and was pleased to hear him emit a startled yelp.

'What's wrong with you?' Jean asked, concerned.

'Hero stabbed me in the leg with her fork.'

Sitting under the table, Hero could have wept. The man had no sense of propriety whatsoever.

'Well, that's nothing to be making a song and dance about,' Jean said comfortably. 'Your father wasn't above throwing something at you if that mouth of yours got too smart for its own good. Never anything that could really hurt him,' she hastened to add, for the benefit of the others. 'Cushions, mainly. Occasionally a book or a piece of fruit.'

Oscar was too busy with his own reminiscing to pay attention to his mother's. 'The New York girl's name was Lola,' he said dreamily. 'She was a lot like the song.'

'She walked like a woman and talked like a man?' Hero said acidly, from underneath the table.

Oscar grinned. 'No. But she did have a dark-brown voice and there was something about her that made me fall to my knees the second I met her.'

Thankfully unseen, Hero's mouth formed a silent 'O!' and she had the urge to pat Oscar's leg better where she had just stabbed it.

'We were in the Meatpacking District, not SoHo,' said Sunday, trying to come to Hero's defence but belatedly realising that she had said the wrong thing.

Everyone looked at her curiously, with the exception of Hero, who was now strongly fighting the urge to stick her fork into Sunday's leg.

'I mean, *we* went out in the Meatpacking District when we visited New York,' Sunday said lamely. 'Me and Hero. Obviously not Oscar.'

'I thought you stayed in Greenwich Village?' asked Pelham.

'We did. But Oscar was talking about going out in New York. So I just thought I should point out that we didn't go out in SoHo. Unlike the song. Can someone please pass me that napkin?' asked Sunday, now sweating profusely.

In silence Toby passed her a paper napkin and Sunday started to chew on a corner, as though to prevent any further unfortunate utterances.

Pelham peered under the table at this point. 'Anything I can do, darling?'

'No, thank you,' Hero said. 'I was just trying to clean my fork on Oscar's trouser leg. I must have slipped.'

Pelham coughed delicately. 'Not really *de rigueur* to clean the utensils on your guest's clothes. Just thought I'd mention it.'

He sat back up and Hero counted to ten, then made her way out from underneath the table with as much dignity as she could muster, determinedly avoiding the beatific smile that Oscar turned in her direction.

Desperate for distraction, Hero started to clear the dirty plates, declining Jean's offer to help. 'No, really,' she said, smiling with genuine warmth at Oscar's bright-eyed mother and wondering how such a nice and apparently normal woman could have brought forth such deranged progeny. 'You're a guest. Have another glass of wine. We won't be a moment.'

Correctly interpreting the 'we' to include herself, Sunday hastily grabbed some plates and followed in Hero's wake to the kitchen.

'I'm going to *kill* him,' Hero hissed, as soon as the kitchen door had swung shut behind them. 'Bringing up the Lola thing. And *no one* calls Pelham Plum.'

'Well, no one but Oscar calls you Lola,' Sunday pointed out, trying to be fair. 'Couples always have names for each other that no one else uses,' she unfortunately added.

Hero almost threw a plate at her. '*Oscar and I are not a couple!* Nor are Oscar and Pelham! And in case you hadn't noticed, Pelham and I use each other's full names!'

'Okay, okay. Hero, just calm down. The dinner party's still achieving what you wanted, isn't it? Oscar might be Pelham's new best friend but it means that he has to accept that Pelham is a major part of your life.'

'I hope so,' Hero said, sounding unconvinced. She scrubbed furiously at a pot for a moment and then said wistfully, 'Do you remember that movie *The Last Supper*?'

'If you mean the movie where the group of friends killed the dinner guest because they wouldn't change their political beliefs by the end of the meal, then yes, I do remember it, and no, you're not allowed to kill Oscar.'

'Oh fine,' Hero sighed. 'I'll just have to hope my cooking does the job, then. And if you get the chance, can you kick Oscar before he gets any blokier with Pelham? They'll be heading outside to urinate in the bushes together before much longer.'

They broke off as Hero's nemesis entered the kitchen with the last of the dirty plates.

'I think I'll just go and check on . . . that thing,' Sunday said, grabbing dessert from the fridge and making her escape as the palpable tension in the room ratcheted up to Unbearable.

'Why are you doing the dishes now?' Oscar asked.

'I like doing the washing up. It calms me down,' Hero said, noisily rinsing the dishes.

Her self-possession was severely ruffled, however, when Oscar came right up behind her and murmured in her ear, 'Oysters, lobster, champagne and now chocolate-dipped strawberries? Are you trying to seduce me, Miss Hathaway?'

'Well, if I am, I'm trying to seduce four other people, including your mum,' Hero retorted, splashing a plate more vigorously into the sink than was warranted and trying to ignore the disastrous effect of his proximity on her composure. 'And *you* brought the champagne. As Sigmund Freud once said, sometimes a banana is just a banana. Not everyone insists on seeing the world as a romantic code waiting to be deciphered. And I happen to like seafood. As does Pelham.'

'Ah, yes. Your boyfriend.' Oscar casually leant back against the counter as he watched her. 'You know, I'm really very glad that you invited me to meet him, Hero.'

'You are?' she said uneasily. 'Why?'

'Because I had my suspicions that he wasn't right for you, and now they've been confirmed.' Hero was speechless as he continued, sadly, 'I'm afraid he really won't do for you at all.'

Hero fought the urge to throw the wet dishcloth at him. 'Based on what?'

'For starters, did you know that he has a recurring groin injury? That's bound to put a damper on things.'

Hero fought back a giggle but found herself growing rather hot under Oscar's meaningful gaze. Trying very hard not to remember what Oscar's groin area looked like, she instead demanded, 'Why did you lie to me?'

He looked genuinely surprised. 'Lie to you? I've never lied to you.'

'You bloody well did. You let me think you were an itinerant bartender and odd-job boy when all the time you're really a successful young entrepreneur.' She eyed him severely. 'I'm very disappointed in you.'

'I don't blame you. Entrepreneur is a horrible job title. It makes me sound like a white-collar criminal.' He paused and added reflectively, 'It sounds almost as bad as venture capitalist.'

She ignored the provocation. 'You led me to believe that you were carefree and adventurous and unconstrained by a conventional career, and all that time you were gunning for *BRW*'s Young Achiever award.'

'Now hold on just a minute,' he protested. 'You called me irresponsible for taking off to New York and working as a bartender. Now you find out that I own a successful company and you're still not impressed. You can't have it both ways.'

'It's not about impressing me,' Hero said sternly. 'All I'm saying is that I think your professional success shows a distinct lack of character. If you had an ounce of integrity, you'd be planning a surfing trip around Sri Lanka in a Kombi van.' And with this rather tangled verdict,

Hero grabbed a stack of bowls and marched back into the dining room, where Jean and Sunday were engaged in animated conversation, while Toby was gamely persevering with Pelham.

'You're a singer, aren't you?' Pelham demanded. 'Let's hear a song then.'

Toby flushed and cleared his throat. 'I can't right now,' he said, not meeting Pelham's gaze.

'Can't? There is no can't. There is only won't,' Pelham shot back, quoting the motivational poster that hung in his office. He would have kept his mouth shut if he had known that he was quoting Yoda, but Pelham remained in blissful ignorance of the source of most of the inspirational quotes that peppered his speech. He was inordinately fond of motivational posters boasting images of heroic firefighters battling fierce blazes or eagles soaring over mountainous landscapes, with captions like: 'Attitude determines altitude!'

Toby looked at Sunday in anguish.

'He can't strain his voice,' Sunday said, frowning at Pelham. 'He can't sing without warming up first.'

'I'm just asking for one ruddy song, not a Carnegie Hall recital!'

'I'll sing if you like,' Oscar volunteered, coming back into the room in time to accurately gauge Toby's discomfort and Pelham's truculence.

'You sing like a sheep trying to gargle,' his mother said fondly.

Oscar grinned at her, not at all discouraged. 'In that case I'll put some backing music on.' He switched on the stereo and the first chords of Marvin Gaye's 'We Got To Get It On' flooded the room. Grabbing his mother, and deaf to her protestations, he twirled her around. Laughing, Sunday pulled Toby up to join them.

Hero sat next to Pelham, who was gaping at the dancers, unsure just how the dinner party had suddenly turned into a lively dance. She smiled and clapped, miserably aware that her boyfriend wouldn't dance with her.

'I'm going to the bathroom,' Pelham said disapprovingly. He made his way stiffly past the others and Hero forced herself to look cheerful, as though she, too, was having fun.

Gasping for breath, Jean pushed her son away and flopped into her seat. 'Get away before you're the death of me,' she panted, pouring herself a glass of water.

Oscar dropped a kiss on top of her head and then held out his hand to Hero in mischievous invitation. Feeling suddenly lighter, within moments she was being dipped and twirled and she started to laugh. As the song came to an end, Oscar spun her into a backwards dip and she gazed up into his eyes, her arms clasped around his neck. Her smile died when she saw the expression in his eyes, and for a long moment they looked at each other.

Then Pelham came back into the room and the moment was over. Oscar helped Hero back up and gave her a mock bow before leading her back to her seat.

Quickly throwing out some inconsequential remark to hide the tumult of her feelings, Hero started to serve dessert. As she handed a plate to Sunday, she became conscious of Jean's gaze upon her. She glanced over and Jean looked away. Hero might have dismissed this intent look but for the fact that for the rest of the night she was aware that Oscar's mother was watching her very closely indeed.

* ✷ *

Pelham was the first guest to depart, citing the need to get up early for a round of golf the next morning. The instant Hero left the room to see him off, Toby, who was shattered after having Pelham yell incessantly at him, retreated to a corner nursing a large scotch. 'What's wrong with him? Is he deaf?'

'No,' Sunday said cheerfully, sitting on the arm of Toby's chair and draping her arms around his neck. 'He thinks you're mad.'

'*He* thinks *I'm* mad? He's been screaming at me all night!'

'Yes, I know. But Pelham is one of those people who speaks slowly and loudly to people who don't speak English. He thinks you're mentally deranged, which is about as useless as being a foreigner in Pelham's book.'

'But why does he think I'm deranged?'

'Oh, because you sang to me in a gorilla suit,' Sunday said airily.

'I didn't sing to you, I sang to Hero. And anyway, that's my job!'

'Forget about him, Tobes. Come on, get up. Jean and Oscar are leaving.' She hauled him up and they followed Jean and Oscar out to join Hero at the front door.

'It was lovely meeting you, Jean,' Hero said sincerely, holding out her hand.

Jean ignored her hand and gave Hero a hug and a kiss on the cheek instead. 'You too, my dear. It must have been sad work for you youngsters to have an old crock like me around, but Oscar insisted. He's a reckless scatterbrain but he does look after me and makes sure I don't get too lonely since his dad passed away.' She looked fondly over to where Oscar was bidding Toby and Sunday farewell. 'Oh, I almost forgot,' she added, handing Hero a large carry bag that held a heavy book. 'Oscar asked me to bring this along for you. Hang on to it for as long as you like. No rush to get it back to me.'

Oscar smiled at Hero. 'Thank you very much for having us,' he said, the merriment in his eyes belying the formality of his words.

He leaned forward and Hero quickly turned her head so that his kiss landed on her cheek.

'Excellent deflection,' he said approvingly. 'A little quicker and I might have got an ear and some hair.'

Despite herself, she grinned. Pushing him out the door, she linked arms with Sunday and they watched until the car's tail-lights disappeared.

'That went well.' Sunday closed the door behind them. Toby headed for the bathroom and she took the opportunity to say, 'Toby's staying the night. You don't mind, do you?'

'Of course I don't mind,' Hero said, thinking she would have minded if her expensive aphrodisiac-themed menu had gone to waste.

'What have you got there?' Sunday asked, peering at the book Hero had taken out of the carry bag.

'Oscar's family photo album,' Hero replied, in a tone of complete resignation.

Curious, Sunday joined Hero as she flicked through the first pages. 'Oh, look at Oscar hugging the donkey! He must have been about eight when that was taken. He's so cute!'

Hero stared bitterly at the photograph. 'If that donkey had had an ounce of feeling for the human race, it would have kicked him in the stomach.' She deliberated vengefully on the recalcitrance of donkeys before flipping the page. 'I can't believe that every single day, children have fatal accidents,' she continued, staring at a photograph of a youthful Oscar strapping on a parachute, 'and yet Oscar seems to have spent his entire childhood consorting with crocodiles and jumping out of planes and, apart from the obvious and extensive brain damage, there doesn't seem to be a damn thing wrong with him.'

'There's *definitely* nothing wrong with him,' Sunday said in a salacious tone as she perved unashamedly at a recent snap of Oscar at the beach, wearing nothing but boardshorts.

Hero shut her mouth abruptly and then shoved Sunday away so that she could look at the photo, too.

'You must admit he has quite a nice body,' Sunday teased.

'Hmph,' Hero answered, in a non-committal tone.

'And personally I think the dinner party was a success.'

'Oh yeah.' Hero gave a hollow laugh. 'It went brilliantly. Let's see, Oscar introduced me to his mother. He and Pelham are new best friends. Pelham wants to enrol me in an etiquette course because he's worried about my table manners, and now I'm looking through Oscar's childhood photos. Yep, everything's just peachy.'

'Jean is lovely.'

'She is,' Hero conceded. 'But Hitler's mum was probably quite nice too. I'm not blaming Jean for her son's behaviour. Although maybe if she'd restrained him more as a youngster, he wouldn't be so uncontrollable now. Actual physical restraints would be perfect.' She smiled dreamily at the enticing thought of manacling Oscar to the wall of a dripping dungeon.

'Well, look on the bright side,' Sunday encouraged. 'Yes, he's bombarded you with romantic gestures. And okay, you spent Valentine's Day with him, and now you've met his mum. But *he* hasn't met *your* parents, and even Oscar can't force you into a wedding dress, or into saying yes.'

Hero shuddered. 'Don't even mention weddings. If Pelham and I ever do get engaged, Oscar will probably try to kidnap him on our wedding day and take his place.'

Sunday gave this scenario her considered opinion, not at all prepared to underestimate Oscar. 'I don't think he would,' she finally pronounced. 'He is sort of insane but I don't think he's criminally violent. He'd be far more likely to convince Pelham to marry a bridesmaid instead.'

'Despite the fact that my bridesmaids would be you and Pelham's sister, Georgia, I still wouldn't be prepared to put it past him,' Hero said mournfully.

Sunday laughed and gave her a friendly shove. 'Cheer up. At least Oscar's only determined to make you fall in love with him. I mean, it's not like he's proposed.'

13

The proposal

Beth stared in horror at the client standing in front of her. 'I beg your pardon, but did you say your name was *Pelham* Grenville-Walters?'

'Yes,' Pelham answered, a trifle impatiently. 'I have an appointment with Oscar Martin at ten o'clock.'

Before Beth could gather her wits, Oscar strode out of his office and greeted Pelham like a long-lost schoolchum.

'Plum!' he boomed, pumping Pelham's hand vigorously. 'Glad you could make it. Come through. Beth, could you please bring us some tea when you get the chance? None of that herbal stuff, of course.' He turned a smile on Pelham, ignoring Beth's astonishment. 'You'd be an English Breakfast man, unless I'm very much mistaken?'

'Actually, I quite like —'

'That's the way, that's the way!' Oscar steered him into his office, finding time to wink outrageously at Beth, who was paralysed with shock.

The door closed behind them, as an unsuspecting Jake walked by.

'Jake!' Beth hissed. 'Oscar's in there with *Hero's boyfriend.*'

'What the hell is he doing here?'

'I don't know – he had an appointment! What should we do?'

Jake looked at the closed door and then at Beth's anxious face. 'Eavesdrop,' he said, without hesitation.

Huddling over Beth's desk, on the count of three, they held their breath as she pressed the intercom button marked 'Oscar: office'.

Pelham was mid-speech. 'So as you know Hero and myself, I thought I might as well come to you for some advice. You can't be too careful in these things. Your company has quite a good reputation, you know.'

'Well, when love is your life's work, failure simply isn't an option,' Oscar said soulfully.

Beth raised her eyebrows at Jake, who shook his head to indicate that he had no idea why Oscar was talking like a motivational poster.

'Exactly!' Pelham said, clearly enthused by Oscar's inspirational aphorism. 'So what do you suggest? How should I propose to Hero?'

At this Jake almost fell off Beth's desk, while Beth's eyes grew round and she put a hand to her mouth.

Inside the office, Oscar eyed Pelham warily. Whatever he'd been expecting, it clearly wasn't this. But when he spoke, his voice didn't betray any emotion. 'Before you think of where and when you want to propose to Hero, you have to consider *why*.'

'Why?' Pelham said, startled. 'Don't I already know why?'

'Do you?' Oscar asked.

'Well, you know. Because I love her and all that,' Pelham said uncomfortably.

Oscar shook his head.

Pelham faltered. 'I'm not proposing because I love her?'

''Fraid not,' Oscar said kindly. 'You're proposing because you're conventional. If what you really felt for Hero was a pure love, untainted by the strictures of societal expectation, then you wouldn't need to marry her.' He leant back in his chair, gauging the effect of this statement on Pelham.

'Hang on just one moment. Are you saying that what I feel for Hero isn't a . . . a grand passion?'

'Exactly.'

Pelham's brow cleared. 'Well, that's fine then.'

'It is?'

'Of course it is. Wouldn't demean Hero or myself by experiencing something so vulgar. Excellent. Keep going, Martin. You're making a lot of sense. So what do I do?'

Oscar was temporarily floored by the idea of someone *not* wanting to be in the throes of a grand passion, but he quickly recovered. 'It's probably the most important moment of your lives,' he mused. 'You have to get it right. Get it wrong and you're looking at a lifetime, and miserable old age, spent with someone who'll never let you forget that you proposed while she was wearing ugg boots.'

'There's no chance of that,' Pelham said. 'I thought I could hire a private yacht and take her sailing in the Whitsundays. And when the time comes to pop the question, I'll moor at a private beach, have food and waiters from a five-star resort waiting, and then propose over a candlelit dinner . . . What?'

Oscar was shaking his head sorrowfully.

'You don't think that's a good idea?'

Oscar steepled his hands together and leant back in his chair. 'If necessity is the mother of invention, cliché is the lonely father of all the unborn children of lost romances,' he said wisely.

'I'm sorry, I don't quite follow.'

Oscar suddenly jerked upright and slammed his fist on the table, making Pelham jump. 'Originality! Do you know why that's so important in love and romance, Plum?'

'Well —'

'What did they teach you at Cranbrook?' Oscar interrupted sternly.

'I went to King's, actually.'

'For once in your life, your place of schooling has no bearing on the situation at hand. Now, as I was saying, originality is the key to making Hero feel unique. Think about compliments. Let's hear one.'

'Hear one what?' Pelham asked nervously.

'A compliment. The more extravagant, the better.'

'Look, I don't think this is really —'

Oscar thumped the table again. 'Necessary? Of course it's not necessary! Food is necessary! Breathing is necessary! But love and its accoutrements —'

'Accoutrements?' Jake whispered to Beth in disbelief.

'— they're *essential*. Unless you think love is a luxury you can live without, let's hear a compliment.'

There was a prolonged silence.

Oscar finally heaved a sigh. 'Okay. Let's start with the easy stuff. We'll do compliments later. Let me hear an endearment instead.'

In Pelham's view, this wasn't much of an improvement, but he knitted his brow and applied himself to intense cogitation. 'Sweetheart?' he finally offered.

'Average. Try again.'

'Darling?'

Oscar shook his head.

'Honeybunch? Pumpkin? Shnookums?' Pelham reeled off with increasing desperation.

Oscar yawned.

'Well, you're the bloody expert,' Pelham said, with justifiable annoyance. 'What would you call her?'

'High Priestess of the Sweetest Idyll,' Oscar answered promptly. 'Goddess Divine Whose Plaything is my Heart.'

Outside, Beth was miming puking into her coffee mug.

'Baby animals always work quite well,' Oscar continued. 'Just make sure you avoid Kitten. One of the most over-used nicknames around. It's right up there with Shmoopy and Bow-wow.'

'Dear god.'

Oscar nodded. 'Exactly. Which is why *you* are not going to refer to Hero as Kitten or Baby Bear or Bunny.'

'I wouldn't dream of calling Hero any of those ridiculous names,' Pelham said, with a disdainful sniff.

'Exactly. From now on you're going to call her Puggle.'

'I beg your pardon?'

'Puggle. It's the correct term for a baby echidna,' Oscar said smugly.

Pelham looked doubtful. 'Are you sure about that? Echidnas are kind of . . . spiky.'

'Yep. Perfect for Hero. All spiky on the outside and – well, she's kind of spiky on the inside, too, come to think of it, but we love her anyway.'

'What do you mean, "we"?'

'I mean you,' Oscar amended hastily. 'But we're a team now, so we're inseparable. I'm you. You're me. We're the royal we.'

'We am?' Pelham said, utterly confused.

'You are. Because you, Pelham, meaning me, are selfless. Remember, selfishness is the father of failed romance.'

'I thought cliché was?'

Oscar flapped his objection away. 'Fine. Selfishness can be the aunt. I'm not interested in the gender and parentage of abstract concepts. Just remember, what is Hero?'

'My little puggle.' Pelham thought for a moment and then said, 'Should I use the adjective "little", or is that incorrect? Does the word puggle presuppose that it's little?'

'I haven't the faintest idea of the desirable weight for a newborn echidna,' Oscar said loftily. 'No doubt there have been some very hefty puggles born to proud parents. Use "little" if you want. It really makes no difference. The important thing to settle is an action plan for your proposal.' He drummed his fingers on his desk as he thought, then snapped them. 'It's quite simple, actually. You just need to save her.'

'I need to save her?' Pelham said blankly. 'Save her how?'

'In the physical sense. To complement the emotional rescue.'

'But, but . . . why?' Pelham was completely at a loss.

He wasn't the only one. Whatever Oscar was up to, Beth and Jake knew that he wasn't following the Serendipity manual on this one.

'Because then she will owe you her life,' Oscar explained patiently to his bewildered client. 'And with that kind of gratitude – well, my friend, with that kind of gratitude comes the best sex of your life.'

Pelham opened his mouth to reply and then stopped as he thought over what Oscar had said.

'And apart from the gratitude that will manifest itself in sexual wantonness and eagerness to please, it's common knowledge that true love depends on the woman seeing you as her hero.'

'Hero needs to see me as her hero?' Pelham repeated.

'Precisely. Hero needs to see you as her knight in shining armour. It's the only way that she's ever going to say yes.'

'But I'm fairly certain she's going to say yes,' Pelham protested. 'We've discussed marriage before.'

'You have?' Oscar said, startled.

'In a very general way. But I'm confident that there's an *understanding* between us.'

'Rule number one. There is not and never will be understanding between men and women.'

Jake opened his mouth to speak, and then remembered that he would be heard in Oscar's office. Grabbing a piece of paper, he scrawled 'We have to stop this!'

Beth nodded. Jumping up, she grabbed his note, ripped it in half and placed the piece that said 'stop this!' on a tea tray. She filled a teapot with scalding water, then, with the tray piled with cups, teapot, milk, sugar and cake, she marched into Oscar's office.

'Your tea,' Beth said, in a tone more appropriate to the public announcement of a papal death.

Oscar shot her a glance and grinned wickedly. 'Thank you, Beth.' He turned his attention back to Pelham. 'Now, as I was saying, it all comes down to the rescue —'

'Sugar?' Beth raised her voice, holding the steaming teapot directly over Oscar's lap in an unmistakably threatening gesture.

Oscar ignored her warning tone. 'No, thanks. Let's see, Pelham, we've had quite a good success rate with the fibreglass shark —'

'MILK?' bellowed Beth, splashing tea aggressively into the cups and still trying to catch Oscar's eye.

'No, *thank you*, Elizabeth,' Oscar said, his tone becoming as steely as hers.

'I must *insist* that you have a slice of cake,' she said, shooting daggers and pushing a plate with the note shoved under the cake towards him.

He accepted the plate, read the note surreptitiously and then crumpled it in one hand. He smiled innocently at Beth and thrust the plate back at her. 'No cake for me, thanks. Watching my weight before the big day, you know.'

'Oh, are you getting married too?' Pelham asked with interest.

Oscar beamed. 'Like you, I haven't actually asked her yet, but I'm fairly optimistic.'

'Well! Congratulations.' He leant forward and shook Oscar's hand.

At the spectacle of Pelham sincerely congratulating Oscar on his forthcoming marriage to Pelham's intended fiancée, Beth collapsed into a chair and stuffed the cake into her mouth in utter resignation.

'Who's the lucky girl? Why didn't you bring her to dinner the other night?'

'She's a scuba-diving instructor,' Oscar improvised, deciding that it would be improper at this delicate moment to mention that he was in love with Hero. 'She's away with a tour group at the moment. Diving with turtles in the Galapagos Islands. It's very popular with Canadians,' he finished, with an inventive flourish.

Outside, Jake was lying back in Beth's chair with a wet handkerchief over his face. Beth limped out of the office with the tea tray and closed the door behind her. Shoving Jake out of her chair, she collapsed and they listened to the rest of the conversation between Oscar and Pelham in defeated silence.

'Now, where were we?' Oscar mused. 'That's right, we're agreed on one thing at least. You do need to take Hero away somewhere. An unfamiliar setting is vital to a successful proposal.'

'My thinking exactly. So as I said, I thought I'd take her to the Whitsundays, just the two of us, and – what?' he asked, as Oscar shook his head once more.

'*Not* a private yacht,' Oscar said firmly. 'And most definitely not just the two of you. You need to go away with a group of friends.'

'Go away with a group of friends to *propose*?' Pelham repeated in disbelief. 'Are you absolutely sure about this?'

In answer, Oscar got up and pulled a file from the bookcase. He flipped through several documents before choosing a spreadsheet. Laying it in front of Pelham, he traced one line with a forefinger, bringing it to rest on a rather impressive set of figures. 'This is our company's turnover for the last financial year,' he said. 'I think I must be doing something right, don't you?'

Pelham's eyes had widened at the column of numbers, and he meekly nodded.

'Right, then. You go away with a group of friends. We just have to decide where. Can you ski?'

'Of course. I was an off-piste lodge champion.'

'Skiing is definitely out,' Oscar said immediately. 'And I suppose if you were going to take Hero on a yacht, you know how to sail?'

Pelham puffed his chest out. 'You're looking at the skipper of the yacht *Beauty*. Took line honours in last year's —'

'No good.' Oscar frowned. He thought for a moment and then his brow cleared. 'Can you ride a horse?'

Pelham shook his head. 'Got thrown when I was just a nipper. Hated the bloody things ever since. I'll tell you this for free, Martin, *never trust any animal that wears shoes*.'

'Er, right,' Oscar said, taken aback by this dictum. 'I'll bear that in mind when we go away on our horse-riding weekend.'

Pelham paled. '*When we what?*'

'That's when you're going to propose,' Oscar said over his shoulder, searching amongst his files for brochures on horse-riding retreats.

'But I hate horses! And I can't ride!'

'That's the whole point,' Oscar said kindly, throwing a sheaf of glossy brochures onto his desk. 'It's extremely important that you look vulnerable. It's a very attractive quality to women.' Seeing Pelham's uneasy expression, he sighed. 'Look, you don't have to believe me. I can give you proof.'

Three seconds later, two paperback novels landed on Pelham's lap. 'What . . . what are these?' he asked uneasily, taking in the title of the topmost novel, *Love Sick*.

'Romance novels.' Oscar peered over Pelham's shoulder at *Love Sick*'s cover, which showed a female doctor tenderly ministering to a handsome patient whose primary affliction appeared to be that he had a jawbone chiselled out of granite. 'Do you know how many of these things sell a year?' He continued without waiting for a response from Pelham. 'Twenty-three million. So they must be on to something, wouldn't you agree?'

Pelham made an inarticulate noise as he put aside *Love Sick* and was confronted by *The Hit List,* the cover of which showed a female guitarist tenderly bending over a handsome pianist whose chest seemed to be sprouting a bath mat through his half-buttoned shirt.

'So that's your homework, Plum,' Oscar said briskly. 'I want you to read these books from cover to cover and make a list of the main points for me. In the meantime, I'll organise our horse-riding trip.'

'*Our?*' Pelham repeated. 'Do you mean you'll be coming along with us?'

Oscar looked surprised. 'Well, of course. You want the best advice that money can buy, don't you? No expense spared? Only a handful of our very special clients get personal service from Jake or myself. I'm going to be right there every step of the way, to make sure that your proposal to Hero goes exactly to plan.'

'It would be a relief to have a specialist there,' Pelham confessed. 'I hadn't realised there was so much to this romance business.'

Bundling his romance novels into one hand, he grasped Oscar's hand in the other and pumped it with real gratitude. 'I'll be in touch. Thanks, Martin.'

'You're welcome, Plum.'

Oscar showed Pelham out and there was a silence as the door closed behind him.

Jake and Beth looked at Oscar, speechless.

'I gather you heard all that on the intercom,' Oscar said, not in the least abashed.

Jake gazed at him mournfully. 'Why the turtle-loving, diving Canadians?' he asked brokenly. '*Why?*' He held up a hand to stop Oscar before he could answer. 'If you'll excuse me,' he said, with great dignity, 'I need to feed the fibreglass shark.'

He stumbled off down the corridor, leaving Oscar to face Beth.

'You're not mad with me, too, are you Beth?' Oscar asked.

'You had better be sure about this girl, Oscar. And what happens if she accepts Pelham's proposal?'

'She won't,' Oscar said. 'I just know she won't.' Seeing that Beth was looking unconvinced, he added simply, 'I can't lose her, Beth.'

Beth paused and her tone softened. 'I know you don't need me to tell you this, but you musn't ever forget that loss is a normal part of life.'

She held his gaze for a long moment, making sure that her words had sunk in, and then moved through to the kitchen with the tea tray, leaving Oscar standing there alone, the colour drained from his cheeks and the customary sparkle in his eyes extinguished.

14

The weekend away

'Pelham? What on earth are you reading?' Hero asked, as she entered the immaculate living room of Pelham's parents' home. Despite earning an enormous wage, Pelham still lived with his parents, as did his sister, Georgia. This lack of independence on her boyfriend's part often bothered Hero, but she could see his point that living at home was economically advantageous, while it gave his parents peace of mind as to his well-being.

Pelham tried to stuff *Love Sick* down the side of the couch, but it was too late. Hero had already glimpsed the lurid cover and she burst out laughing as she registered the title. 'Why are you reading this rubbish?'

Pelham tried half-heartedly to share her amusement. 'I . . . er . . . it's really not that bad,' he said lamely.

'Not that bad?' Hero examined the cover with glee. 'Let me guess, he's a handsome patient and she's a beautiful nurse?'

'Actually, she's a doctor,' Pelham said stiffly. 'My book please, Hero.' He held out his hand.

'Since when have you read romance novels?'

'What difference could it possibly make to you?' Pelham hated being made fun of. His hand was still outstretched.

Noting the stern look in his eye, Hero meekly returned the book, all the mirth draining out of her.

There was a small silence and then Pelham cleared his throat. 'By the way,' he said, diffidently. 'Are you and Sunday free next weekend?'

'I am. I'd have to check with Sun. Why?'

'I was wondering if you'd like to go away somewhere. Maybe the Hunter Valley? I'm happy to arrange accommodation.'

Hero looked at him in surprise. 'You and me and Sunday?'

'Yes. And I suppose we'd better invite that boyfriend of hers,' Pelham said reluctantly. 'Been meaning to ask, Hero, do you think he's quite right in the head?'

'Who?' Hero asked, her mind immediately jumping to Oscar, as it invariably did when questions of mental impairment arose.

'The gorilla bloke that Sunday's seeing. I mean, to turn up at the house of a girl whose name you don't even know and start singing to her first thing on a Saturday morning . . .'

Hero couldn't suppress a grin at Pelham's horror. 'I don't know,' she said wistfully. 'It's kind of romantic, don't you think?'

'It is?' Pelham was taken aback, his introduction to the world of romance having thrown previously held opinions into disarray. 'Well, why the hell did he have to wear a gorilla suit? What's so romantic about a big ape? No.' Pelham shook his head. 'He must be mad. Do you know where he went to school?'

'What does that have to do with anything?' Hero asked tersely.

'King's boy wouldn't do something like that,' Pelham said. 'It's just not done. That's all I'm saying.'

'You can check Toby's educational credentials for yourself, if he ends up coming.' Hero's annoyance with Pelham's snobbery faded as she reminded herself that at least he was trying to reach out to her friends. 'I'll go and phone Sun now.' She put her arms around his neck and kissed him on the cheek. 'Thank you, Pelham.' She paused and then added, almost shyly, 'It means more to me than you know that you're making an effort with my friends.'

She left the room and Pelham sniffed and opened his book, turning the pages in search of where he had left off. Hero was obviously delighted by his idea, he thought, as he tried to stem his eagerness to return to Dr Rogers' steamy supply-room clinch with Mr Otis (wounded shipping magnate). Maybe this Oscar fellow knew what he was doing, after all.

* ✱ *

Two weeks later, Sunday and Hero breathed ecstatic sighs as Pelham negotiated his car up the long gravel driveway lined with plane trees that led to a restored convent now operating as a luxury bed-and-breakfast. The convent was set amongst the rolling hills and vineyards of the Hunter Valley, and the soft golden light of the early autumn afternoon created a peaceful vista. As the car came to a halt outside the imposing façade, with its rows of mullioned windows, Hero gazed out over the grounds, catching sight of a gardener tending to beds of rhododendrons clustered around a small white pavilion that overlooked an ornamental lake.

The peace was cut short, however, by the long list of instructions and requests recited by the owner and concierge, Clarence, most of which concerned the garden, the lifework of his apparently volatile partner, Terry.

Hero was listening patiently when, to her utter disbelief, Oscar strolled into the lobby. 'What the *hell* are you doing here?' she demanded, cutting across Clarence mid-sentence.

'Hero.' Oscar smiled amiably. 'Has anyone ever told you that you look absolutely magnificent when you're being rude?'

'I am *warning* you,' Hero hissed between clenched teeth. 'I can't believe you followed me here.'

'How many times do I have to explain that I can't have followed you when I arrived first?' Oscar pointed out, reasonably. 'It's really not that difficult a concept to comprehend.'

'You followed me here by arriving first when you knew I'd be coming here,' Hero said, a touch incoherently.

Before Oscar could respond, Pelham struggled through the door, bearing two overloaded suitcases. A relieved smile broke across his face as he spied Oscar. 'Martin, you made it! Sorry we're late. We took the wrong exit on the Pacific Highway and ended up going through Toukley and Budgewoi.'

Oscar shook his hand. 'Ah, that'd add at least another forty-five minutes to your trip. I stopped for a cup of coffee in Morisset on the way up. Lovely little town. Have you been there? No? You must visit on your way back.'

Hero interrupted this exchange of pleasantries in a tone that could have cut through solid granite. 'You *knew* he was coming, Pelham?'

'What?' Pelham's smile fled as he realised that he hadn't thought about how to explain Oscar's presence without revealing his plan to propose. 'Er, yes. Sort of. That is . . .'

'We discussed it at your dinner party,' Oscar said affably.

At this point Sunday lugged her case through the door. 'Hello, Oscar,' she said in surprise, and Hero gratefully noted that the treachery didn't extend to her best friend. She revised this opinion moments later as Oscar and Sunday proceeded to greet one another like old friends.

'Here, let me take that for you,' Oscar said chivalrously.

Sunday gratefully surrendered her heavy bag. 'Oh, thank you. I don't know what I was thinking when I packed.'

'Presumably that you might require several bricks to mount your horse,' Oscar suggested with a twinkle.

Sunday laughed. 'Toby will be sorry that he missed you.'

'He's not coming?'

'No, he has a gig tonight. Jazz at the zoo.' Before anyone could comment, she added hastily, '*Not* in costume. He's trying to get his confidence up so he can sing without it.'

'Good place to start,' Oscar said thoughtfully. 'It'll be dark and he'll have the gorillas close by as a sort of comfort.'

'Exactly.' Sunday beamed at Oscar's perspicacity while Pelham looked at them askance. 'Shall we leave our luggage with the concierge and have a drink before dinner?'

There was general acquiescence and Hero watched in disbelief as the three of them, apparently oblivious to her presence, proceeded into what Clarence had grandly identified as the drawing room. In high dudgeon, she headed for the stairs.

Sunday popped her head around the door. 'Hero, don't you want a drink?'

Hero stopped halfway up the stairs, one hand resting on the curving oak of the balustrade. 'No, thank you,' she said icily. 'If anyone wants me, I'll be in my room.'

And with that she swept up the staircase, in what was undoubtedly a magnificent exit.

* ✱ *

Unfortunately for Hero, no one did seem to want her. She waited in dignified outrage for Pelham, Sunday – a maid, for heaven's sake – to come and enquire after her. Finally, after two hours, she got up from the bed, threw aside the magazine that she had not been reading and went downstairs.

Sounds of hilarity greeted her from the drawing room. Pushing open the heavy door, she realised that at least one of her grievances was unfounded. They clearly hadn't started dinner without her – they were still drinking.

'Darling!' Pelham waved a bottle of wine at her by way of greeting, his cheeks unnaturally flushed. Hero had never seen him so relaxed.

'"Hungry Like The Wolf"!' shrieked Sunday as Hero entered.

'No – no, wait – "Crocodile Rock"!'

'Hello, Hero,' Oscar said, drawing up an armchair for her. 'We're thinking up names of songs that Toby might sing at the zoo. Come and play.'

Hero accepted the armchair with an injured sniff. Without glancing at Oscar, she took a glass of the excellent merlot from a rapidly emptying bottle. 'What about "Eye of the Tiger"?' she offered, not wanting to appear a spoilsport just because she was furious with Oscar.

'We've already said that one,' Sunday answered.

'Oh. Then how about "The Lion Sleeps Tonight"?'

There was a small silence.

'We've used that one, too,' Sunday said apologetically. 'We've been playing for a while now.'

'"What's New, Pussycat?"' Hero tried desperately.

'It has to be a zoo animal, Hero. Otherwise it doesn't make sense,' Oscar said, in a kind tone that pushed her annoyance over the edge, into unreasonable fury.

'Oh. That's a shame. Because one of my favourite songs has always been "I'm Gonna Lock My Heart And Throw Away The Key".'

An appreciative smile lurked in Oscar's eyes. 'Really? See that's odd, because I prefer "I've Got You Under My Skin".'

'"Do It The Hard Way",' Hero shot back.

'"Let There Be Love",' he rejoined softly.

Sunday glanced open-mouthed from Hero to Oscar and back again, like a spectator at a tennis match.

Only Pelham seemed unaware of the tense undercurrent. 'You're not playing properly, Hero,' he objected. 'Your songs aren't funny.'

The spell was broken. 'No, Pelham,' Hero said gently. 'It's not funny at all.'

A silence fell and Pelham peered into his empty glass. 'I'm going to order another bottle,' he announced.

'Shouldn't we think about dinner?' Hero suggested, quite unused to seeing him inebriated.

Pelham screwed up his face and flapped his hands to indicate what he thought of that idea, then moved off in the direction of the bar.

'Pelham's really been quite fun tonight,' Sunday remarked, hastily modifying her tactless tone of surprise halfway through the sentence. Meeting Hero's gaze, she added, defensively, 'I just mean he's not usually like this.'

'No, he's not.' Hero's eyes narrowed as she watched Pelham's unsteady progress across the room. She turned to Oscar, who opened his eyes wide in answer to her suspicious glare.

'Me?' he asked, flinging his arms up in a gesture of self-defence. 'You think Pelham being drunk is *my* fault?'

'I'm sure of it,' Hero snapped. 'What did you say to him to make him start drinking?'

'I didn't say anything! Maybe he just realised how good it feels to loosen up for a change. God knows, he never relaxes around you.'

'I *beg* your pardon?'

'Oh, come off it, Hero. It's hardly late-breaking news. The guy spends all of his time trying to impress you. The way he constantly tries to big-note his job and connections, it's all for your benefit.'

'You're confusing Pelham with yourself,' Hero said, through gritted teeth. 'Pelham doesn't require gimmicks and . . . appliances to construct a relationship.'

'*Appliances?*' Oscar choked. 'You make me sound like a whitegoods salesman.'

'You are in a way,' Hero said dispassionately. 'I mean, when you think about it, your business results in a lot of people setting up house together and co-owning refrigerators and washing machines.'

Oscar, who in his more self-indulgent moments liked to think of himself as a modern-day St Valentine, was rendered speechless by this alternative image of himself as a guy in a short-sleeved polyester shirt, wearing a 'Kevin' nametag and earnestly advocating the advantages of front-loader/dryer hybrids.

Before he could respond, however, Hero launched another attack. 'And I don't know where you got the idea that Pelham tries to impress me, because he doesn't.'

'Of course he does,' Oscar said scornfully. 'He's not so uptight when you get to know him. But he seems to feel the need to play the successful businessman around you.'

'That's utter rubbish.'

'Really? Then why is it that for the last two hours, Pelham hasn't once, not *once*, mentioned his work? If you want to know the real Pelham, you should be over at that bar talking to him right now, while his guard's down. Now if you'll excuse me, I'm going to change.' With that, Oscar strode out of the room, leaving an uncomfortable silence in his wake.

'I suppose we all should go and change before dinner,' Sunday said diplomatically.

Hero, who was utterly taken aback at Oscar's severe strictures on her relationship, rounded on her friend instead. 'I can't believe he got Pelham drunk and I can't believe you let him.'

Sunday looked at her in exasperation. 'Hero, I wish you'd get down off your "I hate Oscar" soapbox long enough to shut up and listen to the truth. Oscar didn't get Pelham drunk and he didn't invite himself on this trip. Pelham invited him.'

'*What?*'

'You heard me,' said Sunday, unmoved by Hero's glare. 'They get along surprisingly well. And I'm responsible for Pelham getting tipsy, not Oscar. The poor guy's so stressed about tomorrow, I thought it would be good for him to relax a little before he pro—' She broke off with a sudden gulp.

Hero pounced. 'Before he what?'

Sunday looked around wildly for inspiration, and found none. 'Before he procreated,' she tried weakly.

'Pelham was planning on procreating?' Hero snapped.

Sunday tried a succession of inarticulate noises to convey certainty. 'Uh-huh. Mmmm. Yip.'

'How?'

'How what?' Sunday asked, completely unnerved.

'How was Pelham planning on procreating? Given that he doesn't have a womb.'

'Adoption,' Sunday finally gasped. 'Look, I really need a shower before dinner. I'm sorry I encouraged Pelham to drink, okay?' Without waiting for an answer, she fled upstairs, leaving Hero to stalk the room like a panther deprived of its prey.

Restless, she made her way out on to the wide verandah, where an old-fashioned porch swing stood. Settling herself in its deep cushions, she folded her arms and stared crossly at the beguiling prospect of the countryside swathed in moonlight. Oscar's decisive appraisal that she didn't know the real Pelham, closely followed by Sunday's revelation that Pelham was planning to propose, had thrown her into turmoil.

While she and Pelham had discussed marriage in an arbitrary way, it was a shock to realise that she would have to make an actual, momentous decision the following day. And Oscar's proximity wasn't exactly conducive to clear thinking on the subject.

Lost in confused reflection, Hero was still sitting on the swing when Oscar, wearing a fresh shirt and looking annoyingly attractive, came outside bearing two drinks. He paused and drew in a deep lungful of the night air.

'If you say one word,' Hero darkly threatened, 'just *one* about how beautiful the view is by moonlight or how fresh the country air smells, I swear I will kill you and bury your body under Terry's rhododendrons.'

'I wasn't going to say either of those things,' Oscar said, in an injured tone.

'You weren't?'

'No. I was going to recite a sonnet about the beauty of a woman enraged. Does the same penalty apply?'

'No. I'll bury you alive instead.'

'You know, it's rather more difficult to recite poetry when your nostrils are filled with dirt.'

'My thoughts exactly.'

'Did you have a chat to Pelham?' Oscar asked, wisely deciding to ignore her ferocious scowl.

'No, I did not!' Hero snapped. 'He's still in there talking to the bartender. And that's your fault, too. Don't think I don't know it. Pelham has *never* sprawled over a bar and chatted to a bartender in his life.'

Oscar sat himself down beside her and gently rocked the swing to set them in motion. 'Well, you and Pelham are quite different in that respect. I have a very distinct memory of you chatting to a bartender.' Before she could retaliate, he handed her a drink. 'Here, drink this. It'll make you feel better.'

She looked suspiciously into the tumbler. 'What is it?'

'Scotch on the rocks.'

'I hate scotch. It tastes like medicine. Is there any Baileys?'

Oscar raised an eyebrow. 'Baileys? I never would have picked you for a sweet liqueur kind of a girl.'

'See, that's the problem with you.' Despite her objections to the scotch, she downed the drink in one swallow, grimaced, and then continued. 'You think every single thing about a person has to conform to your exact notion of who they are. Cynical. Sentimental. Romantic. Unromantic. You're incredibly narrow minded. Are you going to drink that?'

Oscar paused, the glass halfway to his mouth. Deciding that Hero's need was greater, he swapped his full glass for her empty one, watching in awe as she dispatched the second drink in the same swift manner as the first.

Setting the empty glasses at a safe distance, he looked her straight in the eye. 'Okay, Hero. What's the matter?'

There was a silence, and then Hero burst out, 'Pelham's going to propose to me.'

Oscar took in her agitation with interest, but wisely decided not to comment on it. Instead, he said mildly, 'How do you know?'

'Sunday told me.'

'I know you're not much given to taking advice from me, but for Pelham's sake, try to act surprised when he asks.'

'Do you really think I'd let on that I knew?' Hero asked, nettled.

Oscar sighed. 'Quite frankly, Hero, I don't know how you're going to react ninety-eight per cent of the time. That first night we were together, you looked at me like you could fall in love with me, but since we met up again it's been nothing but sexually charged tension.'

Hero smiled sweetly. 'That's not true. I've definitely progressed to the numb-to-all-sensation-where-Oscar-is-concerned stage.'

'What's it like?'

'Peaceful. Very peaceful.'

'Well, enjoy it, because it won't last,' he advised. 'The next stage is utter-love-and-adoration-of-Oscar and it lasts for all eternity. Which gives you something to look forward to,' he added kindly.

'By that time I'll probably be married to Pelham, so I'll just have to admire you from afar.'

The combative sparkle went out of Oscar's eyes and he looked at her meditatively. 'I don't think you'll really do it. You don't love him, Hero. I know you don't.'

Hero bit her lip. 'Your mistake all along has been to assume that you know my mind better than I do.'

'I can't let you do it.'

'Luckily for me, I don't need your permission to make decisions concerning my own life,' Hero said composedly.

'In that case, just tell me one thing that I've always been curious about. I know I've asked you this before, but why did you stand me up that day at the Met?'

Heat burned through Hero's cheeks and for one wild moment she considered telling him about that agonising moment of indecision and self-doubt. She had wanted so badly to be Lola, to step forward and take Oscar's hand. But she hadn't. She had turned away.

Oscar watched her fighting for an explanation, and decided to make it easier for her. 'My theory is that there are two Heros.' He smiled. 'Or perhaps there's one Hero and one Lola. Either way, I feel like part of you desperately wants to break free while the other part fights hard for security and stability, whatever the cost.'

'Lola doesn't exist,' Hero said, when she could speak. 'She was never real.'

'See, that's where you're wrong,' Oscar said gently. 'Because I kissed her, and she was very real to me.' He paused. 'The price that you're paying for security is too high, Hero. You'll be miserable with him. You know you will.'

'Oh well,' she said, in as flippant a tone as she could muster, 'I suppose the only way either of us will ever know whether that's true is if Pelham and I actually do get married. But thanks for your concern. And I'm not a very good actor but I promise to act surprised when he asks me.'

'In that case, I suppose I ought to help you practise,' Oscar offered.

'What?' Hero asked, completely disconcerted.

Oscar moved closer. 'It's easy, I'll show you. When Pelham sits next to you in the moonlight, just like I am now, and he turns to you and says he's got something important to ask . . .'

He took her hand as he spoke, and immediately something very peculiar happened to Hero's insides, her heart and stomach colluding in some sort of jumping game, over which she had absolutely no control. It was the scotch, she decided hazily. Had to be the scotch.

Oblivious to the hammering of her heart, Oscar asked, persuasively, 'Hero, will you marry me?'

She tightened her grip on his hand, her eyes dreamy. When she spoke, her voice was little more than a whisper. 'Yes.'

His face was almost touching hers now, and as his lips brushed lightly against hers, she closed her eyes. But then he let go of her hand. When she opened her eyes, she saw that he had settled back in the swing, putting distance between them. She looked at him in bewilderment as he said, lightly, 'Sorry. I know I shouldn't have kissed you but I couldn't resist. Anyway, that was perfect. Look at Pelham exactly like that and he'll feel like the luckiest man alive. You know, Hero, I begin to have hope for your romantic streak, after all.'

He set the swing in motion once again, and as the world rushed forward to meet them, Hero didn't know why, but she felt very much like crying.

15

Riding off into the sunset

To Pelham's dismay, the next morning dawned clear, the blue sky providing the perfect backdrop to what Oscar declared would be a memorable day of exploring the local wineries on horseback.

Hero still hadn't quite recovered from the double shock of discovering that a) Pelham was going to propose to her, and b) Oscar appeared to be the newest and most beloved member of their friendship group. Over the breakfast table, she was equally as dour as Pelham, offering only monosyllabic responses.

'Are you two always this cheerful when you're on holiday?' Oscar asked brightly, smearing a generous amount of marmalade onto his fourth slice of toast. Pelham, whose head was aching and whose stomach was in knots, eyed him with dislike as he managed, with difficulty, to sip a cup of black coffee.

Half an hour later, they were standing in the stable's mounting yard while a frightening woman by the name of Hilary looked them over disparagingly. 'Right, have any of you lot ridden before?' she barked.

Against her will, Hero stood a bit straighter. Sunday, Oscar and

Hero put up their hands. After a brief pause, hating to be left out, Pelham did, too.

Hero looked at him in surprise. 'Pelham, you *hate* riding.'

'Well, yes, but that's not to say I haven't done it before,' Pelham said, cross at having a weakness pointed out in public.

'You're not scared of horses, surely?' asked Hilary, in the same tone of voice that she might have used to say, 'You're not scared of fluffy kittens, surely?'

'Yes. No. That is, I suffered a nasty accident some time ago. I was thrown from my mount,' Pelham said nobly, imparting the impression that he had been severely injured in a *Man-From-Snowy-River*-style leap down a cliff face.

Hero, well aware that the accident had occurred when Pelham was five, and that the steed in question had in fact been a Shetland pony, decided that it was wiser to hold her tongue. Pelham could be very touchy about certain things.

Hilary, however, seemed unimpressed. 'We'll put you on Beazley, then. Even if you do manage to fall off, he's so slow you'd have time to re-mount before he took another step.'

Pelham, caught between relief and humiliation at this announcement, took possession of a plump grey horse who appeared to be napping.

'You. You look sensible. You can take Button,' Hilary said to Hero, indicating a restless stallion who plunged his head and whinnied.

'*Button?*' Hero gulped as the stallion stamped a hoof. 'Are you sure he's meant for a beginner?'

'He's fine,' Hilary snapped, adjusting the saddle on Sunday's horse, Queenie. 'Just give him his head. Don't bolt with him and you'll have no problems.'

'Bolt with him?' Hero queried weakly. 'Why on earth would I do that?'

But Hilary, who had turned to check on Oscar's mount, either didn't hear her or chose to ignore her.

Hero gingerly approached Button, who eyed her coldly. 'Nice horsie,' she said, remembering she'd heard somewhere that horses, like babies, could smell fear. 'Nice Button.'

Button tossed his head again and let out a whinny that to Hero's ears sounded very much like 'you're screwed'. Deciding to forsake pleasantries, Hero swung herself up into the saddle and, after a brief tussle, they were off.

✻

In the late afternoon, they leisurely made their way back towards the stables. The sky was blue, the breeze was warm and the panorama of rolling vineyards simply breathtaking. The delicious picnic lunch that they had eaten, the wines that they had tasted and the beautiful weather and countryside had wrought such a mellowing effect that Hero was almost feeling in charity with Oscar. But not quite. As they ambled through fields of wildflowers, she muttered to Sunday, 'We'll probably have to stop soon.'

'Why?' Sunday asked in surprise.

'To let Oscar skip through the flower-filled meadows.'

Sunday giggled. 'Don't be horrible. Anyway, it would be nice to walk through them.'

'For god's sake, don't go suggesting it,' Hero said in abject horror. 'He'll be supervising a daisy-chain-making workshop before we know it.'

'Come on, Hero. He's not that bad.'

'*Not that bad*? I still don't even know what he's really doing here, Sun!'

As though sensing he was the topic of their conversation, Oscar wheeled his horse around to face them. But whatever he had been going to say was lost when Button, unnerved by this unexpected action, reared in fright. Somehow Hero managed to hang on, but then, as everyone watched in horror, Button bolted.

'I must say, you're very thorough,' Pelham remarked to Oscar, watching Hero career off into the distance. 'But how am I meant to rescue her? Will she slow down? I can't go over a trot, you know.'

Pelham's questions remained unanswered as Oscar took off after the bolting horse. The landscape, beautiful when admired from a sedate trot, was treacherous to a galloping horse. It took several desperate minutes before Oscar started to gain on Button. Swerving his mount to avoid a wombat hole, he cursed Button as the stallion shot into thick bushland. At this pace and with little riding experience, Hero might be sent flying into a tree.

But Oscar had underestimated her fortitude. He caught up just in time to see Hero, with a final, exhausted wrench, bring Button to a quivering standstill.

'Hero! Are you all right?' Oscar was stunned when she turned a face full of fury onto him.

'Are you insane?' she demanded, trembling. 'I could have been killed!'

'What are you talking about?'

'You frightened my horse on purpose!' Hero was white with anger and shock. 'What were you planning to do? Rescue me so I'd be grateful? I suppose it never occurred to you that I could have been thrown?'

Oscar tried to calm her. 'Why don't we dismount and walk the horses back to the others?'

'I wouldn't walk two steps in your company!' Hero snapped, furious to discover that she was on the verge of tears. 'You could have killed me with your stupid stunt.'

'I had nothing to do with your horse bolting!' Oscar said, starting to get annoyed. 'Nothing intentional, I mean,' he amended. 'I did startle Button, but I would never do something like that on purpose.'

'Then why do crazy things like this only ever happen to me when you're around? I think you planned it and bribed Hilary to give me that horse or —' She stopped, aware that she was becoming increasingly hysterical.

Oscar waited while Hero took a deep breath and then held Button's bridle while she dismounted. In silence, they started the long trudge back to the others, leading the horses and pointedly ignoring each other.

'Hero!' Sunday called, as they came into view. 'Are you okay?'

'I'm fine,' Hero said dully. She glanced at Pelham, who was sitting under a eucalyptus tree, looking very white. 'Pelham? What's wrong?'

'He tried to go after you and fell off,' Sunday informed them. 'I think his wrist might be broken.'

Pelham gave Hero a twisted smile as she bent anxiously over him. 'I told you I hate bloody horses,' he murmured.

'Can you walk?'

He nodded bravely and Hero helped him to stand, but it was clear from his pallor that he was in considerable pain.

Oscar, who had remained silent all this time, now spoke up. 'It's a long way back to the hotel, Pelham,' he said kindly. 'And that wrist looks very painful. Why don't you ride home behind me?' He turned to Sunday. 'Will you two be all right if we go ahead? Hero can ride Pelham's horse. You'll have to lead Button, but I think he'll be manageable if no one's riding him.'

'That's a good idea.' In an undertone Sunday added, 'He fainted, you know. I think he's in quite a lot of pain.'

Hero and Sunday helped Pelham up behind Oscar, and the girls watched in silence as they went on ahead. Oscar paused for a moment to turn back and wave a final farewell. The sun was sinking fast and as Oscar and Pelham rode off into the sunset together, for once even Hero would have preferred a more conventional romantic configuration.

$$* \ \overset{\displaystyle *}{} \ *$$

To everyone's great relief, Pelham's wrist was sprained rather than broken. Painkillers, a sling and a short sleep had had a remarkably restorative effect upon him, so much so that, to Hero's alarm, he had started drinking again.

Dinner was an excruciating affair, during which Oscar and Hero studiously ignored one another, Sunday vainly attempted to make light conversation and Pelham recklessly depleted the contents of several bottles of wine.

When the waiter had removed their dessert plates, Pelham managed, with great difficulty, to heave himself out of his chair. 'Goin' to the bar,' he slurred. 'Anyone else want another?'

'Pelham, you've had enough,' Hero said sharply. She followed him to the bar, concerned by his unstable progress. 'Those painkillers you've taken are strong and I really don't think you should be mixing them with alcohol.'

In answer, he waved a bottle of champagne at her. 'Mine,' he said petulantly. 'I'm going to . . .' He hiccupped. 'Have a little stroll. In the moonlight. Very romantic that, hey, Martin?' he called across to Oscar.

'Very.' Oscar watched with amusement as Pelham exited through the French doors for his romantic moonlight stroll, failing to invite his beloved to accompany him. Moments later he could be seen unsteadily wandering down the sloping lawn in the direction of the folly.

'We're very sorry about this,' Sunday said to Clarence, who was supervising the bar and seemed a little flustered at Pelham's state. 'He's not normally like this.'

Clarence sighed. 'It happens more often than you would think. I wouldn't mind so much if it wasn't for Terry's rhododendrons.'

'Terry's rhododendrons?' Sunday enquired, not having been privy to Clarence's earlier monologue on the subject.

Clarence heaved another mournful sigh. 'Flattened!' he declared dramatically. 'On a regular basis. The gentlemen overindulge and then fall off the folly and into the rhododendrons. It breaks Terry's heart. They're prize-winning rhododendrons, you see.'

'Could you not re-plant them somewhere else?' Sunday suggested practically.

Clarence turned huge, surprised eyes on her. 'Oh my heavens, no. That's the perfect spot for them. Just enough sun and shade, exactly the right temperature. No,' he went on sorrowfully, 'if we could just do something about gentlemen landing face-down in them, we'd have the Royal Easter Show blue ribbon wrapped up for sure. Terry loves those rhododendrons more than he loves me.' He ended with yet another forlorn sigh.

Delighting in this ridiculous exchange, and quite forgetting that he and Hero were at loggerheads, Oscar turned to share a conspiratorial look with her. A shadow fell across his face as he saw that he was too late. She was making her way across the lawn in the moonlight, in search of Pelham.

$$\star \; \overset{\displaystyle \star}{} \; \star$$

The pavilion, or the folly, as Clarence and Terry liked to call it, was a charming structure, reminding Hero of the scene in *The Sound of Music* when Liesl danced with Rolf during the thunderstorm. That she and Pelham were unlikely to re-enact one of her favourite movie scenes became abundantly clear, however, when she found her lover sprawled in a patch of moonlight in the middle of the floor.

'Pelham?' Hero said gently, bending over him.

Pelham's flushed face lit up and he patted the floor next to him in invitation. 'Hero! Fancy a drink?'

'No thanks.' She decided it was wise to use gentle persuasion, given his condition. In a friendly tone she said, 'This is a lovely spot, isn't it?'

Pelham looked around disconsolately. 'I suppose so.' He frowned and, after further cogitation, put his finger on what the folly lacked. ''s very far from the bar though.'

Hero was unable to disagree with this assertion so she contented herself with sitting down next to him and humming a few bars from the duet between Liesl and Rolf.

'What's that?' Pelham asked.

'"You are sixteen, going on seventeen",' Hero sang, with a small laugh. 'This place reminds me of a scene in . . . Oh, never mind.' She sighed. Pelham had never seen a musical in his life.

'I'm not sixteen, I'm thirty-three,' he pointed out helpfully.

Hero, however, was lost in pensive thought. 'Pelham,' she said, turning a troubled gaze towards him, 'what's our song?'

With impeccable breeding, he stifled a burp. 'What do you mean?'

'Just that . . . we don't have a song.'

Pelham's brow furrowed. 'What do we need a song for?'

'Oh, you know.' Hero tried to sound light hearted. 'To remind us of each other. To play when I walk down the aisle.' She instantly cursed her choice of words as Pelham remembered what he had been intending to do and rather clumsily dragged himself up onto one knee. Unable to balance, he shifted to both knees.

Hero scrambled to her feet and tried frantically to make him stand up. 'No, I didn't mean —'

He cut over her, determined to speak his mind. 'Hero,' he began, accurately enough, before completely confusing her by adding, 'my adorable puggle.'

'Your what?'

'Puggle,' Pelham repeated. 'Baby echidna. Unless, of course, you'd rather be a polliwog?' he enquired. 'It's another name for a tadpole.'

'I don't want to be either of those,' Hero said grimly, detecting the fell hand of Oscar at work. 'I'm quite happy being called Hero.'

'Oh.' Pelham considered this for a moment. 'Does that mean you wouldn't have liked the fibreglass shark either?'

'The what?'

'Fibreglass shark.' Pelham hiccupped. 'I could have saved you from it.'

'What possible danger could I be in from a fibreglass shark?' Hero demanded.

Pelham tapped his finger against his nose wisely. 'Well, I thought it was unlikely myself. Martin suggested it.'

'Oh, he did, did he?' Hero said, her expression darkening. 'What exactly did he say?'

Pelham screwed up his face in thought. 'Danger,' he finally said proudly. 'Thassit. Had to save you from danger.'

Oddly, Hero felt grief, not satisfaction, at having her suspicions confirmed about the horse-riding incident. 'Well, let's not worry about him right now. Come on, Pelham, let's get you into bed.'

He waved her aside with the hand holding the champagne bottle. 'Hero, you know how I feel about you. Love. Devotion. All that sort of thing.' He stopped hazily and then remembered what he had been going to say. 'So how about it?'

'I'm very fond of you, too, Pelham,' Hero said quickly, trying to forestall an actual marriage proposal. 'But why don't we discuss this in the morning?'

He squinted at her, as though trying to remember something else. 'A-ha!' he said with satisfaction, as it came back to him. 'Can you hold this for me? Bloody sling.'

'Of course,' Hero said distractedly. She took the champagne bottle as Pelham fumbled in his pockets with his good hand. Withdrawing a ring box, he clumsily handed it to her.

'For you,' he said, unnecessarily. 'Try it on. Here, I'll hold the bottle.' He watched as Hero opened the jewellery box. Nestled within was a sparkling diamond ring.

'It's beautiful,' Hero said, wondering why she felt like crying.

Pelham tipped his head back to drain the dregs of the champagne. Discovering that the bottle was empty, he threw it on the floor where it rolled with a clatter under a bench. Taking the ring out of the box, he put it on Hero's finger.

'There,' he said with satisfaction. 'Bit big, but we can have that fixed.'

Hero gazed at the enormous jewel on her finger, wondering why it was that instead of the unfamiliar jewel looking out of place, she felt as though her hand no longer belonged to her. 'Pelham, why don't you stand up and I'll help you to bed? We can discuss this in the morning.'

Pelham frowned in concentration as he struggled to his feet. 'Does that mean you'll marry me?' he asked, swaying ever more dangerously.

Hero guided him towards the marble stairs, and fumbled for a response. 'I . . . I —'

But before she could provide a definite answer, Pelham pitched headfirst over the side of the folly, landing unconscious in Terry's prize-winning rhododendrons.

* ✳ *

'Morning,' Sunday said brightly, as Hero and Pelham made their way towards the breakfast table.

Pelham winced at her cheerfulness.

'Coffee?' Sunday said, rather more loudly than was necessary, feeling the churlish urge to extract a measure of vengeance for Pelham having shouted that time at Toby.

Hero, who had spent a sleepless night alternately fretting and fuming, not the least because she was utterly outraged at Oscar's interference in her relationship, ignored everyone as she poured a glass of juice.

'Good morning,' Oscar said, lowering his paper. 'How's the wrist, Pelham?'

He got no response, for at that moment Sunday spied the ring on Hero's engagement finger and shrieked. 'Oh my god! You're engaged?'

Hero looked down at her hand. She had been so terrified of losing the enormous jewel that she'd decided the safest place to keep it was on her hand. She raised her gaze to see everyone's eyes riveted on her.

Pelham stared at her, stunned. 'Did I . . . ?'

'You did,' Hero said faintly.

'And you . . . ?'

There was a paralysed pause. Hero refused to glance in Oscar's direction as she replied, 'I did. I mean I do. I will.'

Pelham's expression cleared. After a momentary pause, Sunday jumped up to hug Hero and then made her way over to Pelham to congratulate him.

Only when she was certain that Pelham was occupied did Hero allow herself to look over at Oscar. He met her gaze squarely, and she flushed and fought the urge to look away. He inclined his head slightly, then rose to shake Pelham's hand and congratulate him on securing the girl of his dreams.

16

The romance of elephants and large erections

Beth and Jake peered through the window into Oscar's office. Since the disastrous weekend away, they had been extremely anxious about him.

'Go and talk to him,' Beth hissed at Jake.

'You go and talk to him.'

'Why me?'

'You're better at that kind of stuff than I am.'

'I've already tried. He just hugs me, tells me not to worry and then goes quiet again.'

'I hate it when he goes quiet,' Jake said, with deep feeling. 'It's so unnatural.'

'I know. Which is why you're going in there now.' Beth gave him a small shove in the direction of the closed door. 'Go on.'

'Fine. But no listening in on the intercom,' he warned.

She crossed her heart and waved him in. After gently knocking, Jake pushed open the door.

Oscar was in the customary position he'd adopted since Hero had become engaged to Pelham. Reclining in his chair, hands clasped around the back of his head, he was looking intently at the ceiling, as though the answers to all of his problems could be found there.

'Oscar? It's me, mate. Jake.'

Oscar slowly came out of his deep reverie and blinked. 'Why are you talking like I'm in a coma?'

'Because you pretty much have been in one for two weeks now, since – since, well, you know,' Jake stumbled, wishing Beth were there.

'Since Hero got engaged to that prat,' Oscar said, succinctly.

'Yes. Since then. We're worried about you. Me and Beth. You seem so preoccupied.'

Oscar waved one hand to dismiss his concerns. 'I'm just thinking a lot.'

'About Hero?'

'Of course about Hero.'

'Well, that's good,' Jake said encouragingly. 'It'll be much easier to get over her if you put in the hard yards now and, er . . .' He fumbled for the best phrase and then, with a triumphant flourish, produced, 'Achieve closure.'

Oscar frowned. 'Get over her? *Achieve closure?* Jake, what are you talking about? I don't *want* to get over Hero – I want to be with her. I know the real Hero, and however hard she's trying to be someone else right now, I know that she isn't going to marry Pelham.'

'Have they called off their engagement?' Jake asked, startled.

'Not yet. But they're bound to. I mean, she can't marry both of us. It's illegal. And immoral. Hero's very big on ethical behaviour. Probably still giving herself a hard time about kissing me the night before she accepted Pelham's proposal,' he finished fondly.

Jake choked but stopped himself from saying anything further.

'So I'm re-thinking my strategy,' Oscar continued. 'I want it to be perfect, of course. The central problem, I've just realised, is that I have too much competition.'

Jake was struggling to keep up with him. 'What do you mean? How many other men have proposed to her?'

'I'm not talking about other men. I'm talking about her best friend, Sunday.'

'You think Sunday wants to marry Hero, too?' Jake asked tentatively, wondering why it was that in Oscar's company he so often felt as though he were being led into the heart of a sandstorm. Blindfolded. By a delusional guide who could only communicate though a primitive form of grunts and tongue-clicking.

Oscar looked at his long-suffering friend sternly. 'Jake, are you quite all right? You're acting very strangely.'

'*I'm* acting strangely? You're the one who seems to think every bloody person in the world, including her best friend, wants to marry Hero.'

'Will you stop blathering for one minute and listen to me? I don't think that Sunday wants to marry Hero but I do think that they've already done pretty much all of the romantic things together. When I went over for dinner, I saw all these photos stuck to the fridge. Sunday and Hero at the top of the Empire State Building at night. On a sunset cruise in Hawaii. At the Eiffel Tower and the leaning tower of Pisa.'

'Why don't you take her to the revolving restaurant at the top of Sydney Tower?' Jake suggested.

Oscar eyed him with displeasure. 'Of all the tacky, *obvious* places. Why would you even suggest something like that?'

'Well, she likes tall buildings, doesn't she?'

'Says who?'

'You just said so yourself. From the sound of it, wherever there's an immense erection, there's your girl.'

'Jake, shut up and pay attention. I want to give Hero the most romantic moment of her life, but when you live in Australia, you can't just whisk someone away for a romantic weekend in Paris or Barcelona.' Oscar collapsed back into gloom.

'You could take her to Melbourne or Brisbane,' Jake offered doubtfully.

Oscar eyed him with loathing. 'I'm not even going to respond to the Brisbane comment. And as for Melbourne, what exactly do you think we'll do once we're there? Shop for black clothing? Drink coffee in pavement cafes and talk about how European it is?'

'How did Pelham end up proposing to her, then?'

Oscar sniffed. 'Initially he wanted to take her to the Whitsundays and have the staff prepare a dinner for them on a candle-lit table set up on a private beach.' He shook his head. 'Can you believe anyone could be so clichéd? Lucky he asked for my advice.'

'So what happened?'

'He got pissed and did a face-plant into the gay concierge's prize-winning rhododendrons.'

Jake digested this. 'And she still said yes.'

'Yes.' Oscar frowned. 'It's the only bit that doesn't make sense. I just can't believe that she really loves him.'

Jake cleared his throat. He desperately wanted to point out that Oscar didn't *want* to believe that Hero loved Pelham. But looking at the state of his friend, somehow he couldn't quite bring himself to do it. Instead he asked, 'So what are you thinking of doing?'

'I'm not sure, but it has to be something incredible and romantic and original. It has to sweep her off her feet.'

Jake applied himself to the problem and then, with a triumphant cry, he strode to the filing cabinet and pulled out a pamphlet, which he threw down in front of Oscar. 'You can hire an elephant,' he said excitedly.

'Who can?'

'You can. Actually, anyone can. It's fairly expensive but it can be done.'

'Why would I want to hire an elephant?'

'For Hero.'

'Where does the elephant come into it?' Oscar asked patiently.

'I can't think of everything!' Jake said, exasperated. 'You have to put in a bit, too. Perhaps you could sit on the elephant.'

'Both of us, or just me?'

Jake considered. 'I think it would be better if it were both of you. Otherwise, if you were on the elephant and she was on the ground, you might have to shout and Hero might not find that very romantic.'

'Shouting from the top of an elephant doesn't sound very romantic,' Oscar agreed. 'Er, could you just clarify for me again – what exactly is romantic about the elephant in the first place?'

'It's not the elephant, per se,' Jake said, with great dignity. 'It's the *gesture*. It's a grand gesture.'

'Oh.'

'It's the *size* of the elephant that makes it romantic,' Jake continued, warming to his topic. 'And the fact that elephants can be difficult to procure.'

'You just said that anyone can hire an elephant.'

'Well, yes, but you have to research it. Anyway, that's not the point. Why do you think so many men propose at the top of tall buildings?'

'So they can jump off if she says no?'

'Because it's *symbolic*. Standing at the top of a tall building, it's like saying you've got the world at your feet. An elephant, sky-writing – they're all big, grand gestures that say love is limitless.'

Oscar was staring at his friend in awe. 'Jake, that was beautiful. I think I want to marry you.'

Jake glared at him. 'Go ahead, laugh. But you've been sitting here for two weeks staring at the ceiling. At least I've come up with a decent suggestion. What have you come up with?'

Oscar looked at him with surprising calm. 'Something just occurred to me, actually. I'm going to do what every Aussie male does when he's confronted with the big issues in life.'

'What's that?' Jake asked suspiciously.

Oscar beamed. 'I'm going to ask my mum.'

'Mum? How did Dad propose to you?'

'He didn't really,' Jean said, reflectively. 'Once we'd been together for about a year, it was pretty much taken for granted that we'd tie the knot. Things were different in those days.' Emerging from a pleasant reverie, she looked over at Jake, who had been cajoled into accompanying Oscar for moral support. 'How *is* Beth, Jake?'

Jake looked startled. 'She's fine, Mrs Martin. Same as always.'

'Numbskull,' Jean said. 'You haven't a clue, have you?'

Jake looked helplessly at Oscar, who shrugged.

'Mum, forget about Jake and concentrate on me. Hero's engaged to Pelham and I have to stop her, but I don't know how.'

'I suggested an elephant,' Jake interjected, in an ill-fated attempt to win Jean's approval.

'And pray what would Hero want with a nasty, smelly beast whose steaming dung is the size of your head, Jake?' Jean enquired.

Jake gulped. 'It's the gesture,' he said meekly. 'It's grand.'

Having reduced Jake to the level of shame-faced schoolboy, Jean turned her gaze on her son. 'I know you felt very strongly about Hero when you met her in New York,' she said gently. 'But Oscar, has it occurred to you that Hero might have changed?' She let this sink in, before continuing. 'And you've changed, too. Back then you were —'

'I know how I was back then,' Oscar interrupted, in a voice that signalled he wasn't prepared to discuss it further. Seeing that Jake had averted his gaze and that his mother was looking anxious, he softened. 'Look, I know this seems crazy,' he said, running one hand through his already dishevelled hair. 'But I'm not clinging on to some dream of a girl that I made up years ago. Hero's real, and she's about to make a horrible mistake with her life. And it's partly my fault,' he added shrewdly. 'I bet you anything that I goaded her into accepting Pelham's proposal.'

'Whatever her motivation was, it's her decision to make,' Jean pointed out.

Oscar looked at her despairingly. 'Mum, you liked Hero. And you met Pelham. Do you really think I should just let her marry him without even trying?'

Jean heaved a deep sigh and gave in. 'I don't care how much you boys make from that company of yours, I can tell you this. If I know anything about the matter, Hero doesn't want elephants or marching bands or sky-writers. Just tell her how you feel.'

'I've already done that,' Oscar pointed out. 'And it hasn't got me anywhere. If I'm going to compete with Pelham, there's no point in being sensible and responsible. I tried just being friends with Hero, so we could get to know each other, but now that they're engaged, I don't have the luxury of taking things slowly. And Hero's overdosing on reality as it is. The real Hero's like me – she's a dreamer and a romantic. But between them, Pelham and the stubborn Hero are burying her alive.'

'Why are you so sure you know the real Hero?' his mother asked suspiciously. 'You can't tell me you got all that insight into her character from having fantastic sex with her in New York.'

'Mother!'

Jake made a choking noise and clapped his hands over his ears while Oscar looked at his mother, outraged.

'Oh, as if you didn't sleep together,' she said dismissively. 'Now answer my question. Have you been reading her diary?'

'Not exactly,' Oscar said evasively, wishing that his mother wasn't so alarmingly telepathic, and trying not to think of Hero's postcard in case she somehow picked up on it. 'Look, just trust me on this. If I'm wrong, she'll go ahead and marry Pelham. But if I'm right, I know that she'll respond. All I need help with is the context. So what do you consider romantic?'

Jean didn't have to stop to think. 'The fact that your father and I were married for thirty-seven years and every single morning he brought me a cup of tea in bed,' she said wistfully.

Oscar leaned over and kissed her cheek. 'I think I get your point. But I don't have thirty-seven years to change Hero's mind.' He stood up to leave. 'By the way, if someone did want to propose in the traditional manner, do you know if he's meant to get down on his right or his left knee?'

The mischievous sparkle returned to Jean's eyes. 'If I were you, Oscar my love, I'd get down on both of them and say something nice about her shoes while you're down there.' She paused and then added, 'I liked Hero very much. And I'm sure your dad and . . . and everyone who loved you, they'd all be very happy if things worked out between you.'

Oscar looked at her for a long moment. 'Thanks, Mum.'

They said their goodbyes and left. Only then did Jean allow the tears that she had been holding back to roll gently down her face.

17

Orange quarters and turtle doves

Oscar looked up in surprise as Toby was ushered into his office. 'Hey, what are you doing here?'

Toby shook his hand shyly. 'I came to ask if you were serious about that offer of work. I've been practising singing without the gorilla suit and I think I'm almost ready to do it in public and in daylight,' he added in a rush.

'Absolutely. I've convinced my colleagues of the romance of singing telegrams, so you can start up the new department. Give your details to Beth and she can add them to the system. By the way, are you busy right now?' He waved Toby to follow him down the corridor to where Beth sat at reception.

'Not really,' Toby answered, struggling to keep up.

'Excellent. You can accompany me on a fact-finding mission. Beth, I'm going out for a couple of hours. You can call my mobile if you need me.'

'Of course,' Beth said calmly. 'Where are you going?'

But Oscar was already making his way towards the carpark. Toby shrugged at her and smiled helplessly before following in Oscar's wake.

'Where are we going?' he asked, sliding into the passenger seat of Oscar's car.

'The exhibition centre at Darling Harbour. The bridal fair at the exhibition centre, to be exact.'

'Oh.' Toby thought this through. 'Why?'

'Research,' Oscar replied briskly, starting the engine.

'Research?' Toby hesitated and then asked, 'This doesn't have anything to do with Hero, does it?'

Oscar grinned. 'I've been racking my brains for weeks, trying to think of a way to get through to her, and I just can't seem to come up with the perfect solution. I need romantic inspiration.'

'But isn't Hero getting married to Pelham?' Toby said in confusion.

'They're *engaged*, Toby,' Oscar said severely. 'It doesn't necessarily mean that they will get married.' Seeing that Toby was still looking bewildered, he elaborated. 'Engagements are like sending a canary down a mine shaft. It's a trial run. If the canary comes back twittering, then the miners can proceed to the hidden treasures.'

'So marriage is the treasure and you don't want Pelham to have it?' Toby asked, trying very hard to see where this was going.

'God, no. Pelham is welcome to his own treasure, just as long as it's not Hero. No, I just want Pelham and Hero's canary to snuff it,' Oscar said cheerfully.

'Oh.' Toby was silent for a moment. 'What does this have to do with the bridal fair again?'

'Ideas. Inspiration.'

'But you're not going to get original ideas from a bridal fair,' Toby protested. 'There'll just be an endless huge room filled with stands for wedding dresses, tuxedos, reception centres and bands for hire. I mean, how complicated can getting married be?'

⋆ ✱ ⋆

'Butterfly releases are stand number thirty-five. Take the far right-hand aisle and turn left at the bagpipes display, go past the teeth-bleaching demonstration and wedding-dress conservation box salesman and it's right next to the cupcake-wedding-cake versus croquembouche cook-off. Next!'

The harassed guide at the information stand greeted Oscar and Toby, who were staring around the enormous exhibition hall with mouths agape.

'Straight to aisle forty for you two. Next!'

'Wait a minute, how do you know what we're looking for?' Oscar asked.

'Specialists in lesbian and gay weddings are in aisle forty.'

'Oh. Thanks. But we're not marrying each other.'

'You're not?' The guide looked around, as though expecting to see their errant fiancées hiding under the 'Win The *Australian Idol* Second Runner-Up As Your Wedding Singer!' raffle table.

'Nope. Is there anyone that specialises in wedding sabotage?'

'I beg your pardon?'

'Sabotage,' Oscar repeated. 'You know, averting a marriage because you can see that the couple are making a terrible mistake.'

'I don't think sabotage is listed. But let me check.' The guide consulted an enormous index of the fair's participants. 'Let's see, I guess that would be under "s". Hmmm, napkin rings, orange quarter suppliers . . .'

'Orange quarter suppliers?' Toby repeated in surprise.

'Yes, it's for people who want an AFL-themed wedding. They're very popular nowadays, especially in the country towns. The groom wears the guernsey, shorts and footy boots and the bride throws a footy for the single girls to mark, instead of a bouquet.'

'But can't you just cut up your own oranges?'

'You could,' the guide said, in a distant tone that conveyed her view on the cheapness of preparing one's own orange quarters. 'Now, where was I? Ah yes. "Pagan rituals, pageboy discipline, personalised stationery, priests".' She shook her head sadly. 'It skips straight from "roses" to "tiaras and turtle doves". I'm sorry, boys, there's no "sabotage", although I must say it's an excellent idea. But since you've already bought your tickets, why don't you go in and look around anyway?' She leant in and whispered, 'Anecdotally, I've heard that just attending this fair can break up engagements, so you never know, you might be in luck.' She smiled mistily at them and then abruptly bawled, 'NEXT!'

A little daunted, Oscar and Toby plunged into the predominantly female crowd. Every so often a male, wearing a hunted expression and clutching several showbags filled with advertising material, shot them a desperate, pleading glance before trailing off in the wake of his excited womenfolk.

'What are we looking for exactly?' Toby asked.

'I'll know it when I see it,' Oscar replied enigmatically. 'Hey, do you think Hero would like a star?' He paused at a stand that promised to name a star after your beloved, presumably for an intergalactically negotiated sum.

'Dunno. What's she going to do with it?'

'I could buy her a telescope, too, so she could look at it,' Oscar said, warming to the idea.

'She'd probably use the telescope to keep a lookout and run away when you come to visit.'

'Good point. Okay, forget the star.'

Toby halted in front of another stand. 'Why are there so many signs using French words?' he wondered aloud, gazing at the '*L'amour in the Time of Calories*' stall.

'French is considered a romantic language, I suppose.' Oscar headed towards a jewellery stand where he was greeted by an immaculately groomed woman sporting a red velvet suit, a fox stole over her shoulders and an alarmingly bouffant blue hairstyle.

'*Bonjour, monsieurs,*' she announced in a broad Australian accent. 'My name is Pearl. Jewels were my destiny. When it comes to engagement rings, I consider my happy role to be that of the gatekeeper to paradise.'

Seeing nothing amiss with this greeting, Oscar promptly shook her hand and congratulated her on her elevated role in life, while Toby simply goggled and tried to avoid the beady glass stare of the fox.

'Ah,' Pearl cooed, seeing Oscar's gaze drawn to a beautiful ring of pink and white diamonds. 'Now that one is very elegant. Perfect for the sophisticated lady with smaller hands. What shape are your fiancée's hands?' she earnestly probed.

'Hand-shaped,' Oscar replied, startled, leaving aside the fact that he didn't have a fiancée. 'What other shapes are there?'

She smacked him playfully, and to Toby's great distress, the fox head bounced up and down on her shoulder. 'Naughty! You know what I mean. It's very important that the ring you choose reflects your *chérie*'s personality, as well as symbolising your relationship.'

'Do you have anything in granite?' Toby enquired.

'Shut up, Toby,' Oscar hissed.

'Why?' Toby asked, widening his eyes in mock surprise. 'It's the perfect choice. It symbolises Hero's attitude towards you, as well as the rocks in your head. Perfect, if you ask me. Of course, it will have to be quite a small piece of granite. There's not much room left on Hero's engagement finger these days,' he explained to a bemused Pearl.

'Shut *up*, Toby,' Oscar repeated, loudly enough to catch the attention of a nearby woman who had been deep in frustrated conversation with a cowering girl wearing a headset and carrying a clipboard. Her eyes narrowed as she sized up Toby and Oscar, and in a moment she was upon them.

'Good afternoon, my name's Moira,' she said briskly, holding out a hand to shake. 'I'm in charge of the catwalk parades but we've had a little problem with some of our male models and we need extras for the next parade. It starts in ten minutes. Are you interested?'

'You want us to get up there?' Toby asked in horror, looking at the long catwalk set up in the centre of the room. 'Not a chance.'

'We'll pay you five hundred dollars for fifteen minutes,' Moira said, adding, 'each.'

'What happened to the real male models?' asked an interested Oscar.

'Kilts. Very large safety pins,' she replied tersely.

'Uh-uh.' Toby shook his head emphatically. 'No way. Thank you very much for asking but there's no way in hell we're getting up there.'

Toby turned to walk away, but Oscar grabbed his arm. 'Wait a minute, Toby. This could be the perfect opportunity for you.'

'What are you talking about? I'm a singer, not a male model!'

'Yes, but you're a singer who finds it hard to sing in public without your gorilla costume. Don't you see? This would give you excellent practice. You don't even have to sing – you just wear a suit and walk in front of a crowd.'

'Will I be wearing a suit?' Toby demanded of Moira.

'Yes. Well, maybe a kilt,' she disclosed reluctantly. 'But we've worked the safety pins out now and there's a St John's ambulance officer on standby.'

'We'll do it,' Oscar said.

Toby emitted a protesting yelp but it was too late. Oscar was already pulling him in Moira's wake, deaf to Pearl's last-ditch attempt to sell him a ring with the heartfelt cry of, 'But *monsieur*! *Waitez-vous!*'

'Oscar, stop it!' Toby objected, dragging his feet. 'Hey, why do you want to do this so badly?'

'It'll be fun,' Oscar threw over his shoulder. 'We can pretend we're in *Zoolander*. We'll have our own walk-off.'

Toby followed reluctantly, protesting all the way and still not quite believing that Oscar was doing this to help him overcome his stage-fright. And in this Toby was quite correct, because while he'd been giving Moira his first, firm refusal, Oscar had seen something that Toby hadn't: Sunday and Hero, and an older woman who had to be Hero's mother, making their way through the crowd.

* ✶ *

'Mum, I don't need a wedding planner,' Hero said patiently, for the third time.

Unsurprisingly, Hero had an ulterior motive in allowing her mother to coerce her into attending the bridal fair. She had been about to reject the invitation out of hand when it occurred to her that she might get some good story ideas for the magazine. Having had five ideas rejected kindly but firmly by Sasha the previous week, she was starting to feel desperate.

Coralie tried to hide her disappointment at her daughter's stubbornness. 'Well, if you're sure, darling. But there are a thousand and one details that are so easy to overlook, and the planner over there is offering a bonus grief-counselling session.'

'It's a wedding, not a funeral! Why would anyone need grief counselling?' Hero demanded, waiting for Sunday, who had stopped to admire a floral display, to catch up.

Hero's mother looked uncomfortable. 'Apparently not every parent-in-law feels that they're gaining a daughter. Some just feel like they're losing a son.'

'Are you referring to Gloria and Norman?' Hero said icily, naming Pelham's admittedly difficult parents, who had the unfortunate habit of referring to Pelham as their 'first-born'.

Coralie pursed her lips and murmured something that sounded like 'mmm-whff'.

'I'll have you know that they were *delighted* when Pelham announced our engagement,' Hero said, suppressing the memory of Gloria's startled cry, which had been closely followed by the pressing of a linen handkerchief to her lips and the immediately expressed desire to lie down in a darkened room. Norman had said, 'Harumph!' This was about as much as anyone ever got out of him, but Hero was firmly of the opinion that this 'harumph!' had been uttered in a celebratory tone of parental pride.

Thankfully, Hero's mother was distracted by a shirtless, bow-tie-wearing stripper who announced that his name was Chad and handed her a pamphlet on hens' night harbour cruises with a rather smarmy wink. Within thirty seconds, Coralie had completely discomfited the young stud by confiding how, in her day, prior to the invention of the booster gel cup, girls had had to stuff their bras with tissues – said while glancing knowingly in the direction of his crotch. By the time she moved on to sage words of advice regarding ingrown chest hair, Chad's brash exterior was in tatters, but he was conscious, too, of feeling pleasantly molly-coddled in a way he hadn't experienced since he was eight.

Hero and Sunday had strolled on without waiting for Coralie. Taking advantage of their privacy, Sunday asked, 'Is your mum quite okay?'

'As okay as she ever is, I guess. Why?'

'She keeps asking me what Sigourney Weaver's *really* like. I must have told her ten times that I've never met Sigourney Weaver. In fact I didn't even know who she was until your mum explained.'

'She thinks you're saving Rwandan mountain gorillas with Sigourney Weaver.'

Sunday thought this through. 'Is this anything to do with Toby and his gorilla suit?'

'Of course it is. Just go along with it, Sun. It's probably less complicated in the long run. Where is Mum, by the way?'

'She's still at the hens' night stand.' Sunday glanced over with interest. 'She seems to be getting a pole-dancing lesson now. Should we do something?'

'There's nothing we can do. She's always been uncontrollable, but I think she's getting worse. If you ask me, parents should be encouraged not to retire,' Hero continued disapprovingly. 'It's very bad for them.'

Sunday giggled. 'I love your parents. I never did find out how their Bollywood Valentine's dinner ended up.'

'It was horrible,' Hero said, shuddering. 'They called each other Raj and Sunita for a month afterwards. And apparently the neighbours complained because they kept breaking into song in the new pergola.'

'It's nice that they're so in love after all this time, isn't it?' Sunday sighed.

'Yes, and they've never needed to spend thousands of dollars to prove it.' In disgust, Hero took in the manic bustle surrounding them. 'This place isn't about love and romance, it's all about bloody money. Where weddings and commercial transactions are concerned, it usually involves Russian brides and the internet, but all this is even worse.'

Sunday frowned at her. 'Don't be so cynical.'

'Cynicism's got nothing to do with it.' They stopped by a travel agent's desk and Hero picked up a brochure. 'Look at this – a week-long honeymoon in Fiji costs double what a normal week's holiday in exactly the same place costs. Thousands extra for satin sheets and roses on arrival and a couple of strategically placed candles. It's all such a rip-off.'

'Yes, well, a honeymoon's not a holiday, is it, dear,' the man in charge of the stand snapped, plucking the brochure out of Hero's hand. 'And most people are happy to pay a little extra to ensure that the most magical and special time they'll ever spend with their chosen soul mate is perfection.'

Hero ignored him and continued with her tirade, gesturing at the other stands to support her argument. 'And the lengths women go to for a single day! Facials, diets, waxing, teeth bleaching. What's next? Disposable Botox injections?'

'Aisle four,' interjected a passing woman with a very tight forehead.

'And all of it preying upon people's emotions and weaknesses and insecurities. It's horrible. They're vultures.' Hero stopped in her tracks and her eyes gleamed as it occurred to her that this could make an excellent article for *Angel*. She could even see the title: 'For Love *And* Money'.

'The people here don't look like they're being preyed upon,' Sunday argued, watching a woman nearby laughing with her bridesmaids as they attempted to waltz with a professional instructor.

'Well, they are,' Hero said firmly, as loud music suddenly blared out of the overhead sound system. 'And furthermore —'

Whatever Hero had been going to say was lost as Sunday clutched her arm in a painful grip. '*Hero!* Is that —' she gasped.

Hero followed her gaze to the catwalk. '*Oh my god . . .*'

There, at the back of the catwalk, splendidly attired in a ruffled white shirt and green tartan kilt, was Toby, launching a last-ditch attempt to escape. 'I have funny knees,' he hissed miserably at Oscar.

'Everyone has funny knees, Tobes. Knees are meant to be knobbly. They're protruding bits of bone.'

'At least yours are even. Mine are lopsided.'

'Will you please stop going on about your knees? We're walking out there, doing a full turn, holding a standard hand-on-hip pose with a backwards chin to right shoulder, then walking back in half-time. And that's that. Consider it your interview for your new job with Serendipity. Now go.' Oscar adjusted Toby's sporran and gave his petrified friend a small shove.

To the jaunty strains of 'Achy Breaky Heart', they made their way out on to the catwalk, following in the wake of a cowgirl-styled bride, complete with white rhinestone-trimmed boots and a cracking whip.

Toby trudged grimly ahead, looking neither left nor right. Oscar, however, was playing the crowd like a pro, winking cheekily at admiring girls, completely comfortable with the kilt swishing gaily around his knees.

He scanned the crowd until he located Sunday and Hero, who had come to a dead halt with mouths wide open. Oscar grinned and, oblivious to a squawk of protest from Toby, jumped agilely from the stage and dropped onto one knee in front of Hero.

'What's that idiot doing?' the floor manager muttered into her headset.

Moira looked intently at the crowd, who were lapping it up. 'Just go with it,' she ordered. 'Tell the girls backstage to hold off on their cues. Signal the other models to keep up a little show.'

Hero, meanwhile, was staring dumbstruck at her kilted nemesis, who had possessed himself of one of her hands.

'Marry me?' he asked, his eyes twinkling at her outrage.

'No!' she hissed. 'What on earth are you doing here?'

'Kill the music,' Moira commanded, sensing a genuine drama. The music abruptly stopped and the entire crowd turned to look at Hero, whose cheeks were burning as Oscar, to ripples of laughter, proceeded to get onto both knees.

'Will you marry me?' he asked again.

A contented sigh rippled through the crowd.

'NO!' Hero shouted.

The crowd looked at her disapprovingly and the sigh changed to a disgusted murmur.

'I'll marry you, darlin',' a nearby woman offered, casting Hero an indignant look that clearly said 'spoilsport'.

Knowing that Hero was close to imploding with rage, Oscar cast her one final look of merriment and then shuffled, still on his knees, straight to Hero's mother.

Oscar repeated his offer and, blushing with delight, Coralie accepted. With considerable effort, he hoisted her into his arms and carried her in triumph backstage. Utterly lost for words at the spectacle of Oscar carrying off her mother, Hero also had to suppress the exasperating truth that her predominant emotion was envy. Toby and the cowgirl bride, who had taught him how to boot-scoot while Oscar held his side-show, also exited as the entire crowd, minus one, thunderously applauded.

As the hubbub died down and the parade continued, Hero said loudly, 'Well, I couldn't say yes, could I? I'm already engaged.' The few people who bothered to listen shook their heads and gave her a wide berth, treating her like a serious killjoy. She could have wept with frustration.

'Shall we go and find your mum?' Sunday asked, when she had stopped wolf-whistling and cheering her beloved.

'No. She's probably ringing Dad to tell him the good news about her engagement,' Hero said acidly.

'Why didn't you just say yes?'

'Say *yes*?' Hero repeated in horror. 'Are you mad? He would have held me to it!'

'I don't see how,' Sunday said reasonably. 'It was only a bit of fun. I think you're starting to take things too seriously, Hero.'

'I *know* him,' Hero said bitterly, pushing through the crowd towards the transportation section. 'If I'd said yes and then tried to back out, he'd probably charge me with some arcane law involving breach of promise.'

'He probably would,' Sunday said, stopping to stroke a blinkered horse who was a proud employee of Carriages of La Elegance. 'But honestly Hero, he has to give up sometime. He can't *force* you to stand in front of a celebrant and say yes.'

'I wouldn't put it past him to find a way,' said Hero. 'The man just appeared wearing a kilt in the middle of a bridal-fair catwalk and carried off my mother. With, I might add, the assistance of your boyfriend, who up until now I thought was a sensible, reliable human being.'

'You kind of have to admire Oscar's persistence and ingenuity,' said Sunday, in a wistful voice.

'You can call it that. I prefer to call it obsession and desperation.'

'It is kind of romantic, though. You could never imagine Pelham doing something like that.'

'Thank god,' said Hero, feeling unaccountably annoyed that love for her would never motivate Pelham to behave that extremely.

At that moment Coralie swooped on them. 'Darling! Did you see me? One moment I was in the animal aisle – it was lovely. They have horse-drawn carriages and all kinds of birds, including swans and doves, and there were some depressed-looking kittens they've trained to carry engagement and wedding rings, like Mr Jinks, the cat in *Meet the Parents*.'

'Your point, Mother?' Hero said, in a tone of weary resignation.

'Well, anyway, I looked over and saw that *lovely* young man on his knees in front of you. Why did you say no?'

'I'm already engaged. That's why we're here, remember?' Hero said dampeningly.

'Oh yes. To Pelham. Well, still. And then he proposed to *me* – did you see us? It gave me quite a thrill, I must say. Took me right back to the day your father proposed on the Ferris wheel at Luna Park. Of course, the child in the car behind us was throwing up hot dog everywhere but no one can tell me that it wasn't magical.' She paused to draw breath. 'It's odd that he singled you and then me out, isn't it? I had a quick chat to him just now, but he didn't say his name.'

Sunday opened her mouth to reply but stopped, quelled by a

forbidding look from Hero.

'He's no one, Mother,' Hero said firmly. 'He's absolutely no one.'

18

The secondhand wedding dress

'So how was the bridal fair?' Pelham asked, lowering his newspaper as Hero and Sunday entered the house.

Sunday, who was feeling unwell, most probably due to the amount of wedding cake samples she had consumed, waved at Pelham and promptly disappeared into her bedroom to lie down.

'It was okay,' Hero answered, banishing the memory of Oscar down on one knee in front of her, surrounded by a crowd of excited females. 'I was getting ideas for the dress mainly.'

'But you'll be wearing Mother's dress,' Pelham said absently.

'I'll be what?'

'Of course you will. Mother would be very hurt if you didn't, Hero.' He saw the look on her face and hastened to add, 'It will be altered to fit you, of course.'

A vision of Pelham's mother, habitually dressed in pastel twin-sets, with a string of pearls around her neck and stiffly frosted hair, floated through Hero's mind. Gloria dressed well and expensively but she also looked like – well, like Pelham's mother. Hero couldn't help feeling that there was something a little bit wrong with looking like the groom's mother on your wedding day. 'But what if I don't like it?' she asked lamely.

'You will,' Pelham said. 'It was imported from Paris. Cost a fortune.'

'I'm sure it was very expensive,' Hero said, with as much patience as she could muster. 'But that's not the point. What if I don't *like* it?'

'Well, there's no point arguing about that now.' Pelham stood and folded his newspaper. 'You haven't even seen the dress. I'll let Mother know you'll be dropping by sometime this week to try it on. I'm sure that as soon as you have it on, you'll love it.'

$$* \overset{\textstyle *}{} *$$

Hero stood before the long mirror in the upstairs spare room of Pelham's parents' North Shore home, the dress falling in waves of softest satin around her.

'We'll have to let it out,' Gloria said, a trifle smugly. 'Of course, I was a *lot* younger than you when I married Pelham's father.'

Hand sewn, hand beaded, hand embroidered and trimmed with hand-made lace, there was no denying that the dress was beautiful. But Hero felt as though all those unseen hands were tightening around her throat, cutting off her oxygen. She fought for air and then, knowing there would be a fight ahead, said, 'Gloria, it's a beautiful dress. It's just . . . it's not me.'

To Hero's surprise, Gloria smiled tolerantly. 'You're marrying my first-born. My Pelham. You're going to be one of us.'

Unaccountably, an image of Jean entered Hero's mind. Jean, with her fashionable but comfortable clothes, who didn't look like an eastern suburbs princess or a North Shore lady who lunched. Jean, who looked like herself and had laughter lines deeply etched around her eyes. Hero looked at Gloria's smooth visage. There wasn't a single laughter line to be seen. Although that didn't necessarily indicate an absence of humour, it was more likely that Gloria had stocked up on supplies in aisle four at the bridal fair.

Gloria surveyed the dress thoughtfully. 'I'll have my dressmaker, Rita, do the alterations. It's a long way over to Double Bay, but she's by far the best in Sydney. Now do be careful taking it off, Hero. You almost put your foot through the train before.'

Hero stepped gingerly out of the dress. Despite the warmth of the mid-autumn day, she shivered as Gloria tenderly packed the dress back into its box.

* ✳ *

Hero looked up in surprise from her morning cup of tea as Sunday presented her with an envelope tied with a white gauze ribbon. 'What's this?'

'Your engagement present. I'd kiss you but I don't want you to get whatever it is I've got.'

'Are you still feeling sick?' Hero looked at her friend with concern, noting her pallor.

Sunday waved off her concern. 'I'm fine. I've just got some bug I can't get rid of.'

'You should go to the doctor. You've been unwell for almost a week now,' Hero scolded, as she untied the ribbon. The envelope contained a voucher with Hero's name elegantly inscribed in calligraphy on a dotted line. '"Welcome to the world of Davina Findles",' Hero read aloud.

She reached the next line and her eyes widened in dismay. '"Fortune teller",' she finished faintly.

'It's the same woman I went to last year. Remember?'

'You mean the one who said you'd be getting a pet? Despite the fact we're not allowed to keep animals in this house?'

'She didn't tell me I was going to get a pet. She said that I was going to forge a loving bond with an animal, which you said was both criminal and —' Sunday stopped short and went quite pink in the face. 'A loving bond with an animal,' she said, in a strange, high-pitched voice. 'Hero, *Toby's gorilla suit*!'

'Oh, come off it. You know what horoscopes and fortune tellers are like. They make such vague predictions, you can make them fit virtually any circumstance.'

Sunday was resolute. 'You can say what you like, but you'll see. Let me know when you're free and I'll make an appointment for both of us.'

'Okay,' Hero said, trying to sound enthusiastic. 'And thanks, Sun. It's a lovely engagement present. Now make sure you go to the doctor, okay? It's a bit early for a winter cold.'

'Yes, Mum,' Sunday said cheekily.

19

Revelations

Two weeks later, Hero hung back as they neared the fortune-teller's premises in Glebe. 'I'm still not sure about this, Sun.'

'What aren't you sure about?'

'Well, the thing about fortune tellers is that what they tell you might come true, because it's fate, but equally you could make it come true because what you think is going to happen happens because you've already thought it would.'

'I have no idea what you just said. All I know is that if it was good enough for the Oracle of Delphi, it's good enough for me,' Sunday replied comfortably. 'Anyway, I'm open to all different sorts of spirituality.'

Hero snorted. 'Spirituality? Tarot's just a deck of cards.'

'You know, your problem is that you close yourself off to anything that you don't understand or that can't be explained rationally.'

'Yes,' Hero said. 'It's because I'm a human being. Our ability to reason explains why we're running the planet and ferrets have to answer to us. Well, reason *and* thumbs,' she added, handsomely.

'If you're going to go in with a closed mind, it won't work,' Sunday said flatly.

Hero sighed. 'Fine. I'll try.'

She meant to try. She really did. But unfortunately the first thing that greeted her was an enormous sign: DAVINA FINDLES: TAROT, CLAIRVOYANCY, HOROSCOPES, CONTACT WITH THE OTHER SIDE (PETS INCLUDED), PALM AND TEA-LEAF READING.

'What? No ectoplasm?' Hero muttered, just low enough that Sunday couldn't hear.

They made their way up a creaking wooden staircase, into an atmosphere redolent with incense. A small sign hung from a closed door off the waiting room: THE UNSCIENTIFIC ART OF CRYSTAL-BALL GAZING IS NOT A SERVICE THAT IS OFFERED SO PLEASE DO NOT ASK AS REFUSAL OFTEN OFFENDS.

'Now, if she had a crystal ball she could tell who was going to ask for a crystal-ball reading and she could refuse to see them so she wouldn't offend them,' Hero pointed out.

'Shut up!' Sunday hissed.

'I'm just making a point. A little bit of foresight, Sun. Sometimes it's all that's required in this sort of delicate situation.' Hero looked up from her inspection of a brochure touting the merits of chakra realignment to see that Sunday was suddenly looking very pale. 'Hey, are you okay?' she asked in alarm.

Sunday made her way unsteadily over to the window and flung it open. Breathing deeply, her colour gradually returned to normal. 'It's just the incense,' she said, flapping Hero's concern away. 'It's a bit strong.'

'It's not that strong,' Hero argued. 'This has been going on for weeks. If you don't go to the doctor in the next day or two, I'll drag you there myself.'

Before Sunday could reply, the door was flung open and Davina Findles appeared.

To Hero's disappointment, she wasn't wearing a purple caftan embroidered with silver zodiac signs. Rather, Davina, whose age it was impossible to guess, was dressed entirely in black: a black woollen skirt was topped by a black crocheted shawl fastened around her hips, and a black organza scarf was wrapped in tight loops around her throat. Pushing a clump of rust-coloured hair off her forehead, she regarded them through kohl-rimmed eyes that continuously blinked.

Sunday came away from the window. 'Davina? Hi, I'm Sunday. You might remember me – you made an *excellent* prediction for me the last time I was in. And this is my friend, Hero.'

A faint expression of recognition flickered across Davina's face. She nodded at Sunday, then spoke in a heavy accent that might have been Eastern European, or the result of a past career at a theatre restaurant. 'You are ze vun who vas going to become intimate wiz an animal, are you not?'

'That's me.' Sunday flushed with pleasure. 'It came true,' she disclosed in a rush. 'We're very much in love.'

Davina held up one hand to forestall further disclosure. 'Pleez. Do not say any more. I do not vant ze details. Zey may make me sick.' Sunday subsided and Davina blinked myopically. 'Vich of you is first?'

'Can't we go in together?' Hero asked, not savouring the prospect of facing Davina on her own.

Davina shook her head so vehemently that the glasses perched in her bird's nest hair threatened to fall onto the floor. 'No! Ze fortune telling is very intimate. If ze future is to reveal itself to Davina, zere must be privacy.'

Hero quickly waved Sunday in. 'You go first, Sun.'

'You sure?'

'Positive. I'll wait right here.'

'Okay.' Eagerly, Sunday followed Davina into the smaller room and the door closed firmly behind them.

Hero took a seat, growing increasingly impatient as she tried to discern the muffled conversation from the other side of the door. At one point she heard Sunday loudly exclaim. With a complete lack of shame, Hero pressed her ear to the door but she couldn't hear more than the odd word. Disgruntled, she returned to her seat and flicked unseeingly through a copy of *Past Imperfect, Future Conditional*, not a French grammar book, as she'd first thought, but a fortune-tellers' trade magazine. She was startled to realise that Brad Pitt and Jennifer Aniston were going to get back together again, until she realised that the magazine was several years old.

When Sunday finally emerged from the inner sanctum, looking slightly dazed, Hero jumped to her feet. 'Well? What did she say?'

Sunday didn't quite meet her gaze. 'Lots of things,' she mumbled. 'I'll tell you later. After your session.'

Davina's room wasn't at all what Hero had expected. The fortune teller was seated at a red-velvet draped table with a deck of tarot cards in front of her. There was a heavy smell of incense in the air, but a quite ordinary-looking computer sat on a desk and one corner housed a wardrobe that looked as though it might have come from Ikea. Next to it hung a framed poster reading, WHAT LIES BEHIND US AND WHAT LIES BEFORE US ARE SMALL MATTERS COMPARED TO WHAT LIES WITHIN US. Hero couldn't help thinking that this was a rather odd choice of message for a fortune teller to display. She committed it to memory anyway, knowing that Pelham would add it to his collection of aphorisms, homilies and inspirational quotes.

'Haff you chosen vich magic carpet you prefer to visk us into ze future?' Davina asked throatily.

'I beg your pardon?'

Davina tried again. 'By vot means do you vish to experience ze revelation?'

'What are you talking about? Do I have to turn my mobile phone off?'

'Yes. You do,' snapped Davina, clearly displeased by this business-like approach to her mystical scene-setting. 'And I also must tell you zat zis session is being taped. You vill be given ze tape of your reading ven you leaff.'

'Thank you,' Hero said politely, double-checking that her mobile was switched off.

'Hiff you are *quite* ready?'

'What? Oh sorry. Go right ahead. Shoot.' Hero sat back and crossed her arms, waiting for Davina to begin predicting.

But instead Davina glared at her. 'Ze true psychic does not *shoot*. Now, for ze sird time, do you prefer ze tarot, ze tea leaves, ze palm reading or ze astrological chart?' She pronounced 'astrological' with a tremendous rolling of the r.

Hero shrugged, resisting the urge to ask for the crystal ball. 'Whatever. Cup of tea might be nice.'

'Very well. Ze tarot cards it is,' Davina hissed, with a certain amount of un-seer-like vindictiveness. 'You vill shuffle ze cards, pleez.'

Hero shuffled, trying not to breathe in the incense fug too deeply. She already felt somewhat heavy headed.

'Now cut zem into zree piles. Representing ze past, ze present and ze future.'

Hero did as she was told and Davina picked up the first pile.

'You had a happy childhood,' Davina began, 'and zere seems to be a significant female presence in your early years.'

'That would be my mother,' Hero said, bored. 'Look, can you skip the past, please? I'm not really interested in hearing whatever you managed to find out about me from Sunday. And I'm sure she told you that this reading is my gift for getting engaged to Pelham, so we may as well skip the present, too. Can we go straight to the future, if you don't mind?'

Davina glared at her as though tempted to call off the entire reading, but then, gathering her professionalism around her like a star-spangled velvet cloak, she haughtily pushed two sets of cards aside and began to lay out the third pile.

Expecting the same cries of simulated amazement and wonder from Davina that had accompanied Sunday's reading, Hero was almost annoyed as the fortune teller laid the cards out in total silence, her only reaction a tiny crease between her painted-on eyebrows.

'Well? What is it?' Hero asked finally, unable to bear the suspense.

'It is very odd. I haff never seen ze cards like zis before,' Davina began, with what seemed to be genuine puzzlement.

'I'm sure you haven't,' Hero said derisively.

'Vell, you are not going to marry . . . Vot did you say your fiancé's name vos?' Davina asked, stung to frankness by Hero's abrupt manner.

'Pelham.'

Davina pursed her lips and looked at the cards again. 'It does not make sense,' she muttered. 'Unless . . . vot is his full name?'

'Pelham Grenville-Walters,' Hero said. 'Vot – I mean, *what* does his name have to do with anything?'

Davina looked at her triumphantly. 'It is as plain as zat haughty, turned-up nose on your face. You are going to marry a man whose first name begins with "O".'

'All right,' Hero said slowly. 'Very funny. How much did he pay you?'

'Who?' asked Davina, bewildered.

'You know exactly who I'm talking about. Is he here now?' She flung up the cloth covering the table and peered underneath. Stalking across the room, she flung open the cupboard door, half expecting to see Oscar hiding between the coats.

'Young lady, I vould be grateful if you vould take your seat so I can finish your reading. I haff no idea vot zis is about but —'

'You know *exactly* what I'm talking about!' Hero yelled in frustration. 'I'm talking about Oscar Martin, who has paid you or charmed you or done something to you to make you read me that fortune and try to change my future! Well, it's not going to work, do you hear me? I don't care what you do, I am going to marry Pelham!'

'I can see zat you are very upset but zere is really no point haffing ze false hope,' Davina said soothingly. 'You are going to marry someone whose name starts with "O". It could not be clearer.'

Several weeks of accumulated frustration and worry about her impending marriage collapsed onto Hero and, to her horror, she burst into tears.

Davina forgot her annoyance and placed a comforting arm around her client's shoulders, exuding a strong smell of boiled cabbage. 'You do seem very set on zis Pelham,' she said worriedly, then her expression cleared. 'You could always buy ze cat and call it Pelham?'

'I don't want a cat called Pelham,' Hero sobbed. 'I want a husband called Pelham!'

'Do you? Vy?'

'Because . . . because . . . he loves me and . . .' She hiccupped and stopped.

'And you love him,' Davina prompted.

'Yes. I . . .' She stopped again. 'That is . . . I'm going to marry him.'

Davina surveyed her for a long moment. 'Zis is not quite ze same, is it?' she said dryly.

Moments later, Hero brushed past a startled Sunday. 'We're leaving,' she said and, without a backward glance, made her way down the staircase.

Sunday looked apologetically at Davina, who shrugged and held out a cassette.

'Your friend has left ze tape behind. Can you make sure zat she gets it? Maybe when she has calmed down a leettle, she vill vont to listen.'

$$*\ \text{\Large *}\ *$$

The following day, Sunday returned home to find Hero sitting on the couch in a darkened room and staring at the wall, a half-eaten tub of ice-cream melting slowly on her lap.

'Hero?' Sunday said, startled. 'Are you okay?' She pulled the curtains open.

Hero blinked but didn't look up. 'I don't know how to fight him any more,' she said dully. 'I'm tired and fed up, and I can fight Oscar but I can't fight the entire world. There's only one of me and he's got a whole army of gorillas and fortune tellers and god knows what else. He even has my mother and my best friend on his side. Hell, he practically has *Pelham* on his side.'

Sunday looked hurt. 'I'm not on his side,' she protested. 'I'm on your side. I'm always on your side, Hero.'

Hero gave her an appraising look, holding her ice-cream spoon aloft. 'Are you?' she asked dispassionately. 'I don't think you are.'

Sunday considered her response carefully, determined to tell Hero the truth but not wanting to say anything that could be construed as critical of Pelham. 'Has it ever occurred to you that being on Oscar's side is exactly the same as being on your side? That maybe it really is fate that you two end up together?'

'Oh, for Pete's sake. People who believe in that kind of crap ring astrology hotlines that charge five dollars a minute. It's how charlatans like Davina stay in business. It has nothing to do with fate or romance or real life or the truth.'

Sunday suddenly looked very odd, but before she could respond, Hero gave her a wan smile. 'Anyway, enough about me. How are you? Did you go to the doctor like you promised?'

'Yes.'

'Is it the 'flu?' Hero asked, putting the lid back on the ice-cream.

'No. I'm fine. I'm just . . . Hero, I'm . . . pregnant.'

'*What?*' Hero dropped the tub of ice-cream.

'I'm pregnant. The doctor confirmed it this morning. I haven't had the 'flu. I've had morning sickness.'

'Oh my god.' Hero sank limply back onto the couch and then sat bolt upright at a new thought. 'Have you told Toby?'

'Yes.' Sunday gave a small smile and swallowed. 'He's thrilled.'

'Well, that's great, Sun,' Hero said gently. 'How do you feel?'

'Not sure. Happy, but scared. Very glad that my new and overwhelming urge to eat paper products is just a natural craving. And Toby and I both want it. It's just so unexpected.' She stopped again and then added, 'Well, it *was* unexpected, until we went to see Davina.'

'What's she got to do with it?'

'She saw it. She told me I was going to become a mother very soon. And all of a sudden my constant queasiness made sense.'

'How pregnant are you?' Hero asked, uneasily quelling the memory of the prediction that Davina had made for her.

'About eight weeks. Toby and I think we might have conceived on the night of the dinner party.'

'Good lord. Those oysters were worth every cent.' Hero mused on this for a moment and then asked, 'So I assume Toby's – *stage-fright* problems are a thing of the past?'

Sunday looked at her in confusion, wondering why Hero was changing the topic. 'We hope so. He's still working quite closely with Oscar to overcome it.'

'He's what?' Hero asked, utterly startled and not wanting to dwell on the image of Oscar helping Toby with that particular problem.

But Sunday had still other revelations. 'Toby asked me to marry him.'

'Oh, my god! Are you going to?'

'I don't think so. Not right now, anyway. I feel like this is big enough as it is. But do you want to know something funny?' Sunday looked shy. 'I know you won't agree, because you don't believe in love at first sight and destiny, but even though this baby wasn't exactly planned, I feel completely sure about the future. About Toby and me, I mean. We might not have known each other for very long, but it just doesn't matter. We're right for each other and we both feel the same way. I think in your heart, you always really *know*.'

'The situation you and Toby are in has nothing to do with me and Oscar.'

'Who's talking about Oscar?' Sunday asked, innocently.

'You were. In a sneaky way. But it's not the same – you and Toby have a proper relationship. I have puppy shrubs, bolting horses and gorillas.'

'The gorilla's mine. Keep your hands off him.'

Hero grinned, and stretched out a hand. 'Can I?'

Sunday nodded.

Gently, Hero placed her hand on Sunday's still flat belly. 'Hello, baby,' she whispered.

They shared an awestruck smile, then burst out laughing. Hero flung her arms around her best friend, her heart bursting with happiness, her desire to sit in the dark and eat ice-cream entirely forgotten.

20

Sexual healing

For the next few days Sunday's news took precedence over all else, but at the back of Hero's mind, plans for revenge against Oscar had started to foment.

Sunday had become used to a certain listlessness in Hero so she was startled to see her one morning with eyes sparkling and an air of determination.

'I've had an idea,' Hero declared dramatically.

'What is it?'

'It's simple. All I have to do is pursue Oscar. I'm such an idiot not to have realised that he won't give up because he thinks I'm a challenge.'

'Let me get this straight. Oscar's been pursuing you for months and you're now so fed up, you're going to pursue *him* so he'll fall *out* of love with you?'

'Yep. What do you think?' Hero watched her friend intently.

'It's so weird, it might actually work,' Sunday conceded.

Hero whooped. 'Okay, first things first. How should I start?'

'You want to do something romantic for Oscar?' Sunday said doubtfully. 'Like what?'

There was a protracted silence.

'This romance thing is actually harder than it looks,' Hero grudgingly admitted.

'That's because you're up against an expert,' Sunday consoled. 'Most people just send flowers to get the ball rolling, but he's got years of experience. It's a bit like trying to sell ice to the Eskimos.'

'Hey, that's not a bad idea. Maybe I could dress up like an Eskimo girl.'

'Toby could lend you his gorilla suit,' Sunday offered.

'Why on earth would I want to borrow that?' Hero demanded. 'That's about the least romantic idea I've ever heard.'

'He was wearing it when we first met!' Sunday said hotly.

'All right, all right. I'm sorry. But I don't think I'll borrow it, if it's all the same to you.' She lapsed into thought and then snapped her fingers. 'Got it. Josie and the Pussycats.'

'The cartoon rock band?'

'Yep. I just remembered that Oscar has a thing for them. Maybe I could dress up in a Pussycat costume.'

'And then what are you going to do?' Sunday asked, curious.

Hero smiled sweetly. 'Easy. I'm going to do the one thing guaranteed to turn Oscar *off*. I'm going to seduce him. Pure sex, no romance: he'll freak out completely.'

'But what about Pelham? You know, your fiancé? I don't think you're exactly meant to seduce other men when you're engaged.'

Hero waved one hand to dismiss her objections. 'I'm not really going to seduce him. I'm going to do just enough to worry him so he rethinks the way he feels about me.'

She departed from the room, humming merrily, filled with schemes and stratagems. Sunday glanced ruefully at the puppy-shaped shrub that Oscar had sent Hero, which had started to flower. 'Is it just me, or are Hero and Oscar getting weirder?'

There was no reply from the flowery puppy so, with a sigh, Sunday tipped her glass of water over it.

* ✱ *

'Where are we going?' Sunday asked Hero as they stepped out of the car and on to Oxford Street on a sparkling Sydney Saturday.

'To a sex shop,' Hero said cheerfully.

'*What?*'

'I've already tried all the costume shops and none of them had what I need. But then a woman in Newtown suggested I try some of the sex shops on Oxford Street. Apparently Oscar's cartoon fetish isn't so unusual.'

As she spoke, Hero opened the door to a discreetly signed establishment. But Sunday didn't follow.

'What are you waiting for?' Hero demanded impatiently.

'I can't go in,' Sunday whispered. 'I feel like my dead grandmother is watching.'

'She probably is. She's probably urging you to buy the strap-on —'

Sunday shrieked and clapped her hands over her ears.

'— miner's lamp,' Hero finished innocently. She gave Sunday a shove through the door. 'Oh, for heaven's sake, I knew your grandmother, too. Don't forget she was a nurse during World War Two and she had six children.'

'What does that have to do with anything?'

'It means that she was a brave and feisty woman who had sex at least six times. I think it would take more than me buying a costume from a sex shop to shock her. Now move.'

They entered the shop, Hero curious and Sunday cowering. A glamorous transvestite, who appeared to be at least nine feet tall, courtesy of towering, sequinned platform-heeled boots, looked up as they entered.

'Good lord,' she drawled, taking in their fresh faces and Sunday's pastel-coloured cardigan. 'Are the Girl Guides doing fetish badges these days?'

Hero smiled. 'Yes. Once we've got our rope-tying badge, then we're allowed to move on to Bondage and Discipline.'

The transvestite eyed Hero appreciatively, obviously deciding that here was an adversary worthy of her time. Adjusting her hot-pink lurex unitard and black fishnets, she proceeded to appraise them with a connoisseur's gaze.

'Wha— what are you doing?' asked Sunday, now completely unnerved after stumbling into an inflatable pony.

The transvestite held out a hand, gesturing for silence. 'I am Madame Callous,' she announced, once she was sure that she had their complete attention. 'Callous with an "o",' she snapped, noting that Hero's lips had twitched. 'And I am discerning your inner sexuality.'

'You're what?'

'I'm discerning your inner sexuality,' Madame Callous repeated calmly. 'It's similar to astrology, only it's a more exact science. Everyone has a sex sign in the same way that you have a star sign.'

'What's your sign?' Hero asked.

'"Open for business",' Madame Callous cackled. She wiped a tear from a heavily made-up eye. 'Oh dear, I never get tired of that one. You see Pandora there?' She nodded at a young woman reading behind the counter, oblivious to all around her. 'She's a masochist.'

'How can you tell?' Sunday asked breathlessly.

Hero snorted. 'You mean apart from the fact she's reading Don DeLillo?'

Madame Callous continued, unperturbed. 'You, dear, definitely have aspects of the whip. There's no doubt it's the mind games that really turn you on. But I'm picking up something else, too . . .' She looked at Hero intently, in a trance. Then her expression cleared and she beamed as she declared, 'You're a lesbian.'

'No, I'm not,' Hero countered. 'I have a male fiancé. Try again.'

'We're talking about your inner sexuality, darling. Your secret desires and fantasies, not the socially acceptable façade that you present to this heterosexually-centric, facist world we live in. Are you sure you've never felt the teensiest inclination to, you know, play tea parties with only the cups?'

Hero considered this. 'Is that a euphemism for having sex with another woman?'

'Naturally. Women are like the open vessel, waiting to be filled. The teapot on the other hand – very phallic. The spout, you see.'

'Oh. Well, in that case, no. I quite like teapots, too.'

'But you do have a thing for Angelina Jolie?'

'Of course I do,' Hero said scornfully. '*Everyone* has a thing for Angelina Jolie. That doesn't make me a lesbian.'

'But I'm definitely picking up very strong feminine vibes here. Do you like dressing up as a woman by any chance?'

'I am a woman.'

'Damn. I keep forgetting. It's been so long since we've had anyone of uncomplicated gender in this shop, it must be throwing off my psychic aura.'

'Hero, stop arguing and go look at the lesbian porn,' Sunday said, all shyness forgotten in her eagerness to be scrutinised. 'Madame Callous, what about me?'

Madame Callous lifted Sunday's chin and gazed deeply into her wide and trusting eyes. She closed her own eyes and moved her hands around Sunday's head, testing her aura. Finally she opened her eyes, shook her head and said, 'Can you bend over and lift your skirt?'

'Can I what?' asked Sunday, taken aback.

'It's a bit like palm reading,' Madame Callous explained reasonably, 'except I need to examine your —'

'Don't look now, Grandma,' Sunday said faintly. 'Go and check on Cousin Gretel.'

'Whatever you are, you're a rarity.' Madame Callous considered Sunday more closely, then snapped her fingers. 'You're not a coprophiliac, are you?'

'What's a copro—' Hero began, but Sunday got there first.

'No. I most definitely am not,' she said flatly.

Madame Callous shrugged. 'Suit yourself.'

'Is there a book or something on sex signs?' Sunday asked, unwilling to give up without confirming her classification. 'Could I learn how to read them?'

Madame Callous waved an airy hand. 'It's a gift, child. You have to be born with it. But if you insist, there *is* a copy of my modest publication on the subject over on the counter. The discount sticker on the front no longer applies,' she added hastily. 'That was a Valentine's Day special.'

Sunday perused the sex signs book while Madame Callous showed Hero where the fantasy costumes were kept, kindly helping her search through the racks of nurses' uniforms and French maid outfits until they reached the cartoon character section.

'Oh my god, you have a Muttley costume!' Hero cried, unsure whether to be pleased or disturbed.

Madame Callous pushed aside two Roger Ramjets and one Foghorn Leghorn. 'I remember when Superman was the most popular costume in stock,' she said, sighing as she recalled a more innocent era. 'And then there was the Ninja Turtles craze.' She shuddered. 'Terrible for business. The shells, you see. Not very manoeuvrable. But people never consider the *practicalities* when they're caught up in a fad. They were like lemmings.'

'Who were?'

'The turtles.'

'The turtles were like lemmings?'

'Exactly. Imagine trying to have sex while dressed like a crime-fighting turtle who behaves like a lemming. No wonder people are so mixed up these days,' she concluded sadly.

Unsure as to the correct response to this observation, Hero simply nodded. With an armful of costumes, she headed into a dressing room and drew shut the purple velvet curtains.

Clutching a copy of Madame Callous's *Complete Guide to Sex Signs: Releasing your Inner Slut*, Sunday settled down on a trapeze swing to read, only looking up when Hero emerged from the dressing room, clad in a skin-tight leopard-print leotard, complete with tail.

Sunday eyed her friend critically as Hero adjusted her cat's ears headband. 'Which one are you?'

'I don't know. Josie, I guess.' Hero reviewed her appearance in the mirror.

'Shouldn't you have red hair, then?'

'Probably. I don't suppose you still have our wigs from New York, do you?'

Sunday shook her head. 'Haven't the faintest clue where they are. Do you want me to ask if they sell wigs here?'

Hero looked uneasily at a man in shiny tracksuit pants who was covertly eyeing her from behind a blow-up doll that, distressingly, had a stubby-holder sunk into its head. As he caught her gaze, he licked his lips. She shuddered. 'Yes, please. I'll just stay in the dressing room.'

Sunday disappeared in search of Madame Callous and Hero retreated to her dressing room, drawing the velvet curtains firmly behind her.

Two minutes later, Sunday thrust a curly red wig into the cubicle. 'I found this up the back,' she said. 'It's the perfect colour.'

Hero set to fitting the siren-red wig, while Sunday settled herself back into the trapeze, swinging herself gently as she returned to her book.

Madame Callous, bustling past with an armful of discounted vibrators, stopped and looked disapprovingly at her. 'That trapeze isn't a toy, you know.'

Sunday looked enquiringly at the sign above her head, 'Sex Toys'. Madame Callous pouted, and Sunday changed the subject to placate her. 'How did you get your name?'

'All the good ones were gone.' Madame Callous sighed melodramatically. 'Madame Vicious, Madame Nasty, Cruella du Vile. Callous was pretty much all that was left. You wouldn't believe the jokes I've had to put up with, about warts and corns and the like.' She looked sorrowfully at Sunday through diamante-studded false eyelashes. 'People can be so unkind.'

The dominatrix mused for a moment on the cruelty of her fellow humans, before snapping back to the present. 'Don't suppose you'd be interested in one of these, would you?' She offered Sunday a boxed vibrator. 'I could do you a three-for-two deal.'

'There's only two of us,' Sunday said, puzzled. 'Why would we need three . . . ugh. Don't answer that. *Please* don't answer that.'

'You could give the spare to a friend, of course,' Madame Callous said innocently. 'Such filthy minds the young ones of today have.'

'Why are they on sale?' Sunday asked, curious despite herself.

Madame Callous looked evasive. 'They're a little bit different from the classic model.'

'In what way?'

'They don't *exactly* vibrate.'

'But they're vibrators. If they don't vibrate, what do they do?'

'They sort of hum,' Madame Callous said hopefully. 'One client said she found it quite soothing.'

'Thanks, but I really don't know what I'd do with it. And don't suggest anything either,' Sunday added, as Madame Callous opened her mouth to reply.

Madame Callous stalked off, muttering under her breath something that sounded like, 'Bloody goddammed crappy humming Taiwanese imports.'

Sunday nodded approvingly when Hero stepped forward with the red wig settled under her furry ears. 'You look exactly like Josie,' she said gleefully.

Hero grinned and swished her tail saucily. 'Good, that's sorted. What have you got there?'

Sunday held up three rattles for her to inspect. 'I found these when I went looking for the wig. Which one do you like best?'

'You're buying your baby a rattle from a sex shop?' Hero asked doubtfully.

'Well, it's not like they're *used*,' Sunday defended herself. 'And they're the nicest ones that I've seen.'

'The yellow one then, I guess. Hey, do you mind waiting a few more minutes? They have lots of sexy underwear and I thought I might try some on. For our honeymoon.'

'Yours and Oscar's?' Sunday teased, before registering Hero's glare. 'Sorry, couldn't resist. But is Pelham a sexy underwear kind of a guy?'

Hero had already moved back into the dressing room with armfuls of lingerie. 'Don't know,' she called through the curtain. 'I've never worn stuff like this before. Why don't you try something on, too?'

Sunday shook her head, forgetful of the fact that Hero couldn't see her. 'No point. Aside from the fact that I won't fit into anything in another few months, poor Toby's had too many bad experiences at hens' parties. If he so much as sees a garter, he starts to sweat. And not in a good way. Are you quite all right in there?' she asked, as a groan emanated from the dressing room.

'I'm fine,' came Hero's muffled voice. 'I just didn't realise these were crotchless knickers and now they're stuck on my – ow!'

Further sounds of heavy breathing and tussling emanated from the dressing room and Sunday had to shake the rattles threateningly to disperse the interested crowd of sexual deviants wandering over to inspect the kerfuffle.

Finally Hero emerged, breathless and red in the face but properly dressed once more.

'Are you okay?' Sunday asked anxiously.

'I think I cricked my neck.' Hero rubbed the back of her neck gingerly. 'I tell you what, some of this stuff is trickier to put on than the clothes in Akira Isogawa. And I'm still not sure whether these are underpants or a hair-tie,' she said ruefully, shaking out the garment that had caused her so much trouble. 'Maybe I'll just get a nice bra and knickers set from David Jones for the honeymoon.' She discarded a bundle of red and white lace knickers with leather trim. 'I'm thinking pale-green satin with bows. Are you going to buy that book?'

Sunday nodded enthusiastically. 'It's really very interesting. And I'm taking the yellow rattle, too.' She smiled at Madame Callous, who had stalked over to ring up their purchases.

Madame Callous raised her beautifully plucked eyebrows at Sunday's rattle but it was Hero's wig that really caught her attention. She paused in the act of ringing it up and looked at Hero with new-found respect. 'Well! Who'd have thought? It just goes to show you never can tell about people.'

'I thought that was the whole point of the book that Sunday just bought,' Hero pointed out. 'That you *can* tell about people.'

Madame Callous sniffed but didn't deign to reply. She handed over their bags and watched as they exited her shop into the bright sunshine. The tracksuit man joined her, looking longingly after Hero.

'I'd stick to inflatable girls if I were you, precious,' Madame Callous warned him. 'You'd be in way over your head with that one.'

'She looked so pretty in her cat costume,' the man said wistfully.

'Darling, the girl is a lesbian with a male fiancé, and judging by what she just bought I'd doubt you could find a website catering to her tastes. And I know you don't need me to tell you how rare that is.' She took his arm consolingly and led him back to the blow-up doll section, where she helped him climb aboard the inflatable pony. 'Trust Madame Callous, poppet. Some people are just too weird for the rest of us.'

21

The seduction

'Where to?'

'Bronte, please.' Hero clambered into the back seat of the cab.

The driver tilted his mirror and caught sight of the cat's ears headband poking out of her handbag. 'Fancy dress party?'

'Yes,' Hero said shortly, pulling her coat tight. Her tail was very uncomfortable to sit on. She moved it to one side and emitted a squeak of disgust as the back of her bare thigh came into contact with something wet and sticky on the seat.

'Unusual thing to go as. An ocelot, I mean,' the driver commented as the cab moved off.

'I'm not an ocelot,' Hero said, hunting through her bag for a tissue to wipe her leg.

The driver looked at her again. 'You have to be,' he said calmly. 'The only branch of the large cat family to have ears that are round with irregular spots *and* stripes is the ocelot. It's a scientific fact.'

'Look, I'm not a ruddy ocelot. I'm Josie from *Josie and the Pussycats* and I just sat in something disgusting. You should clean this back seat.'

The driver put his tongue between his teeth and shook his head. 'Look like an ocelot to me,' he said resentfully, under his breath.

Hero might have looked like an ocelot but she was feeling like a hooker. She wrapped the coat around her even more tightly and swivelled to see what she had sat in. It felt horribly like chewing gum, but it had a wet, softer texture that she didn't even want to try to identify.

Ten minutes later, she was ringing Oscar's doorbell. As the taxi disappeared, she had the sudden paralysing thought that her prey might not be home but thankfully, after just a moment, she could hear footsteps approaching and then the door opened.

'Hero!' Oscar said, clearly startled. 'What are you doing here?'

'Can I come in?' Hero asked without preamble, all attention focused on removing the disgusting mess from the back of her thigh.

Oscar looked bemused but opened the door wider and she found herself in an airy Art Deco flat with high ceilings and big windows overlooking the lights of Bronte.

'May I use your bathroom?'

'Of course,' Oscar said, still looking at her curiously. 'It's through there, off the bedroom.'

He indicated a door and she gratefully fled. Locking the bathroom door behind her, she grabbed a wad of tissues, soaked them and scrubbed at the back of her thigh, all the while trying to shake the daunting feeling that there could not have been a more inauspicious beginning to a seduction.

Taking a deep, calming breath, she reminded herself of her anger over the horse-riding incident. If she honestly wanted Oscar out of her life for good, she had to start doing something about it now. If she couldn't change fate, she thought, hanging her coat on the back of the bedroom door, then she might at least be able to change Oscar's mind.

She set her cat's ears headband over her wig, ready and armed to go into battle. But then something on Oscar's bedside table caught her eye.

Unable to quite believe it, Hero bent down and picked up the creased and faded postcard from the Metropolitan Museum in New York. The image was etched into her memory, but even more familiar was the handwriting on the reverse. It was hers.

She read the words that she had written all those years ago. Words never meant for anyone else's eyes.

I want to remember always how I felt the first time that I stood in front of this painting. Alive and overcome with the beauty and possibility of the world. Certain that fate had brought me to this moment for a reason.

And I want to believe in true love again. I want to be in love like I was before.

I'm so frightened that I'll settle for less.

Hero stood quite still for several moments – so still, she could feel every beat of her heart as it pumped blood through her body. What was her postcard doing in Oscar's bedroom? She felt naked, as though someone had ripped a page from her diary and put it on display.

'Hero? Are you all right in there?'

'Fine.' Her voice cracked slightly and she gathered herself together. 'I'm fine. I'll be right out.'

Hero returned the postcard to its original position, propped against a photo frame, and then bent down to take a closer look. The photo showed a smiling Oscar, his hair ruffled by the breeze. She recognised the location, Nielsen Park, one of her favourite places in Sydney. What she didn't recognise was the pretty girl wrapped tight in Oscar's arms.

'Hero, I'm counting to three, and if you're not out by then I'm coming in to check on you,' Oscar warned, through the closed door.

Hero jolted out of her trance. 'No, I'm coming right out,' she called, casting one final look over her shoulder to make sure there was no evidence of her snooping. Although why she should be worried about being thought a snoop when he was clearly a postcard thief, she wasn't sure.

Oscar was in the kitchen, pouring two glasses of wine. When he turned, the words of welcome died on his lips as he took in her cat's ears, leopard-print leotard and her tail, which was hanging limply between her legs. Belatedly remembering her plan, Hero twirled it in what she hoped was a saucily fetching manner.

'Ah, Hero?' Oscar cleared his throat, his eyes never leaving the movements of her tail. 'What are you doing?'

'What do you mean, what am I doing? What does it *look* like I'm doing?' Hero gazed at him expectantly.

Oscar made a Herculean effort to concentrate on her face. 'It looks like you're, um, twirling your tail. And what were you doing in the bathroom all that time?'

'Never mind about that,' Hero said, unwilling to bring up the unsexy subject of having an unidentified substance from the back seat of a taxi stuck to her thigh. 'More to the point, what do you think of my costume?' As he continued to gaze speechlessly at her, she said crossly, 'I'm Josie. From *Josie and the Pussycats.*'

'Oh.' He paused and then, seeing more was clearly required of him, added in a plaintive tone, '*Why?*'

'Because I'm seducing you!' Hero snapped. Her nerves, already frayed by the chewing-gum incident and the discovery of her post-card, not to mention the photograph, tightened further at his refusal to be immediately reduced to a quivering heap of lust by her outfit. She forced herself to stay calm. 'I know you have a thing for the Pussycats,' she said, taking a step towards him.

He backed away. 'Oh. Well, thanks. But maybe you could put your coat back on and we could watch a DVD instead.' His voice wavered under her predatory gaze. 'Or we could play Scrabble. Or I could show you my holiday photos from New York.'

'But why would we want to waste time when we could be in bed?' She smiled and took another step towards him.

Instinctively, Oscar took another step back, until he was pushed up against the kitchen bench.

Taking advantage of the fact that he had nowhere left to run, Hero fastened one well-manicured hand around his wrist in a vice-like grip.

He tried to shake her off. 'Hero, stop it! What the hell has gotten into you?'

She looked at him innocently. 'I thought this is what you wanted?'

'No, it is not! Well, it is,' he amended, honestly. 'But not like this.'

She let go of his wrist and picked up a glass of wine. She took a sip, then said, flippantly, 'Look, Oscar, I'm about to get married and I realised that this is my last chance for a fling. Take it or leave it.' She was satisfied to see that he looked dumbfounded.

'You'd really cheat on Pelham with me, for the sake of a last-ditch fling?'

'You sound shocked,' she said, in a smooth tone that didn't quite mask an underlying bitterness as she thought of the framed photo beside his bed. 'But people are unfaithful to their partners all the time.'

'Other people might be, but somehow I don't think you're one of them. So why don't you tell me what this —' his wave encompassed her costume '— is really all about.'

'It's about sex,' she retorted bluntly. 'The opposite of romance.'

'Sex isn't the opposite of romance,' he objected.

'Will you *please* just shut up for once and let me finish?' Hero begged. 'I am not in the mood to hear more of your theories on romance and love.'

'Sorry,' he said, contritely. 'Go ahead. You were talking about sex.'

'Yes. I was. And I've decided that I'm a big enough person to admit that there is something between us —'

'Perhaps it's your tail?' he suggested.

She glared him into silence again. 'Whatever it is, it's purely physical. So I thought we might as well get it out of our systems before I'm married.'

He mulled this over and then nodded decisively. 'Fair enough. Do you want to be on top?'

Hero choked on her wine. '*What?*'

'I thought I should check your personal preferences,' he said kindly. 'Otherwise we can just go for it, like we did in New York, and figure it out by instinct.'

Hero took a deep swallow of wine to fortify herself. 'You mean – you *want* to?'

Oscar looked surprised. 'Of course I want to. I'm a bloke. You just offered me no-strings-attached sex. You're dressed like an ocelot. What more could I possibly want?'

'But . . . but . . . where's the romance?' Hero flailed, feeling as though she was rapidly losing control of the situation.

'I could light some candles,' he offered. 'Or we could have a bath together. Although judging by how long you were in the bathroom before, you've probably already had one.' Clearly enjoying the reversal of roles, now he gripped her wrist, a wicked light in his eyes.

Hero was still holding her wine glass in her other hand, so when Oscar leaned in to kiss her, she couldn't push him away. At the back of her mind, she was dimly aware that she didn't really *want* to push him away. But just before his lips touched hers, she managed to mutter, 'My postcard.'

Oscar stopped and looked at her intently. 'What?'

Hero cleared her throat and carefully placed her glass on the bench. 'My postcard,' she said, in a firmer tone. 'The one of the Picasso painting. I lost it in New York, but I just found it again.'

For the first time since they'd met, Hero saw Oscar at a genuine loss. He actually looked guilty.

'Oh.' It was his turn to clear his throat. 'You saw that, then.'

She nodded and folded her arms, determined not to let him off the hook.

He ran a hand through his hair. 'I can explain.'

'Please do,' she said, satisfied to see him wilting under her steely tone.

He shuffled his feet. 'It fell out of your bag, that night we were together. And it caught my eye. I love that painting. You know that. I still have the print I bought in New York.'

'Don't change the subject.'

'No.' He hung his head. 'Well, I know I shouldn't have but I turned the card over and read what you'd written.'

Hero's cheeks burned but she said nothing.

Oscar looked up and smiled ruefully. 'I could say that I was intending to give it back to you the next day, but the truth is that even back then I was scared I wouldn't be able to hold on to you. And I didn't have a photo of you, or anything. So I . . . I kept it.'

Deep mortification meant that Hero failed to catch the intensity in Oscar's voice. 'So all of your *antics*, your certainty that we're similar deep down – it's all because of a few throwaway lines on the back of an

225

old postcard?' She forced herself to sound amused. 'Oscar, what I wrote is like bad teenage poetry. Sometimes, in private, people write down drivel. It doesn't mean anything.'

It was as though he hadn't heard her. 'Who were you in love with, Hero?' he asked softly. 'What happened to the person you were truly in love with? Why have you ended up with Pelham?'

The hurt from all those years ago rose up inside her once again. When she met Oscar's gaze, he was dismayed to see the shuttered look in her eyes.

'His name was Elliott,' she said coolly. 'While we're sharing, who's the girl in the photo beside your bed? Your sister?'

He flinched at her sarcastic tone. 'No. She's not my sister.'

'Ex-girlfriend then? Or perhaps she's your current girlfriend?' Hero waited for his response, and in that pause Oscar – fatally – faltered.

Overcome by the memory of Elliott's infidelity and the raw humiliation of Oscar having read her postcard, a torrent of bitter words spilled out of Hero. 'Oh god,' she said, trying to sound light-hearted but succeeding only in sounding savage, 'you're *exactly* like Elliott. You two should get together some time – you could compare notes on how to romance women before treating them like dirt. You know, I never got the chance to ask Elliott this, so I'll ask you. What is it that excites you about hurting us? Is it the chase, or is it ego? Do you just hate to think that there could possibly be one woman out there who can resist your romantic crap?'

The colour had drained out of Oscar's face. As he met Hero's contemptuous gaze, she felt almost frightened by the grief in his eyes.

A heavy silence fell between them, cut by the ringing of the doorbell.

Hero suddenly remembered her unconventional attire and clutched her hands protectively in front of her cleavage. 'You didn't tell me you were expecting guests!'

'You didn't give me time to tell you anything,' he pointed out shakily.

'Get rid of them!'

'I'm not getting rid of my mother.'

'*Your mother?*' Horrified, Hero snatched off her cat's ears and dashed to the bedroom to retrieve her coat, just managing to gather her composure as she heard Jean and Oscar greeting one another at the door.

With what dignity she could muster, Hero strode out into the living room to greet Jean, her coat firmly buttoned to her chin. But Jean's warm smile of welcome faded into a quizzical look.

With a feeling of dread, Hero tentatively gazed downwards, in the direction of Jean's gaze.

Her tail was still firmly in place, dangling between her bare legs.

22

Looking into the future (again)

'Pelham! What are you doing here?' Hero stopped dead in the living-room doorway and pulled her coat more tightly around her, thankful that she had shoved her tail and headband into her bag.

'Waiting up for you, of course. Where were you?'

'I, er – milk,' Hero improvised. 'We needed milk. But they were closed.'

'You're a regular pussycat, the way you go through milk,' Pelham said fondly. He looked at her more closely as she winced. 'You look a bit odd, Hero. Are you okay?'

'Absolutely. Couldn't be better,' Hero gabbled, desperate to escape to her room to change. 'Has Sun gone out?'

'No. She's in her bedroom with Toby. I think they're having an argument.'

'Sunday and Toby are arguing?' Hero said in surprise. 'They never argue.'

The falseness of this statement was immediately borne out by the slamming of the front door as Toby exited in high dudgeon, followed moments later by loud clattering noises in the kitchen.

'Never mind them right now, Hero. There's something I need to bring up with you.'

Pelham looked uncomfortable and Hero wondered uneasily whether he had any idea where she had been. She almost laughed with relief when he waved Sunday's copy of *Complete Guide to Sex Signs: Releasing Your Inner Slut* at her.

'I found this in your bedroom,' he said gravely.

'It's not mine, it's Sunday's,' Hero retorted. 'And stop treating me like a thirteen-year-old boy. That book's no more smutty than some of those romance novels you've been reading lately. I picked up *Love Sick* and quite honestly, what went on in that supply cupboard has made me concerned for the hygiene standards in hospitals today and —'

'Yes, all right,' Pelham said hastily, displeased that his latest hobby had entered the conversation. 'Nevertheless, you might consider me old fashioned but I don't think *publications* like this ought to be left lying around where anyone can see them. You'll give people the wrong impression of the sort of person you are.'

'What sort of snoop is going to be prowling round my bedroom and going through my things?' Hero retaliated, aware that she was a hypocrite of the first order. 'Oh, I don't mean *you*,' she said hastily, as Pelham's back stiffened. 'But really, Pelham, it wasn't on display on the coffee table.'

'Thank heavens,' Pelham said with fervour. 'If Mother ever saw this —'

'Yes, well, she won't,' Hero snapped. As usual, the mere mention of Gloria made her tense. 'Look, it's really not as bad as you think.' She took the book from his grasp and coaxed him on to the couch next to her. 'See here? That's a whip. That's me – I'm into mind games.

And then there's the coprophiliacs. That's Sunday's sign.' Hero peered hard at the illustration. 'It looks kind of like ice-cream, or a mound of whipped cream. Maybe it means that Sunday's into kinky things with whipped cream.'

'Yes. That's exactly what it means,' Pelham said hastily. Despite himself he was drawn to the book. 'What's this?'

'That's my other sign. I'm a lesbian, too,' Hero said, as she continued to stare with furrowed brow at the coprophilia illustration. 'You know, you'd think if it was cream or ice-cream, it would be in a container of some sort or a cone but —'

'*You're a lesbian?*'

'Apparently. There's no need to look like that,' Hero said kindly, taking in Pelham's disturbed expression. 'I'm just a lesbian on the inside. According to Madame Callous, I'm really a heterosexual facist.' As the silence stretched on, Hero asked in surprise, 'Well, what's wrong with you? I thought you'd like it that I'm a lesbian. Isn't that a common male fantasy?'

Pelham was trying to sufficiently compose himself to speak. 'So all this time . . . and I thought you were just being sweet, letting me rent the *Tomb Raider* DVDs over and over again . . .' Too choked up to continue, he fell back into silence.

'Pelham, I am not a lesbian,' Hero said firmly. 'And I can prove it. We can go back to the shop together and get a more accurate reading.'

'How do you do that?'

'I just have to bend over and pull up my skirt and let her . . . oh, for Pete's sake.'

Pelham had clapped his hands over his ears and started to loudly hum the *Chariots of Fire* theme.

Two minutes later, following Pelham's exit, which hadn't been quite as loud as Toby's (Pelham would never dream of doing anything so common as slamming a door) but had been equally as irate, Hero entered the kitchen. Sunday was seated at the kitchen table, making an ice-cream sandwich out of two sheets of white A4 paper. Without a word, Hero took a spoon from the drawer and joined her, slapping the copy of *Sex Signs* down on the kitchen table.

'What did you fight about?' Sunday asked morosely.

'Me being a lesbian,' Hero answered, lifting a heaped spoon from the tub. 'You?'

'Me being a coprophiliac.'

'Have you found out what it means?'

'Er, I have an unnatural love of copra. They're dried kernels of coconut,' Sunday hastily confabulated, reasoning that Hero didn't need to know the sordid details. 'Very hard to come by, unless you live in Malaysia.'

'But what do you *do* with them?' asked Hero curiously.

Sunday shrugged. 'Buggered if I know.'

'What do you *want* to do with them?' Hero persisted.

'I don't know! Eat them? I'm going through a very hard time right now, Hero. I've just discovered that I'm a sexual deviant and I'm probably going to lose my relationship over it, so could you please not keep asking me for specifics?'

'I'm not exactly mainstream either,' Hero reminded her stiffly. 'And Pelham's probably going to break up with me, too.'

Sunday dismissed Hero's problems with a sniff. 'That's different. You like girls. Boys love that.'

Hero shook her head. 'Only in their fantasies. In real life they want us to love the teapot, not the cup, if you get what I mean.'

'You mean the bucket is a fantasy but the watering really has to be done with a hose?'

'Exactly.'

'Or the space shuttle is quite comfy but the rocket launcher is more exciting?'

'You can stop now.'

Sunday subsided and they both sat in silence for a moment.

'Sun?'

'Yes?'

'What if we're not really who our sex signs say we are?' Hero lifted her head defiantly. 'We've gone through life so far being straight and unattracted to coconut by-products, so why do we have to change now?'

'They're our *sex signs*,' Sunday said sternly. 'You heard Madame Callous, it's like star signs.' She paused and then added in a threatening tone, 'You're not going to tell me that the fact I'm an Aquarian and you're Saggitarian means *nothing*?'

'Well, not if you look at me like that, I'm not.' Hero frowned thoughtfully. 'But maybe it's like astrology in other ways. I mean how you're an Aquarian with an Aries ascendant, which makes you forgetful *and* demanding. So for example I could be a lesbian with —' Hero stopped and scrabbled through the book for inspiration '— an inclination for frottage.'

'What's frottage?'

'It's when someone rubs up against you on a tram or train,' Hero explained, after scanning the definition.

'Can it happen on any form of public transportation?'

Hero consulted the book again. 'I guess so. Although monorail frottage seems extra creepy for some reason.'

'I never knew there were so many ways to get aroused,' Sunday said, in a tone of voice that suggested she would have been happy to remain in ignorance. 'Speaking of which, how did the big seduction go?'

'I think I had chewing gum stuck to my thigh. I saw a photo of his girlfriend and then his mum turned up,' Hero summarised.

'*Oscar has a girlfriend?*'

Hero tried to sound nonchalant. 'Maybe. It might have been an ex-girlfriend. Whoever she is, he still feels strongly enough to keep her photograph on his bedside table.' Hero thought of telling Sunday about the postcard, but decided against it. She felt incredibly tired and confused and she didn't want to analyse the whole thing all over again right now.

'Are you sure it wasn't his sister or a relation?' Sunday asked, still shocked.

'Positive.'

'It doesn't necessarily mean that he's still in love with her,' Sunday said, sensibly.

Hero gave her a withering look. 'How many photos of your ex-boyfriends do you keep in a frame next to your bed?'

'Okay, it's a bit weird, I admit. Did you ask him about it?'

'Yes.'

'What did he say?'

'He didn't say anything. He didn't have to say anything. He had guilt written all over his face.'

'Hero, I'm so sorry.' Sunday leant over and gave her a hug.

Hero laughed shakily and pushed her away. 'For what? If you're thinking that this is Elliott history repeating, then forget it. I'm not in a relationship with Oscar, remember?'

But you are in love with him, Sunday thought. There wasn't much point in pursuing this, though. Hero would never admit to it, least of all now. 'So what happens next?'

'Nothing, I hope. I doubt Oscar will persist with me now that I've seen straight through him. Which, thankfully, means that I don't have to dress up in this costume ever again. Still, I suppose I should have known my plan would never work. I'm just not that sort of person.' Hero sighed. 'Anyway, it doesn't matter any more. Once I'm married, life will go back to normal.'

'But it won't be how it has been, even if Oscar does disappear,' Sunday said slowly. 'I mean, when you're married to Pelham, you'll move to the North Shore and I'll probably never see you again.'

'Don't be ridiculous. We haven't discussed where we're going to live yet. Maybe we'll end up over this side.'

Sunday snorted. 'Pelham *hates* this side of the harbour. You're going to disappear into Mosman, I just know it.'

'I'll still work in Darlinghurst,' Hero said, trying not to acknowledge the stab of dismay she felt at the idea of living in Mosman, close to Pelham's parents. 'Have you and Toby discussed where you're going to live?'

'If we move to Canberra, we can probably afford to buy a house,' Sunday said glumly.

'*Move to Canberra?* But that – that's worse than Mosman!'

'I know.' Sunday slumped. 'But Toby thinks children should grow up in a house with a garden and we can't bloody well afford to buy anything in Sydney.'

'Bringing up your kids in a nice environment is important, but bringing them up on their own planet is important, too,' Hero pointed out. 'You can't move to Canberra, Sun. Have you actually been there? Nothing's open after ten o'clock at night! Moving to Canberra is like moving back in with your parents.' She stopped short, belatedly remembering that Pelham still lived with his parents.

Sunday was concentrating on her own problems. 'Well, it's not like we'll be going out dancing every night with a baby, is it? No,' she continued, in a tone of despair, 'this time next year, Toby and I will be living in Canberra and trying to convince ourselves that Lake Burley Griffin is actually very scenic, and you'll be living on the North Shore with Pelham and playing mixed doubles once a week with Gloria and Norman.'

Hero and Sunday looked at each other, aghast as this vision of their bright futures unrolled before them. And then, as if on cue, they burst into tears.

23

Naming rights & wrongs

While Sunday and Toby made up fairly quickly after their argument, a small but definite rift had set between Pelham and Hero. Hero thought him uptight and hypocritical, while Pelham was worried by Hero's interest in the crass topics in the sex signs book, and he had no hesitation in laying blame for this at Sunday's door. It was therefore with the noble intention of easing Sunday's bad influence on Hero that Pelham and his mother created a hectic schedule of wedding-based appointments and meetings, all designed to keep Hero busy, and away from Sunday. Thus it was that Sunday and Toby found themselves alone in the house once again on a Saturday afternoon.

Sunday looked up from her notebook and smiled as Toby handed her a cup of herbal tea and a sandwich.

'Are you still trying to make a list of baby names?'

'Yes,' Sunday sighed. 'It's a lot more difficult than I thought it would be.'

'Why don't you read out the contenders so far?' Toby settled back on the couch, his arm around her.

'At the top of my boys' names shortlist, I've got Evelyn, Hyacinth, Jody and Shirley.'

Toby sat bolt upright, almost spilling his tea in the process. 'Sun, you must have the lists mixed up. That's the girls' names.'

Sunday looked surprised. 'No, they're all boys' names.'

'You want to call our son *Hyacinth*?'

'Yes,' Sunday said eagerly. 'In Greek mythology, the sun god Apollo fell in love with Hyacinth, who was exceptionally beautiful. One day they were playing discus and Apollo accidentally killed him, but then he transformed the blood that had flowed from his wound into a flower, which he named Hyacinth,' she finished dreamily.

There was a dead silence and then Toby spoke. 'So you're going to name our son after a beautiful gay boy who was crap at sport and turned into a flower?'

Sunday scowled. 'I happen to think it's a beautiful story,' she said with dignity.

'It is a beautiful story,' Toby agreed, trying to remain calm and rational. 'But if you call our son Hyacinth in real life, he's going to spend his entire teenage years with enough blood coming out of his nose to create a commercial harvest of his namesake. And the same goes for Evelyn, Jody and Shirley.' He allowed this to sink in and then said, encouragingly, 'There must be some other names that you like?'

'I do like the name Hannibal,' Sunday admitted. 'After the third century BC Carthaginian general, you know.'

'I didn't know. And I'm sure he was very brave and made the Carthaginian people proud. But unfortunately the name has been used again since then.'

'In a book?'

'And a movie.'

'It was a blockbuster, wasn't it,' said Sunday gloomily, preparing for the worst. 'Is he some sort of action hero?'

'Kind of. He was highly intelligent.' Sunday looked pleased, but then Toby continued, 'He was also a cannibalistic serial killer.'

Sunday looked aghast. 'They named a *cannibal* after one of the greatest generals of the pre-Christian era?'

Toby nodded.

'Well, maybe I could still call our baby Hannibal,' Sunday said defiantly. 'After all, I've never heard of this horrible film till now.'

'Sun, in your world, they're still speaking Latin and assuming that Christianity is a passing fad. Our son, on the other hand, will have to live in the real world and he'll have to put up with his schoolfriends wearing protective head gear every lunchtime.'

'What does that mean?'

'The movie Hannibal ate someone's face off,' Toby informed her.

'He ate someone's face off?' Sunday repeated in horror.

Toby nodded again.

Shakily, Sunday put a line through Hannibal. She stared dejectedly at her depleted list.

'Which girls' names do you like?' Toby asked, trying to divert Sunday's thoughts from cannibalistic serial killers back to newborn bundles of innocence.

'Hersilia, Perlopia or Melpomene,' Sunday reeled off.

'Good grief. Sun, if we must have something classical, why not Cassandra or Persephone?'

'Persephone means "bringer of death",' Sunday informed him icily.

Toby sighed and flipped through her baby name book in search of alternatives. 'Well, Melpomene was the muse of Tragedy. You know, at this rate we may as well go ahead and call her Bad News.'

Luckily for Toby, the doorbell rang at this moment. After shooting him a cross glance, Sunday got up to answer it and re-entered moments later with Oscar in tow.

'Hello, Oscar,' Toby said in surprise. 'What are you doing here?'

'I've come to return something to Hero. Is she home?'

'She's gone out,' Sunday said tactfully, deciding there wasn't much point in elaborating that Hero was at a fitting for her wedding dress. 'We were just having a cup of tea. Would you like one?'

'If it's no trouble.'

'Of course it's not. Toby, would you mind making Oscar a cup of tea?'

'Herbal or normal?' Toby asked.

'Normal, please. White with one.' Oscar sank into an armchair, dropping a plastic bag by his side. He caught sight of the baby name book lying discarded on the couch and asked in alarm, 'That's not the reason Hero's marrying Pelham, is it?'

Sunday couldn't help laughing at the idea of Pelham having a shotgun wedding. Gloria would probably shoot both Hero and Pelham, before turning the gun on herself. 'No,' she said. 'It's mine. Toby and I are having a baby.'

'Bloody hell! Congratulations!' He sprang up and Sunday submitted to being kissed and fussed over. 'Is that why you're eating a sandwich made out of paper?'

Sunday nodded. 'I have cravings for paper all the time. But only white A4, for some reason. I ate the front page of the newspaper the other day and it made me feel quite sick.'

'Huh.' Oscar shook his head in disbelief at the rapid pace of Sunday and Toby's relationship. 'You know, I have got to speak to Jake about hiring Toby as more than just a singer,' he said, with deep feeling. 'He's the fastest mover I've ever met in my life. I mean, look at Hero and me – we're still at the erotically charged animosity stage, while you and Toby are about to become parents. Unbelievable.'

'Hero's animosity towards you might lessen if you tell me about the photo of the girl next to your bed,' Sunday said, deciding to throw caution to the winds.

Oscar shot her a sharp glance and then shook his head. Although he was smiling, Sunday noticed that for the first time since she'd met him, there was a guarded expression in his eyes.

'Sorry, Sun,' he said. 'I have every intention of explaining, but I think it's only fair that I tell Hero first.'

Before Sunday could push further, Toby entered, bearing a cup of tea.

Oscar jumped up to shake his hand. 'Congratulations, Toby! I just heard the news. That's fantastic.'

Toby beamed. 'Oh. Thanks. I suppose it all seems very sudden.'

'Not at all. Sometimes you just know, don't you?'

Sunday and Toby looked at each other and smiled.

'Yes. I suppose you do,' said Toby happily.

'I understand perfectly. That's exactly how it was when I met Hero.'

Toby didn't know where to look, but Sunday spoke up in exasperation. 'Oscar, please don't take this the wrong way, because only the fact that I've grown quite fond of you enables me to say this, but you do realise you have rocks in your head?'

Oscar nodded. 'Quite a few people have told me that already.'

'Hero's engagement to Pelham is real. You're not planning on objecting during the wedding, are you?' she asked in alarm.

'Sunday, can I ask you something?'

'What?'

'Have you given Hero your honest opinion of Pelham?'

Sunday reddened and looked defensive. 'Hero's my friend. I will always support her.'

'See, that's what I don't understand,' Oscar said thoughtfully, between sips of his tea. 'Pelham and Hero are patently not right for one another. He's too uptight for her and she turns him into a bigger bore than he really is. But no one except me seems willing to point this out.'

'But you have no idea what Hero went through —' Sunday stopped and then bit her tongue, furious with herself.

Oscar was looking at her shrewdly. 'So tell me. All I know is that his name was Elliott. And however bad it was, there's absolutely no reason for her to ruin the rest of her life because of him.'

'I'm not going to betray Hero by discussing her relationships with you!'

Oscar took sympathy on her heated state and smiled. 'Calm down, Sun. I'll change the subject. How are you going with names for your baby? Or is it a secret?'

Toby spoke up in a desperate tone. 'What would you think if you met someone called Hannibal?'

'That their nickname would undoubtedly be Cannibal,' Oscar said cheerfully.

Toby looked triumphantly at Sunday, who in turn looked downcast. 'It's not as easy as just picking a name from a book,' she retaliated. 'For starters, we have to think about whether we're going to have more than one child.'

'Why?'

'Well, what if we have a naming theme? We have to think about it now.'

'What *are* you talking about?' demanded Toby.

'I'm talking about Hero's family. They're all named after characters from Shakespeare,' she explained, seeing Toby and Oscar's confusion. 'Hero is named after a character in *Much Ado About Nothing*. Her sister in London is named Portia —'

'*The Merchant of Venice*,' Oscar supplied helpfully.

'And her younger brother, Laertes, lives in Melbourne. But they all got off easy compared with her older brother.'

'I didn't know Hero had another brother,' Toby said, surprised.

'That's because he works for the UN and he's always being sent somewhere war-torn or ravaged. Hamlet's been in Aceh for eight months now.'

'Ha ha.'

'No, really. He's been in Aceh for ages.'

'Hero has a brother named *Hamlet*?'

Sunday nodded. 'Hero doesn't see him very much. He was never really around, even when we were kids. He's always been a bit of a loner.' As Toby and Oscar continued to stare at her in disbelief, she added, in an aggrieved tone, 'I don't know why you're looking at me like that. It could have been worse. Our next-door neighbours were really religious and they named all their kids after different popes. At dinnertime you'd hear them yelling at Gelasius and Boniface, and the twins Hyginus and Hilarius, that if they didn't finish their sprouts they wouldn't get any Neapolitan ice-cream. Anyway, it was because of our weird names that Hero and I became friends straightaway. When everyone else in the play-ground is called Sarah or Kate, you find each other pretty quickly.'

'In that case, you should call your baby Hannibal and just cross your fingers that he ends up sharing a sandpit with Genghis Khan,' Oscar suggested.

'Maybe this is a good opportunity for you to get more in touch with the modern world, Sun,' Toby said, glaring at Oscar. 'After all, you don't want our child getting laughed at by the other kids because it's spinning wool while they're playing computer games.'

'Carding wool,' Sunday murmured, absentmindedly picking up Hero's abandoned copy of *Marie Claire* and flicking through it. 'The children were given the job of carding the wool. Women were the spinners. But maybe you're right.' Her attention fixed on a captioned photograph and she gave a cry of delight. 'It must be fate! I've found a *lovely* name, and it's *very* modern.' She showed them a page filled with celebrity photographs.

'You want to call our child Puff Daddy?' Toby asked, in an accent of abject horror.

'Don't be ridiculous. I want to name it Bennifer,' Sunday said happily.

'*Bennifer?*'

'It's the perfect name for a boy *or* a girl,' she declared, heaving herself off the couch. 'I'm starving. I'm going to have some more Vegemite on A4. Anyone else want some?'

'No, thanks.'

Oscar waited until she had left the room and then turned to Toby. 'Should we explain how the name Bennifer came about?'

Toby was still looking pale. 'We'd have to explain who Ben Affleck and Jennifer Lopez are, and then we'd have to tell her about Ben Affleck and Jennifer Garner, and by the time we were finished she'd be even more confused and Ben would probably have moved on to Jennifer Aniston anyway.'

'Fair call. And it's so hard to explain how bad *Pearl Harbor* was.'

'And *Maid in Manhattan*. And don't even start me on *Elektra*,' Toby said with feeling. Agitated, he picked up the *Sex Signs* book from a pile of books on the coffee table and thumbed through it unseeingly.

Oscar looked at him with respect. 'Hey, you're pretty good on bad movies. You should come down to the DVD store some time and meet Quentin.' Before Toby could ask who Quentin was, Oscar unfolded himself from his chair. 'I'd better get going. Can you tell Hero I dropped by?'

Sunday had re-emerged from the kitchen with a paper sandwich in hand. 'Sure. Is that plastic bag for her?'

'Yep, she left something on the floor of my bedroom the other night. Gave me a shock when I stepped on it, I can tell you.'

Sunday tipped the bag upside down and the curly red wig from the sex shop tumbled out. She picked it up with a fond grin. 'Don't you think it's kind of like the one she wore in New York?'

'Kind of,' Oscar answered. 'Except this one is a merkin. Where *did* she get it?'

'What's a merkin?' Sunday asked, perching the wig on her head for fun. 'Is it something to do with a meerkat?'

'Not really. It's the name for a wig made out of pubic hair —'

Before he could finish, Sunday screamed, snatched the wig from her head and threw it away. Then she launched herself across the room at Toby. They fell to the ground in a brawling heap as Sunday tried to grab the sex signs book from him.

'NO MORE! GIVE IT TO ME! I – DON'T – WANT – TO – HEAR – ANY MORE!' Clasping the book, she shot over to the farthest corner of the room, panting furiously and looking positively hunted.

'It's okay, Sun, just calm down,' Toby said anxiously.

'IT'S NOT OKAY! I don't want to know any more. I don't want to know about frottage or meerkats —'

'Merkins,' Oscar interposed.

'— or one hundred and one things to do with a frozen frankfurter and a tub of strawberry jam —'

'Eew,' Oscar said, screwing up his face. 'Mixing sweet and savoury is just plain wrong.'

Sunday ignored him, sweeping on with her tirade. 'And Hero and I most definitely do not want to do unnatural things with coconut kernels or teacups, so if you'll excuse me, I am going to get rid of this book!' She hurled it out of the open window to show that she meant business. 'And now my boyfriend and I are going to *make love*.' She paused and added defiantly, '*In the missionary position*.' She swept from the room, throwing a regal, 'Come, Toby!' over her shoulder.

Toby was looking awed by Sunday's dazzling display of rampant conservatism.

'You heard her, Toby,' Oscar said kindly. 'You have to come.'

Toby stood up, and although a faint blush stole into his cheeks, he proudly straightened his shoulders, sniffed his underarms for luck and strode from the room to make love to his beloved in the most unimaginative way possible.

$$\star \; ^\star \; \star$$

When Hero returned home from her dress fitting, she was exhausted and irritated by Gloria's ceaseless stream of thinly veiled criticism. Sunday's bedroom door was closed, so Hero couldn't ask her why the living room looked as though a brawl had taken place.

She sank down onto the couch and sprang up again as she made contact with something soft and hairy. Surprised to find her Pussycat wig, she looked around the room for answers. It was then that she spotted the Picasso postcard she had last seen sitting on Oscar's bedside table. Next to it was a single sheet of paper, torn from Sunday's notebook.

I came around to explain. I'll call you tomorrow or (if you want) you can call me.

I'm not giving up, Lola.

For a very long time Hero sat there, letter in hand, trying to work out whether she ought to interpret Oscar's words as a threat or a promise.

24

The wedding planner

More than a week had passed since Oscar's visit to return the wig, and for the first few days Hero had resolutely blocked his calls and attempts to see her. She kept reminding herself that photographs of pretty girls on his bedside table had absolutely nothing to do with her anyway. But now he had gone quiet, and to say that she was uneasy would be an understatement. Oscar on the romantic rampage was one thing, but Oscar being quiet and invisible after making a declaration of action was unnerving in the extreme.

Unable to concentrate on work, Hero rang the only person that she hadn't heard from lately and who knew both Oscar and herself.

'Mum? It's me. Listen, this might sound odd, but you haven't had any telephone calls or visits from strange men, have you?'

'You mean your Uncle Arthur?'

'No, Mum. I don't mean Uncle Arthur,' Hero said flatly. 'I just wondered whether —' She broke off, wondering how to proceed without alarming her mother. 'Has anyone tried to talk to you about me getting married?'

Coralie's voice instantly brightened. 'You mean your Aunt Edna? As a matter of fact —'

'No, Mum, I don't mean Aunt Edna!' Hero practically shouted.

There was a small, hurt silence. 'Well, you *asked*,' her mother said huffily. 'So I don't see why you're shouting at me.'

'Mum, please,' Hero begged, 'has anyone who isn't family approached you to discuss my wedding?'

'You're being very odd. And I haven't the slightest notion what you're talking about.'

Hero felt a sense of overwhelming relief, tempered with something that was almost disappointment. She had been so sure she was learning how to read Oscar. 'Sorry,' she muttered.

'That's okay, darling. Perhaps you should take up yoga before the wedding. I'll get you a pamphlet. I can give it to you when I see you on Sunday afternoon.'

'Sure,' Hero said dully. And then, 'Wait a moment. Sunday afternoon? What's happening on Sunday afternoon?'

Her mother exhaled in exasperation. 'We're meeting with your wedding planner at our house at two o'clock. Honestly, Hero, you're getting very forgetful lately.'

'Wedding planner?' Hero said, confused. 'But I don't have a . . .' She groaned, wondering how it was that Oscar continuously out-manoeuvred her. It was probably because he had a lifetime's experience of being a psychopath whereas she was merely normal. 'Let me guess,' she said heavily. 'My wedding planner's name is Oscar.'

'Of course it is, darling,' Coralie said, puzzled. 'He rang to arrange the session two days ago. He sounds very charming,' she added, in a tone that instantly alerted Hero to her match-making mode. 'I thought it might be nice for Portia to meet him when she flies back for the wedding.'

'He's gay,' Hero lied, unaccountably annoyed at the idea of Oscar and her sister being set up.

'Oh.' Her mother was momentarily disconcerted. 'Well, perhaps he'll be nice company for Hamlet at the wedding. We've only spoken on the phone, but I swear he could charm the birds out of the trees, that one. And you know how morose Hamlet can be. The last thing we need is a long face at the wedding, but I'm sure Oscar would brighten him up.'

'What on earth are you talking about? Oscar is not coming to my wedding!'

'Of course he is, sweetheart. How is he meant to ensure that every-thing runs smoothly if he's not there? Honestly, you're so scatterbrained sometimes that it really makes me wonder.'

✳

Hero arrived at her parents' rambling, country-style house that Sunday afternoon at a quarter past two, spoiling for a fight. It was raining and Oscar's car was already parked in the driveway, under a dripping euca-lyptus tree. She pushed open the front door and followed the sound of voices down the hall, past the dozens of framed family photographs, to the large living room that opened on to the overgrown garden. Taking a deep breath, she peeked through the door. Prepared for the worst, she nonetheless stopped short at the sight that greeted her astonished gaze.

Oscar was seated on one of the comfortable couches, balancing a cup of tea in one hand and a photograph album on his knees. Hero's mother was laughing at something he had just said, while her father was searching through his record collection and throwing comments over his shoulder. But it wasn't only this scene of cosy familiarity that caught Hero by surprise. It was the table in the centre of the room, covered by a crisp white linen cloth and laden with dainty china and an afternoon tea of chicken sandwiches, raspberry friands and (Hero almost fell over in shock), unless she was very much mistaken, *cucumber sandwiches*. She glanced around to check that she was in the correct house, and at that moment her mother looked up and saw her.

'Hero, darling! Did you get caught in traffic? Come in. I've just been showing Oscar some photos of you when you were at school,' she said in a guilty rush. 'You remember Oscar, don't you? He's the lovely young man from the bridal fair. Isn't it a coincidence?'

'Isn't it just,' Hero said drily.

Oscar met Hero's glare with his usual twinkling smile. 'I'd stand up but I'm terrified that I might drop something,' he said by way of greeting.

Hero ignored him and made her way over to her father. 'Hello, Dad,' she said, dropping a kiss on his cheek. 'What are you looking for?'

'Hello, love. I'm hunting out "Lola", by the Kinks. We were talking about it and I know I've got a copy somewhere.'

'Try your iPod,' Hero teased him, suppressing the urge to fight with Oscar over his sly introduction of 'Lola' in front of her parents. She was determined to save her ammunition for the main battle.

Her father snorted. 'Don't you iPod me. This record collection will be worth a fortune one day.'

'Mmm,' Hero said, flicking through the albums. 'You'd better be careful, Dad. If my inheritance includes that Neil Sedaka album, I might be tempted to bump you off.'

'Philistine,' he replied affectionately.

Hero seated herself on the chair furthest away from Oscar, watching as he flipped his way through the photo album. She could tell that her mother was in her element – Oscar was exactly the sort of lively young man that she approved of.

'Which photo are you looking at now?' She looked over Oscar's shoulder. 'Oh,' she said in a disappointed tone. 'Yes, that's a nice one of the whole family but it's a shame Hero looks so severe.'

Despite herself, Hero flinched. She didn't have to see the photograph to know that it was the family portrait taken when she was thirteen and trapped in that awful, gangly stage. The rest of her family were laughing and looking relaxed; Hero had her hair in tight plaits and resembled no one so much as Wednesday from *The Addams Family*.

Coralie tut-tutted at her. 'I don't know why you couldn't smile a little.'

Hero felt compelled to defend her younger self. 'I was thirteen, Mother, and I had braces.'

'I think it's a good photo of you,' Oscar said.

Hero laughed derisively.

'I do,' he reiterated. 'You do look serious, but you don't look miserable. I bet you spent lots of time reading by yourself and always looked after your younger brother.'

Startled into silence by this accurate assessment, Hero said nothing. Coralie, who had assumed that Oscar was a kindred spirit, given his antics at the bridal fair, looked surprised at his approval of Hero's solemn demeanour. Before she could say anything, however, Hero's father stood up and brandished a record triumphantly.

'Got it!'

'Please don't put it on now,' Hero begged.

Support came from an unexpected quarter. 'She's right, Theo. We have so much to discuss,' said Hero's mother.

Outnumbered, Theo gave up. 'Shouldn't Pelham be here?' he enquired.

'There's no need.' Hero took a deep breath and decided to end this farce right then and there. 'Mum, Dad, Oscar's not a wedding planner. He's been lying to you. He's trying to worm his way into your good books because you're my parents and he wants to be with me.'

Her mother and father looked at her in confusion.

'I don't understand, Hero,' her father said slowly. He turned to Oscar, a grim expression on his face. 'Is what my daughter says true? Are you some sort of imposter?'

In silence, Oscar pulled out a business card and handed it to Hero's parents.

Coralie's face brightened as she read it. 'Of course he's a wedding planner, Hero. He told me he worked for Serendipity when he rang to make today's appointment.' She turned to Oscar, impressed. 'But I didn't realise you were the boss! There was an article on you and your partner —'

'Jake,' Oscar supplied.

'That's it, Jake, in the Saturday magazine supplement a few months ago.' She turned to Theo. 'They're the ones who do all the lovely romantic things.'

Oscar tried to look modest and failed utterly. 'That's us.'

Hero's mother nudged Theo in the ribs. 'Here, you take this card,' she said playfully. 'I think you should give him a call next week.'

Theo coughed in embarrassment but kept the card.

'Could we get back to the point, please?' Hero demanded, in a voice that dripped ice. 'Technically, wedding planning may be amongst the services that his company offers, but the fact remains that I did not hire him.'

Her parents looked from Hero to Oscar and back again. 'Is that true?' Coralie asked.

Oscar met her gaze directly. 'Yes.' There was a pause and then he added, 'Pelham hired me.'

Hero looked at him, dumbfounded.

'Very thoughtful of Pelham,' said Hero's mother, seizing on a rare chance to sincerely approve of Pelham.

'You're lying,' Hero accused Oscar, springing to her feet.

'Hero!' her father said, shocked.

Oscar, however, remained unmoved. 'I'm not, Hero. I can prove it.'

From his leather satchel, he pulled out a signed contract and with growing fury Hero recognised Pelham's precise signature.

'Pelham hired *you* as our wedding planner?'

'And as his general, er, romantic adviser.'

'Meaning what?' Hero bit out.

'I . . . assisted, I suppose you could say, in your engagement,' Oscar confessed.

'So that weekend away – you were there to *help* Pelham?'

Oscar nodded.

That he'd gone out of his way to deceive Pelham only made Hero more furious. 'Pelham might have hired you but I *know* you. Somehow you convinced him to listen to you. You want to ruin our relationship and this is your way of doing it!'

'Hero, you're being irrational,' her mother remonstrated. 'Why would he want to cause trouble between you and Pelham? He's a professional.'

'He's a professional liar!' Hero shouted. 'And he's doing it so that I'll break up with Pelham and go out with him instead, and I won't, I won't, I won't!' She just managed to refrain from stamping her foot but it was a near thing.

'Whatever the rights and wrongs of this situation you had better stop carrying on like Veruca Salt this instant,' her father said sternly. 'Or I'll send you to your room.'

'I'm an adult and I don't live here any more!' Hero snapped. 'You can't send me to my room!'

'Just try me,' Theo said grimly.

Coralie intervened, looking puzzled. 'But darling, this makes no sense. Why would Oscar want to date you? He's gay.'

'I'm not gay,' Oscar said. 'Who told you I was?'

In silence, they all turned to look at Hero.

'Hero, did you lie to me?' her mother asked, in a tone of disappointment that was far worse than anger.

Hero tried to hold her chin up and defiantly return their gazes, but the overwhelming injustice of being branded a liar, while that modern-day Machiavelli turned her parents against her, was too much.

She pounced on safer ground from which to vent her fury. 'I'm not the only hypocrite here. Since when do you make cucumber sandwiches, Mum? When I was five, you fed us pakoras and laksas. You've never made a white-bread sandwich in your life!'

Coralie looked hurt. 'I just thought . . . you seemed to like them that time Gloria had us over for afternoon tea and . . .'

'You're not Gloria!' Hero's shame at exploding at her mother caused her to completely lose self-control. 'Why would you think for a second that I want you to be like her?'

Hero's mother looked at her for a long moment. 'I don't think you want me to be like her, darling,' she said softly. 'I think you want to be like her.'

Hero felt as though she'd been winded. *'Like Gloria?'* she gasped. 'You think *I* want to be like *Gloria*?'

At this point Hero's father made an almost imperceptible movement with his head. Catching the gesture, Oscar nodded and they slipped unnoticed out of the room, leaving Hero and her mother alone.

'Well, maybe not the pearls and the Botox,' Coralie conceded. 'But even when you were a little girl, you had conservative tastes and you liked things calm and orderly, the way they are at Pelham's parents' house. I remember it used to drive you mad, how messy we all were. Your bookshelf was the only one in the house that was nicely arranged – you had it all organised according to size and genre. And I'll never forget the birthday party when you made me buy horrible frozen sausage rolls and party pies and you wanted to play pass the parcel. Do you remember?'

'I remember,' Hero said shortly. It had been her ninth birthday and she was just old enough to be aware of the differences between her family and those of her friends. She had been terrified that her mother would serve unrecognisable Indian sweets or put on weird South American music and teach them all how to dance. She had just wanted to be like everyone else. And the party had started off just as she'd planned, until somehow her family had taken over, like they always did, and instead of playing pass the parcel and having three-legged races, Hero's friends ended up playing African bead games and eating baklava while she sat on her bedroom floor and cried. All these years later, she could still remember the pain and humiliation of being over-looked at her own birthday party.

'So I can see the attraction that Pelham's family have for you,' Hero's mother finished.

If Hero had glanced up and seen the expression of sadness on her mother's face, her anger would have drained away and she would have gone over to hug her. Instead, she gazed unseeingly through the French doors to the rain-soaked garden beyond, unconsciously clenching and unclenching her fists.

Coralie watched her and decided that things couldn't get much worse. She took a deep breath. 'Don't marry him, Hero.' Now Hero did look up, but her mother's gaze was no longer sad, it was steady. 'I've never heard you and Pelham laugh together. Not once.'

The flash of fearful acknowledgement in Hero's eyes confirmed everything Coralie had suspected. But before she could say anything further, Hero snatched up her bag. Without a word, she left, slamming the front door behind her.

Coralie sat on the couch, listening to the sound of her daughter's car receding into the distance. Theo and Oscar tentatively stuck their heads around the door.

She patted the space on the couch next to her. 'Come and sit down, Oscar,' she said, mustering a smile. 'Because if you don't mind, I'd like to know exactly what's going on between you and my daughter.'

25

For love and money

It was to prove a shame, for many reasons, that Hero didn't go home and burst into tears that afternoon. If she had relieved her emotions, she most probably would have calmed down by the next day and rung her mother to apologise.

But she didn't. And as Sunday spent that night at Toby's, Hero was unable to relate the story to her friend and benefit from her considered opinion on the matter. Instead, she spent the greater part of Sunday night tossing and turning, fury increasing as she piled up memory upon memory of Oscar's outrageous behaviour. By the time she made it to work on Monday morning, heavy-eyed and still incensed, she had completely lost any perspective and was utterly hell-bent on seeking revenge.

Sasha looked up in surprise as the door to her office was flung open with considerable force.

'I have an idea for an article,' Hero announced, without preamble. She paused for dramatic effect and then said, '"For Love *And* Money".'

Sasha raised an eyebrow. That was a good sign. It meant that Hero had succeeded in catching her interest.

'An investigation into industries that ruthlessly exploit the love-lorn. Internet dating. Matchmaking services. Fortune tellers.' Hero took a deep breath. 'And companies like Serendipity.'

'Serendipity?' Sasha said sharply. 'I thought they had a good reputation?'

'That's exactly my point. They do have a great reputation, but what's it really all about?' Hero started to pace around the office.

'You're going to tell me, aren't you?'

'It's about cynicism,' Hero said, ignoring Sasha's dry tone. 'The complete antithesis of romance. It's about exploiting collective clichés about romance and love in order to deprive the socially inept of their hard-earned cash.'

'Have you broken up with Pelham?'

Hero looked indignant. 'Just because I suggest a story exposing the exploitation of romance does not mean that I'm bitter about my own failed love-life!'

'So have you?' Sasha asked, unmoved.

'No, I have not!'

There was a long pause. 'Then why is it that I get the distinct feel-ing that this story is personally motivated?' Sasha mused.

Hero shifted uncomfortably but met her boss's gaze defiantly.

Sasha nodded briskly. 'Okay. Go ahead with it. Let's see, today is the twelfth. How quickly do you think you can turn it around?'

'Why?' The team at *Angel* worked at least three months ahead of schedule, so Sasha's question was unexpected.

'We've got space in the June issue. A writer's let us down so I could slot your article in, providing you can write it in the next few days.'

'I – er – of course.' Hero cursed under her breath. With all the wedding-related appointments that Pelham and Gloria had planned, the last thing she needed was extra work. But having waited so long to have a piece published, she could hardly say no.

'Right. Then go for it. But Hero?'

'Yes?'

'If it turns out that any of the people or companies you're investigating have, let's say, a genuine motivation, then they had better not end up in your article.'

Hero turned Sasha's own gesture back on her, raising one eyebrow. 'The New Romantics are *very* eighties, Sasha.'

Sasha smiled at her gently. 'But cynicism is so nineties. And if I say we're having an eighties revival, why then, Hero my love, we are.'

Hero was triumphant as she exited Sasha's office. She was going to get back at Oscar once and for all, and she was going to use her own methods, not his. It would be a professional hit and it would end this twisted romance, once and for all.

⋆ ✶ ⋆

In the interests of fair and balanced journalism, Hero had formally requested, and been granted, an interview with Oscar and Jake, despite Jake's fervent protestations. At twenty-five past nine the following morning, Oscar made his way to Jake's office to drag his unwilling partner to the meeting.

'What are you looking so bloody pleased about?' Jake demanded, shooting a look of annoyance at Oscar. 'Mate, she works for *Angel*. We pull in a lot of business from there. If she flays us, it could hurt the company badly.'

'She's not going to flay us,' Oscar said confidently. 'Now hurry up and come to the conference room.'

'How do you know she won't?' Jake groaned and looked at Oscar pleadingly. 'For the love of god, *please*, I beg of you, *please* don't try to charm her any more! We'll end up bankrupt *and* in prison.'

Oscar looked affronted. 'I wouldn't dream of trying to charm a client.'

A glimmer of hope shone in Jake's eye. 'You wouldn't?'

Oscar shook his head virtuously.

'Wait a minute, what do you mean by *client*?'

But Oscar was already making his way towards the door.

'Oscar! I thought that weekend away was a one-off. Don't tell me her fiancé is still on the books?'

Oscar turned and smiled wickedly at his long-suffering friend. 'I'm Hero's wedding planner. How can she assess our business properly unless she experiences our services first hand?'

'WHATEVER YOU'RE UP TO, STOP IT!' Jake bawled down the corridor after him. 'DAMN YOU, OSCAR! I FORBID YOU! DO YOU HEAR ME?'

Oscar waved a hand in acknowledgement but kept walking, merrily whistling.

Jake collapsed back into his chair. Without him having to ask, Beth silently entered the room and handed him a cold towel to place on his overheated brow. To Jake, she had the aspect of a celestial comforter and, to her utter surprise, he grabbed her hand and kissed it passionately. As he then took refuge under the towel, he was unable to witness the slow blush that crept up her cheeks and the soft expression in her eyes before she quietly closed the door behind her.

✳

'Is your obvious disdain for my company linked to your personal hostility towards me or is it the result of your general anti-romance position?'

The interview had only been going for ten minutes and already Jake was wishing that he had made his objection about attending rather more forcefully. He felt like a spectator at a Palestinian–Israeli tennis match.

'I don't believe that I'm anti-romance,' Hero shot back. 'I just don't find the particular brand of romance that you sell attractive.'

'What's wrong with it?' Oscar countered.

'What's right with it? Your clients are outsourcing their personal lives. They're paying a professional to orchestrate some of the most important milestones in their lives. Personally, I would question the sincerity of my partner's feelings if he had to pay someone else to devise a way to express how he feels about me.' Realising that she had walked straight into a trap, she bit her lip, furious with herself, but Oscar was gracious enough not to point out that Pelham had done exactly that.

Instead he said, 'You seem to think our clients come in, plonk down their credit cards and leave it all up to us. That's not the way it works at all. We sit down and talk to them about their partner, and then devise a tailormade strategy, something that reflects who they really are. Some people simply don't know how to be romantic and they ask us for help. All they want is to have a day, or a moment, that's pure escapism, that lifts them out of their daily lives.'

Hero snorted and pointedly turned to Jake. 'All right then, let's hear about these so called "tailormade strategies".'

'Well, we use balloons,' Jake said, running a finger around his collar and wondering why the office seemed so warm. 'Ranging from small, helium-filled ones printed with a personalised message to sunrise balloon-trips over the eastern and northern beaches.'

'Things filled with hot air,' Hero wrote in her notebook, then looked up at Jake composedly. 'What else?'

'Er, flowers of course. Sky-writing. Gourmet food hampers.'

Hero listed these strategies under the heading 'EPHEMERA'. She then placed her open notebook on the table, under Jake and Oscar's noses.

'Now, look here,' said Jake, flustered, 'you're twisting everything I'm saying.'

Hero looked at him in surprise. 'No, I'm not. All of those things *are* ephemeral – they don't last more than a few days. In the case of sky-writing, it only lasts five or ten minutes at most, in the best conditions. Isn't that right?'

'Well, yes, but —'

'And balloons *are* filled with hot air, and to be frank so is your colleague.' She stood up. 'I think I have everything I need.'

Thankful that the ordeal was over, Jake fled, mumbling something about Beth needing him.

As Hero gathered together her things, Oscar's voice cut in, his amused drawl showing that he was completely unaffected by her barbs. 'Have *you* ever been on a balloon ride with someone you love, Miss Hathaway? Or a picnic? Or a sailboat at sunset? Because if you had, you'd know it's the memory, even of something as fleeting and simple as a bouquet of flowers, that's the true gift.'

'There's absolutely no need to remind me that you prioritise escapism and dreams over real life. I'm well aware of that fact.'

'You're not hearing me. Dreams and romance are a part of real life, and real love.'

'Just because I don't subscribe to your financially motivated conception of romance, it doesn't mean I'm incapable of love,' Hero retaliated.

'Oh really? So what does it feel like?'

'What?'

'What does being in love feel like?'

'You're being ridiculous.'

'No, really. You've abused my company in person and you're about to do it in print, so I think it only fair that you tell me, off the record, what it feels like, in your expert opinion, to be in love.'

Hero was silent, and when she looked up, her cheeks were flushed. 'I know that this won't accord with your unrealistic notions of love but . . . he makes me feel safe.' She left the room abruptly, before Oscar could respond.

Oscar raised his coffee mug in salutation. 'Well, that's unfortunate, Hero,' he said softly, 'because you can take it from me, the one thing love cannot do is keep your beloved safe.'

26

Knowing an ocelot by its stripes

'I don't know.' Geoffrey was leaning against his desk, holding Hero's Pussycat costume at arm's length. 'I've always thought that if I were a cat, I'd be an Abyssinian or a Russian blue, something exotic. This costume has a whiff of tabby about it.'

'That's only because I sat in something in a taxi,' Hero said. 'Look, Geoffrey, it really doesn't make much difference to me. I just thought you might like to have it. If you don't, I'll give it to the City Mission op shop.'

Geoffrey pursed his lips and held up a commanding hand. 'I didn't say I didn't want it. I'm just thinking things through. William Baker says that you have to make *considered* choices,' he added, his haughty veneer slipping as he imparted this nugget of wisdom from one who was as a god to him. William Baker was the stylist who'd purchased Kylie Minogue's gold hotpants at a London market for the reputed sum of fifty pence, thereby attaining a rank in Geoffrey's pantheon above Patricia Field, the legendary stylist from *Sex and the City*, and only a few degrees below Kylie herself. 'Can you put it on?'

'Now?' Hero sighed as Geoffrey nodded. 'Why do you have to see it on? It's going to look different on me than it will on you.'

'That's for sure,' Geoffrey said smugly, patting thighs that were admittedly firmer and slimmer than Hero's. 'But William Baker says —'

Hero groaned loudly, cutting him off. 'If you promise never to mention William Baker again, I'll make you a present of that Diane von Furstenberg dress I bought in New York.'

Geoffrey clasped his hands together. 'Really?'

'I'll even pay for the alterations. Now, do you want this costume or not?'

'Put it on and then I'll decide.'

Muttering peevishly, Hero disappeared into her office and emerged several minutes later in the leotard with the dangling tail. She had drawn the line at putting on the cat's ears headband, which she held in one hand.

'Happy now?' she asked, doing a twirl as Geoffrey critically surveyed the possibilities of the outfit.

At that moment, the intercom on his desk buzzed. Such was the power Sasha had over her staff that Geoffrey promptly scurried back behind his desk and sat upright, the model of a dutiful assistant, even though Sasha couldn't see him.

'I want Hero in my office. Now,' Sasha snapped.

Startled at her boss's irate tone, Hero answered for herself. 'I can be there in two minutes, Sasha.'

'I said now.' The intercom cut off.

Without stopping to change, Hero made her way swiftly to Sasha's office. It was one of the benefits of working for a women's magazine, she reflected, that one could wander through the office in a leopard-print leotard, complete with tail, and not a single person would afford you a second glance.

Sasha impatiently gestured for Hero to sit down and then flung Hero's copy across the desk. 'What the hell is this?'

'My story,' Hero said warily, recognising the printed pages.

'Second page. The highlighted paragraph. I'm assuming you have proof?'

Hero didn't have to look. 'Yes.'

'Because,' Sasha continued, as though Hero hadn't spoken, 'I know you would never deliberately assert anything that could irreparably damage a successful business and leave us open to claims for damages, libel or lost revenue.'

'You're right. I wouldn't.'

Sasha leant back in her chair and looked Hero over. 'You know, something doesn't sit right. The rest of the article is fine. But Serendipity has an excellent reputation.'

'Sasha, it's all crap. They commercialise romance and love and they're making a fortune out of it. Their ethical policy doesn't mean a thing and I have proof that they will contravene it when it suits them.'

'Show me the proof.'

'You're looking at it,' Hero said quietly. 'It's me.'

Sasha's eyebrows shot up. 'You?' In one of the lightning-quick deductions for which she was famed as much as feared, she put it all together. 'Cardboard cut-out guy? Who the hell is he?'

Hero took a deep breath. 'Oscar Martin. The founder of Serendipity and one of its two owners. He's pursued me for months, using his company's resources, despite knowing that I have a boyfriend who's now my fiancé. He's flouted his own company's policies at every turn.'

'What about entrapment?' Sasha asked sharply. 'Is there a possibility that you could be accused of encouraging his breach of ethics?'

'I did every bloody thing I could to discourage him,' Hero said, with rancour. 'Nothing worked.'

'Have you had any sort of personal relationship with him?'

Hero flushed. 'Years ago.'

'So there's been nothing between you since?'

'We kissed once, not long ago,' Hero admitted reluctantly. 'But it was a mistake.'

Sasha drummed her fingers on the desk while she processed Hero's information and then shook her head decisively. 'I'm sorry, Hero. I can't run it.'

'Why not?'

'Because Serendipity is one of our biggest advertisers,' Sasha said bluntly.

'A moment ago you were worried about ethics!'

'I still am. But I'm not going to run this story and lose a major account and possibly put you and the magazine in a position where we can be sued. I'll run the article without the Serendipity material, or not at all.'

'I guess it's not at all, then,' Hero shot back. 'I assume that your refusal leaves me free to sell it to another publisher?'

Sasha inclined her head graciously. 'Of course. But in case you change your mind about cutting the story, I'll brief Karla,' she said, naming the features editor. 'I'm flying to Milan tomorrow so she's overseeing the corrections to the June and July editions.' She paused and added, 'But if you want my opinion, Hero, which I know you don't, I'd put that article in a locked drawer and give the key to someone else until you've thought it over.'

Ignoring this advice, Hero grabbed her article and strode out in a filthy temper.

It was a few minutes later when Sasha noticed something long and furry lying on the floor. Picking up Hero's cat's tail, she dangled it musingly. 'Looks like you just lost all of your nine lives, my girl.'

27

Serendipity

'New edition,' Geoffrey sang, throwing the June *Angel* on Hero's desk.

Hero looked at it listlessly. Normally she was happy to spend hours assessing articles, poring over them for mistakes, looking for ways to make each story better, but as her wedding approached, even work had lost its stimulation. She'd tried to convince herself that this was normal, that every bride was consumed by their wedding, but deep down she was fairly certain that most brides-to-be didn't place apathy at the top of their list of predominant emotions.

She couldn't help thinking that much of her indifference was due to the unpublished story sitting in her desk drawer. Reluctantly, she'd taken Sasha's advice and tucked it away. Therefore she was still unpublished, unable to wreak revenge on Oscar, and unenthusiastic about her wedding. All of which was making her very grumpy indeed.

Picking up the magazine, she flicked through it in a desultory fashion.

Moments later, a high-pitched scream brought Geoffrey running, rather impressively, in six-inch stilettos.

Hero's face was white as she mutely waved the magazine at him.

'Hero? What is it?' Geoffrey asked, genuinely alarmed. 'Did that new stylist team a Supré top with a Wayne Cooper skirt? I'll kill her. And then Sasha will kill her again.'

Hero shook her head, fighting for composure.

Geoffrey took the magazine and skimmed the article she pointed at. 'Sasha ran your story,' he said, puzzled at her distress. 'Aren't you meant to be celebrating?'

'I don't understand,' Hero whispered, jabbing again at the offending pages with a finger. 'How did this get in?'

Geoffrey looked at her in utter bewilderment. 'I emailed it to Karla, of course. Hero, what's *wrong*?'

'It wasn't meant to go in,' Hero wailed. 'It's a mistake.'

'But it's a great article. Although it didn't quite have the effect you intended,' he admitted. 'After reading the proof, I made an appointment with Davina. You won't believe what she told me. Apparently my soul mate is a man who lives in the country. I mean, *me*? In the *country*? Moleskins and R.M. Williams boots! *No heels*? Can you imagine?'

Hero wasn't listening. She had snatched back the magazine and was re-reading her article, hoping against hope that it had been edited, that the references to Serendipity had been removed. But they hadn't. Sasha had been in Milan for the past three weeks and hadn't foreseen that a direct order could ever be disobeyed. And now, thanks to Geoffrey and Karla, the whole horrible, slanderous piece was in.

And it was horrible, Hero thought wretchedly. She had been angry when she wrote it, so angry, and the references to Serendipity dripped with venom. It was her first published article and it was a hatchet job. She was probably going to be fired, she realised. Somehow that didn't seem so bad compared with facing Oscar.

'Geoffrey, I have to make a phone call,' she said, her mouth dry and her voice cracking. She cleared her throat. 'Could I have some privacy, please?'

'Sure.' To Hero's surprise, Geoffrey poured her a glass of water and then gave her a swift hug. 'It's probably not as bad as you think,' he said kindly.

Hero, who had never thought that Geoffrey cared the slightest bit about her, was touched and smiled gratefully at him. He left her alone and she took a sip of water. Then, with trembling hand, she dialled Oscar's mobile number.

She was almost weak with relief when her call went straight through to his voicemail. She started to leave a halting message when she was distracted by raised voices in reception. Before she had time to gather herself, the door to her office was flung open and Oscar stood at the threshold.

Hero took one look at him and her heart wilted. She had never seen him angry before. And he was clearly not just angry but in a towering rage.

To her immense surprise, Geoffrey flung himself in Oscar's path. 'You're not allowed in here without an appointment,' he said dramatically.

Oscar didn't take his eyes off Hero's face. 'Get out of here, Geoffrey,' he said, his voice betraying no emotion. 'Now.'

Geoffrey couldn't quite hide his pleasure that Oscar had remembered his name, but he stuck to his role as protector. 'Never!' he declared.

Hero was now firmly convinced that Geoffrey was rather hoping to be manhandled by Oscar, who had evidently come to the same conclusion. He shot Geoffrey an annoyed glance and then said, quite pleasantly, 'Geoffrey, if you don't exit this office and close the door behind you within the next ten seconds, I will throw you out, and believe me, I will not do it gently.' He paused, and then added, awfully, 'That dress you're wearing looks like it would tear very easily.'

Geoffrey gasped and drew the folds of his vintage chiffon flapper dress protectively around himself.

Hero gave him a wan smile. 'It's okay, Geoffrey,' she said. 'Go.'

'I'm sorry. If I'd worn my floral pinny today, it would be different, but this dress was an absolute *find* and —'

'Really, Geoffrey, it's fine. Thank you for trying.'

Geoffrey trailed out, contenting himself with shooting a vicious look at Oscar, who shut the door firmly in his face.

Oscar turned to face Hero, a rolled-up copy of *Angel* in one hand. 'Had you forgotten that advertisers receive an advance copy?' he asked sharply.

'No, I —'

He cut over her coldly. 'You know, I owe you an apology.'

Hero was utterly startled. 'You . . . what?'

'Yes, I do. I'm extremely sorry that I never listened to you all those times you tried to convince me that we weren't right for each other. You were right – I should have left you to rot with your materialistic, insufferable boyfriend a long time ago.'

Hero cringed as he hurled the insults at her, praying that the storm would abate so that she could try to explain.

'You kept telling me that you weren't the person I fell for all those years ago, and I just kept on believing that deep down you really wanted to be that person. But I was wrong. Deep down you're the sort of person who is capable of *this*.' He threw his copy of *Angel* across her desk and Hero flinched. He glared at her. 'Well? Are you going to say anything? Anything at all?'

Hero tried to speak but the words refused to come.

Oscar stared at her in disgust and then made his exit, slamming the door behind him.

But Hero hardly heard him leave. She was curled up tight inside herself, burning with shame, miserably aware that the pain she had sworn she would never endure again had somehow found her once more.

28

Grace

By eight o'clock that evening, Sunday was seriously concerned. A tear-stained Hero had related the whole woeful tale, and despite several hours filled with cups of tea and Sunday's soothing words, she was no nearer to being comforted.

As Sunday plied her friend with another handful of tissues, the doorbell rang. Hero froze. 'If it's Oscar, I don't want to see him,' she whispered hoarsely. 'Please, Sun, I just can't.'

Sunday patted her as one would a frightened child. 'I'll get rid of whoever it is,' she said gently.

However, she broke her promise. After a few moments' muted conversation, two pairs of footsteps came down the hall.

Hero looked up in trepidation, then gasped in shock. 'Jean!'

'Hello, Hero,' Oscar's mother said comfortably, bustling into the room.

Sunday discreetly slipped away, closing the door behind her.

Hero promptly burst into fresh sobs. Gathering her up in a motherly hug, Jean petted her until the storm abated, nodding wisely as something that sounded like 'I didn't mean to' was repeated over and over again.

'Of course you didn't, love,' Jean said, hugging her tighter and rocking her back and forth. She let Hero cry until the sobs threatened to become hysterical. 'That's enough now,' she said, in a crisp tone. 'I came here to tell you something.'

'That . . . that you read my article and you hate me?' Hero gulped pathetically.

'I did read the article, but no, I don't hate you. And neither does that son of mine.'

'Yes, he does,' Hero wailed, fresh tears rolling down her cheeks. 'And so he should. I did a horrible, vicious thing.'

'Knowing my son, I'm sure you were provoked,' Jean said dryly. 'Listen to me, Hero. Do you know how long Serendipity has been operating?'

'No,' Hero said, surprised out of her lamentations by this unexpected question.

'It'll be coming up to two years soon. Oscar convinced Jake to be his business partner after he returned from New York.'

'Oh.' Hero dabbed at her face with a tissue, unsure as to where this conversation was going.

'Before he left for New York, he worked as a solicitor.'

'*Oscar is a lawyer?*' Hero forgot her misery as she tried to equate the image of the bartending romantic with the corporate lawyer.

Jean nodded proudly. 'He's a very good one, too. He was working for one of the big firms in the city and doing extremely well.'

'He's a *lawyer?*' Hero repeated again, still flabbergasted by the idea that someone as contemptuous of convention as Oscar was once a representative of the law-abiding.

Jean raised her voice a fraction, to override Hero's astonishment. 'Do you know why Oscar was in New York when you met him?'

'Not really,' Hero said, feeling uncomfortable. 'I assumed he wanted to escape from a nine-to-five existence.'

'That is what he wanted, but not for the reasons that you think. He quit his job and went away two months after Grace died.'

'Who?'

Jean sighed and the sadness in her face suddenly made her look much older. 'I thought as much. He hasn't told you about Grace, has he?'

'No.' Hero was suddenly finding it hard to breathe.

'That's typical of Oscar.' Jean took in Hero's bewilderment, and then delivered what she had come to say. 'Hero, Grace was Oscar's fiancée.'

'*His what?*'

'His fiancée,' Jean replied calmly. 'She died in a car accident, almost four years ago. They were going to be married that December.' She allowed Hero a few moments to absorb this and then said, 'Part of Oscar's rationale for setting up Serendipity was to make sure that people seized the day, that they remembered to take time for the people they love.'

'So . . . so he set up the company for her?'

'She was definitely one of the motivating reasons, yes.'

'But he never told me about her,' Hero said, groping her way through these startling revelations. 'He never even mentioned her. Not once. He . . . he must still find it painful to talk about her.' She stopped, overcome with horror at the realisation that she was *jealous*. She clenched her fists, digging her nails into her palms. She hadn't thought it was possible to hate herself more after the publication of her article, but she was discovering that there were new-found depths to which she could sink. She was actually jealous of an unknown girl who had been dead for almost four years.

Jean had been watching her closely and had a very good idea of where Hero's thoughts had taken her. 'My dear, I'm sorry to be blunt but for someone who is about to be married to a person you're clearly not in love with, you seem to have a very high level of romantic idealism. The fact that Oscar has been in love before doesn't make him any less able to love you. You're not competing with a ghost, if that's what you're worried about.'

Hero swallowed hard and then asked, in a small voice, 'Jean? What was she like? Grace, I mean.' She stumbled over the unfamiliar name that had suddenly become such a significant part of her own story.

A small, sad smile played on Jean's lips. 'I think you should ask Oscar. It would do you both good to talk about her.'

$$\star\ \textbf{\Large *}\ \star$$

On the afternoon of the following day, Oscar knelt down and brushed away the leaves that had fallen on the simple plaque set into the earth.

'Hey Gracie,' he said softly, laying aside his bouquet of white cherry blossoms and rolling up his sleeves. Pulling a cloth from his knapsack, he cleaned the plaque and removed withered flowers left by a previous visitor. He arranged the cherry blossoms, then sat back on his heels and took a deep breath.

'Grace, I need to talk to you. The thing is, I met someone. But now it's all fallen apart.' He faltered as his throat closed up. 'I was going to ask you if it was okay. Your parents said it's what you would have wanted, that you'd want me to be happy and get on with my life, but I just don't know what to think any more.' A breeze had sprung up and he felt its gentle caress as he fought back tears. 'It doesn't mean that I don't love you any more, Grace, it's just that you're like a beautiful memory now and Hero's real and here and —'

He stopped, battling for control as the letters engraved on the plaque swam before his gaze. Grace Jane Harris. Twenty-six years old.

'I tried so hard with her. But it didn't work. She just wouldn't see it.' He stretched out a hand to trace the outline of Grace's name. The finality of the cold letters struck him anew.

For one of the few times in his life, Oscar was filled with utter despair. Grace was long dead and nothing he had done had changed Hero's heart. Instead of falling in love with him, she had turned on him and betrayed him in the most public way possible.

He had been wrong about Hero all along.

The breeze blew again, a little stronger this time. A cherry blossom petal detached itself from the stem and floated through the air, landing on his cheek like a kiss.

Closing his eyes, Oscar made a wish, then blew the petal into the warm spring air.

'Thanks Gracie,' he whispered. He picked up his knapsack and strode off into the late afternoon light, the petal catching the sun's dying rays as it spun and danced in the breeze.

29

Playing tennis with Freddy

Hero and Pelham's new wedding planner was named Ashleigh Burton-Smythe. Ashleigh wore beige tailored jackets with skirts, never pants, spoke in a soothing voice that made Hero feel like a three-year-old and tilted her head to one side in a compassionate listening pose whenever anyone said anything that she didn't agree with. Gloria was very much taken with Ashleigh and her suggestions. Hero, on the other hand, very much wanted to throw a swan sculpted out of ice at Ashleigh's perfectly groomed head.

'Hero, did you check the final alteration to the hem of my dress?' Gloria asked, as they assembled at her house for yet another interminable meeting. Her tone was long-suffering, conveying that she asked for so very little and yet continued to receive nothing.

Hero snapped out of her thoughts. 'Uh, no, Gloria. Sorry. I haven't had a chance to try my – your – *the* wedding dress on again. I've been so busy with work and all the wedding things . . .' She trailed off lamely.

Gloria heaved a sigh and exchanged a speaking glance with Ashleigh. 'If it's not *too* much trouble perhaps you could try it on in the next day or so? My dressmaker books out well in advance and if we need further alterations done before the wedding we might run into problems.'

'Yes. Of course.' Hero couldn't bear the disappointment in Pelham's eyes; he never refused or forgot any of Gloria's commands and couldn't fathom anyone else doing so. Instead, she focused on the awful family portrait hanging above the marble fireplace. Pelham appeared to have no chin and Gloria's fingers looked like sausages, but the artist had once painted a governor-general's family and that had been enough for Gloria, who had instantly commissioned a similar work.

'Well then,' Ashleigh said, in the falsely bright tone that made Hero long for the aforementioned frozen swan. 'We've only a few weeks left before the wedding, so let's discuss the music, shall we?'

Ashleigh, Pelham and Gloria launched into an animated debate as to the best choice of bridal waltz, while Hero stood at the floor-to-ceiling windows and stared out at the grey skies and wind-whipped water of the harbour. It was the middle of June and the bitter conditions matched her mood exactly. She had left several messages for Oscar but he hadn't returned her calls. She had even gone around to his flat, but there had been no answer when she knocked on the door. She had considered going to Serendipity, but couldn't quite get up the courage to walk into the workplace that she had denigrated so publicly. She had unfairly jeopardised the jobs of all the staff and couldn't imagine that she would be made to feel welcome, assuming that they allowed her in at all. Besides which, the thought of Oscar raging at her again, but in public this time, made her feel positively sick.

Listening with only half an ear to the conversation, Hero toyed with the idea of suggesting they waltz to 'Closer' by the Nine Inch Nails, just to see Ashleigh's reaction, but then decided she couldn't summon the energy. It didn't really matter what was played, she thought, depressed all over again. It wasn't as though she and Pelham had a special song.

Ashleigh waited until Gloria's pitch for 'I Honestly Love You' by Olivia Newton John ('such a lovely song and she was *so* wonderful in *Xanadu*') had ended and then said, in her well-modulated voice, 'Perhaps I'll give Pelham and Hero a list of popular suggestions and they can choose one for themselves. Now, I just have one last query. There seems to be some sort of misprint regarding the menu. The one I received from your previous wedding planner lists an order for two hundred and forty-nine serves of chocolate biscuit tortoni with Kahlua and King Island cream.' She waited a beat, and then said, 'And one origami cupcake with non-alcoholic chocolate sauce.'

Hero let out a sudden crack of laughter. Pelham and Gloria turned to look at her in surprise. She quickly stilled her smile and attempted to explain. 'It's not a misprint. It's for Sunday.'

Gloria pursed her lips and said to Ashleigh, 'That's the *other* bridesmaid.' She added, in a tone loaded with insinuation, 'The one who's expecting.'

Ashleigh nodded understandingly. 'I completely understand. At any function there are always a few fussy eaters. I did a function recently and there were *three* vegans! It was a nightmare!' Gloria and Ashleigh laughed merrily together, as though catering for vegans was the pinnacle of absurdity.

Seeing the dark expression on Hero's face, Ashleigh abruptly stopped laughing and reassumed her caring persona. 'We can organise a different dessert for your friend, without the Kahlua sauce. Naturally she can't have alcohol, but I'm afraid you'll have to enlighten me as to what an origami cupcake is. I've spoken to the chef and he has no idea how to prepare it.'

'It's not a rare delicacy,' Hero said flatly. 'It's exactly what it sounds like – a cupcake made out of origami. She has cravings for paper, that's all.' She lifted her chin defiantly as Ashleigh and Gloria stared in astonishment. Pelham was simply looking mortified.

'She *eats* paper?' Gloria asked, incredulous.

'Yes.' Hero started to count the seconds and she wasn't disappointed. On the stroke of three, Ashleigh tilted her head to one side.

Pelham laughed nervously. 'Hero's just having a little joke. Leave the menu with us, Ashleigh, and we'll fix that up.' He glared Hero into silence as he took the menu from Ashleigh.

'Well then,' Ashleigh said, head still tilted, 'let's discuss the seating arrangements, shall we?'

Hero looked at Pelham for a long moment and then turned back to the window, staring unseeingly out as the rain started to lash down. Behind her, Ashleigh, Gloria and Pelham continued with their plans for the wedding of the year.

⋆ ✱ ⋆

Hero cursed the Sydney traffic as it crawled to a halt in the downpour. She had exactly ten minutes to reach the dressmaker's and pick up the altered wedding dress, and she knew Gloria would be furious if she failed to make it.

At Double Bay, Hero left her car double-parked and with the hazard lights flashing. Running through the heavy rain, she banged on the glass door of the dressmaker's. For once she was in luck, and several minutes and profuse apologies later, she emerged with the dress, carefully wrapped to protect it from the weather.

Staggering under the dress's surprising weight, Hero ducked her head to avoid the driving rain – and slammed straight into someone who had obviously been employing the same tactic.

Hero was sent sprawling on the slippery footpath while the wedding dress and her bag went in different directions.

'I'm so sorry —' the stranger began, and then said, '*Hero?*'

Hero looked up from her undignified position on the ground. 'Elliott,' she said, in a tone of weary resignation. She had always known that she would run into him again one day. And of course it had to happen during a thunderstorm, when her hair was plastered to her head, her knee was skinned and she felt like bursting into tears.

Five minutes later they were seated in the warmth of a coffee shop, attempting to dry off with napkins. Elliott was a rat and he'd broken her heart, but Hero had to grudgingly admit that he'd retained his ability to sweep her up in his enthusiasm and turn any situation into a mini-celebration.

'That's quite a dress you've got in there,' he remarked, nodding to the enormous bag Hero had draped over two chairs.

'It's my wedding dress,' Hero said, between sips of her hot chocolate, unable to suppress a stab of vindictive delight in imparting this information.

Elliott whistled. 'Congratulations! I can't say that I'm surprised, though.'

'Really? How did you know about me and Pelham?'

'I don't know the guy. But you're the sort of girl who was bound to get married.'

Hero put down her cup and stared at him. 'What's that supposed to mean?'

He held up his hands and gave her the smile that had wreaked such devastation on her all those years ago. 'Hey, don't go getting defensive! I just meant that you're a good catch.'

Hero was positive it wasn't what he'd meant, but she knew it was pointless to argue. Instead she said, 'So what about you?'

'You mean marriage or settling down?' He laughed. 'Not a chance. I like my freedom too much.'

'But what happened to Jasmine?' Hero asked, hating herself for remembering the girl's name.

'Who?'

'Jasmine.' Exasperated by his blank look, she added, 'The girl I found you in bed with when we were going out.'

Elliott had the grace to look ashamed. 'Oh, you mean Kelly. That was nothing. I tried to tell you at the time that it wasn't worth blowing up into something big, but you wouldn't listen.'

Hero stared at him for a very long moment. The girl's name had not been Kelly. It had most definitely been Jasmine, because part of what had hurt Hero so much was that she had known her. She was suddenly willing to bet that Elliott had slept with a dozen other girls besides Jasmine while they were in a relationship. How could she have been such a blind idiot?

Hero suddenly wanted to laugh and cry at the same time. She had spent *years* nursing the wound that Elliott had caused, refusing to even speak his name, and now here he was, right in front of her, and all she felt was relief that she had escaped him. And maybe just a fraction of desire for revenge.

Thinking quickly, she gave him a forced smile. 'I probably did make a mountain out of a molehill.'

Elliott looked taken aback. 'Well, I thought so at the time,' he said tentatively. 'You know, Hero, apart from the dripping hair and the runny mascara, you look great.'

Hero laughed. 'I always look my best when my clothes are see-through,' she said, provocatively drawing attention to the fact that her wet blouse was now transparent.

Elliott leant forward and put one hand over hers. 'Is it true what they say about engaged women getting restless?' he asked softly.

'What *exactly* are you suggesting?' Hero batted her eyelashes, trying not to laugh. Couldn't Elliott see how fake her act was?

'You and me. One last time.'

Hero widened her eyes in surprise. 'Do you mean it?'

He smiled. 'Why not?'

She tried to look confused. 'But what would I tell Pelham?'

Elliott's smile started to slip. 'Why would you tell Pelham?' he asked uneasily.

'But you said you want to try again. If I called off my engagement to Pelham to be with you, I'd have to tell him, Elliott.'

Elliott quickly removed his hand from hers and pushed his chair back. 'Wait just one minute. I wasn't suggesting that we have a *relationship*. I was talking about —'

'Sex?' Hero prompted.

He looked relieved. 'Exactly.'

She held his gaze, her disdain clear to see. 'What on *earth* makes you think I'm like you? That I'd cheat on my fiancé with someone who means absolutely nothing to me?' She stood and picked up her bag and dress. 'You disgust me. And by the way, you know how you always left flowers on my pillow? It doesn't count if you've pinched them from the neighbour's front garden.'

Hero exited the coffee shop, realising on a rush of adrenaline that she had just achieved every bride-to-be's dream – she really had lost an enormous amount of weight in a matter of minutes.

$$\star \, ^{\bigstar} \, \star$$

That evening, in the privacy of her bedroom, Hero sat on the edge of her bed and gazed blankly at the sheathed wedding dress hanging from the back of her door. She sat there for at least ten minutes before finally, reluctantly, slipping out of her clothes. Shivering as the night air brushed over her bare skin, she slowly unzipped the bag and took the dress down from its hanger. Within minutes she was standing at her mirror, staring at herself in the dress she would be wearing when she married Pelham.

A brisk knock sounded on her door and Pelham entered without announcing himself. A grin spread over his face as he took in her dress. 'Hero!' he said with satisfaction. 'You look lovely.'

'What are you doing here? Get out! It's bad luck for the groom to see the bride in her dress before the wedding day!' Hero grabbed her discarded clothes and clasped them in front of her.

'I'm not superstitious and neither are you,' Pelham said, a trifle impatiently. 'Besides, it's not as though it's the first time I've seen that dress.'

'Yes, but you must have seen it on your mother, that's completely different.' Hero paused as something occurred to her. 'Wait a minute, don't you mean you've seen *photos* of this dress?'

Pelham shook his head. 'No. I've seen Mother wearing the dress. She likes to wear it occasionally. Just around the house, you know.'

This struck Hero as a little weird, but she knew better than to utter even the faintest criticism of Gloria. 'What are you doing here anyway? I thought you were busy tonight.'

'I was, but I finished early.' He grinned at her, clearly bursting with news. 'I was putting the last touches to our room. It's finished now, so I thought you might like to drive over to see it.'

Hero instantly forgot all about what she was wearing. 'What do you mean, *our* room? Pelham, you haven't gone and bought somewhere for us to live without running it by me?'

He laughed indulgently. 'Of course not. And it's not really a room. It's the entire top floor.'

'The top floor of where?' Hero asked, bewildered. And then, slowly, 'You . . . you want us to live with *your parents*?'

Pelham nodded, proud as punch. 'Mother and I have been planning the surprise for months. We hired Creswick – you know, the interior designer? I think you'll like what he's done with the wallpaper.'

'But – but Pelham, we never discussed this.'

'Of course we didn't. That's the whole point of a surprise,' Pelham said irritably.

Hero felt as though her life was spinning out of control and she sank down on the bed for support. 'Pelham, we need to talk. Not just about where we're going to live but about . . . lots of things.'

'Like what?'

Hero took a deep breath. 'About us. And our wedding. And everything.'

To her surprise Pelham smiled and came over to sit beside her on the bed. He put an arm around her. 'I was expecting this.'

She looked at him in shock. 'You were?'

He nodded. 'Cold feet. Mother said it's very common. She's been asking me almost every day since our engagement if you'd gotten cold feet yet. Seemed very anxious about it.'

'No. Pelham, you don't understand. I don't think it's just cold feet. I —'

Before she could continue, Pelham clasped her hands and looked at her earnestly. 'The wedding is going to operate like clockwork. And don't worry about afterwards. I know I have strong opinions but I also know that compromise is the foundation of a successful marriage.'

'It is?' Hero asked dazedly, unsure as to where this was all going. She scrambled to marshal her scattered thoughts. 'I mean, you do?'

'I do,' Pelham said firmly. 'And that's why I want to bring up the subject of your bridesmaids.'

To Hero's confusion, he then launched into the tactful, rational speech that he had prepared with Gloria's help. But it wasn't long before the look of complete incomprehension in Hero's eyes brought him to a faltering stop.

'Pelham, what on earth are you talking about? Does Georgia not want to be in the bridal party?'

'My sister? Good god, no. Of course she'll be in the bridal party.'

Hero couldn't help reflecting that Georgia was included as a matter of duty, rather than through any expressed enthusiasm on her part.

'No,' Pelham continued, 'I was thinking more of Sunday.'

'Sunday?' Hero said, utterly bewildered. 'Why wouldn't Sunday be my bridesmaid?'

Seizing this opportunity, Pelham cleared his throat and plunged in. 'Do you think she's the – the most appropriate choice?'

'*She's my best friend!*'

'Darling, I know, but she's five months' pregnant. Won't she kind of . . . spoil the photos?'

Hero looked at him in absolute disgust. 'Spoil the photos?' she repeated, in a deceptively light tone that Oscar would have immediately recognised as being highly dangerous. 'Or are you really worried that my pregnant, unmarried best friend will be by our side in front of all of your friends and family and your father's business associates?'

Pelham flushed. 'I know it's very fashionable to say that anything goes these days, but my parents aren't like yours. Certain things are right and wrong in their opinion and I don't see the need to rub their faces in it, especially not on their first-born son's wedding day.'

'What do you suggest I do? Ditch Sun and get a new best friend?' Hero demanded, standing up in anger.

'Hero, I have to be able to raise legitimate concerns without having you become completely melodramatic,' Pelham said icily. 'I am simply asking you to think over what I've said and then to work out how much value you place on respecting the wishes of my parents.'

Before she could stop herself, Hero retorted, 'Not a lot, if they're such snobs they'd be ashamed of Sunday!'

Pelham started to lose his dignified manner. 'Are you really telling me that you don't care that we'll have a pregnant bridesmaid?'

'Why would I care? She'll be partnered with the world's most boring groomsman!'

'Kenneth and I work together,' Pelham said furiously. 'Do you know who his father is?'

'Of course I know who his bloody father is!' Hero shouted. 'What you seem unable to understand is that I don't *care* who his father is. I choose my friends based on the sort of people they are, not on how much money their parents make.'

'Oh really? Would that include people like your friend Oscar? He's practically insane! I don't know what I was thinking when I went to him for advice. It took me ages to convince Ashleigh and Mother that he was joking about that ridiculous paper dessert.'

'He wasn't joking! And it was a lovely and considerate gesture. But you can't see that, can you?' All of the anger suddenly drained out of Hero, and she finished in a quieter tone. 'All you see when you look at Sunday is potential embarrassment for you and your parents.'

Pelham stood up. 'I'm going now, Hero. I think it will be better if we continue this discussion in the morning, when you've had the chance to calm down.'

Hero wasn't looking at him. She was staring at the huge engagement ring on her finger. Slowly, very slowly, she pulled it off and then held it out to Pelham in her upturned palm.

'What the *hell* do you think you're doing?' Pelham asked, through gritted teeth.

Hero smiled sadly at him. 'We're not going to work, Pelham. I'm sorry I let it go this far, I really am. But we're just too different. You don't understand about Sunday having a perfectly natural craving to eat paper and I don't understand the importance of having business networks rather than friends.'

'You're calling off our engagement because I refuse to allow Sunday to eat paper for dessert?'

'It's not just that.' Hero felt strangely calm now that she had made her decision. 'I'm truly sorry. I think maybe you loved me because you thought I was someone else, someone more like you. But I don't think I'm her after all.'

'That's the most ridiculous thing that I've ever heard.' Pelham's face was unbecomingly twisted with anger. 'I mean, what am I meant to tell everyone? What am I going to tell *my parents*?'

Hero felt an intense stab of irritation. 'Is that all you care about? What Gloria will say?'

'I know you've always found it hard to accept that I value my parents' opinion,' Pelham said, in an ugly voice. 'And I've always understood why, given the sort of parents you have.'

Hero felt rage build within her, such as she had never experienced before in an argument with Pelham. 'What *exactly* are you saying about my parents?' she asked, in a voice that could have cut glass.

'The same thing that you do. That they're unstable and embarrassing.'

'I've never said that!' Hero was shouting again. 'How *dare* you talk about my parents that way! At least they don't have Swiss bank account numbers where their hearts should be!'

'Your parents couldn't afford to have Swiss bank accounts,' Pelham countered coolly. He looked at her for a long, measured moment. 'Think very carefully, Hero, because there's no going back from here. I'm prepared to make some allowance for pre-wedding jitters, but quite frankly, to even say these things this close to our wedding is unforgivable. Is this your final decision?'

Hero focused on Pelham's well-shined shoes and nodded.

When Pelham spoke again, his voice had the same hard tone that Hero had heard him use when making business calls. 'Then there's no point in continuing this conversation. I have no idea why you wasted everyone's time with the wedding arrangements, but no doubt you had your reasons.' He held out his hand. 'I'll take my ring back now and you can return my mother's wedding dress, once you've had it dry-cleaned.'

Hero dropped the ring into his outstretched palm.

Pelham put the ring in his inside coat pocket and then said harshly, 'You know, I can't help thinking that you're calling off our engagement for reasons other than my feelings toward Sunday.'

Hero didn't trust herself to speak, but the image of Oscar flitted into her mind and she was unable to meet Pelham's gaze.

Pelham looked her up and down with contempt. 'I guess Mother was right about you all along,' he said, in a cold voice that made Hero flinch. 'She always said you weren't of our class.'

He turned on his heel and left. Hero waited until she heard the front door close and then her knees buckled beneath her. Fighting for breath, she sat and stared blankly at the Picasso postcard on her dressing table. Several minutes elapsed before she picked it up, re-reading the lines that she had written to herself so long ago.

Two minutes later, the front door opened and shut again. Poking her head out of her bedroom, Sunday called out Hero's name, but there was no answer.

Hero had gone.

30

The other proposal

To Hero's dismay, Oscar's eyes hardened as he opened the door and saw who was standing in the hallway.

'Please.' It was all that Hero could manage to say.

Oscar looked at her for a moment and then, without a word, he opened the door wider.

'Thank you,' Hero said meekly, managing with difficulty to fit the full skirts of her wedding dress through the door. To her great relief, Oscar made no comment on her unconventional attire but merely waved her into the sitting room.

Catching sight of the Picasso print on the wall, Hero regained a little of the courage that had deserted her on the drive over. She turned resolutely to face Oscar, who was standing at a distance from her, arms crossed tightly in front of his body.

'I've called off my wedding,' she blurted.

His eyes widened a little but he made no response.

'It happened just now. We had a fight. Pelham found out about the dessert you ordered for Sunday and he was so disgusted and embarrassed by it and it was such a kind thing for you to have done and then there was that thing he said about —' Hero stopped short, not wanting Oscar to know that Pelham had been ashamed of having an unwed, pregnant bridesmaid.

'All I could think of was *A Room with a View*,' she continued, aware that she was starting to babble but unable to stop herself. 'It was just a little thing but it seemed to show a fatal flaw.'

'You mean how Lucy Honeychurch realised that she couldn't marry Cecil because he wouldn't play tennis with her brother Freddy?'

'Exactly.' Hero sighed with relief at being understood. 'Only I couldn't tell Pelham that.'

'No. I don't think it would have gone down well at all.'

Hero took a deep breath and looked Oscar directly in the eye. 'Why didn't you tell me?' she asked, with difficulty. 'About Grace, I mean.' She watched intently as Oscar's expression changed and was relieved to see that although a fleeting expression of sadness came over him, there was no hint of the raw grief that she had been dreading.

'Mum?' he asked, and then shook his head. 'No, you don't need to tell me. It had to have been her.'

Some of the resistance seemed to drain out of Oscar and he moved across to the couch and sat down. 'I loved Grace very much,' he said quietly. 'And she died not long after my dad. I fell apart, so I took off to New York and worked in bars. I just had to get away from the life we'd had together.'

Hero felt tears welling and she pressed her hands together in mute sympathy. She was dimly aware that she wasn't feeling jealousy or resentment that he had once loved someone else deeply. She only knew that she wanted to comfort him.

'And then, a year later, I met you. We had a one-night stand and then you vanished.' He looked at her ruefully. 'I knew that you had my address – Sunday had written it down. But you stood me up that day at the Met and you never contacted me.'

'You liked me because I wasn't me,' Hero managed. 'You only noticed me in the first place because I was a redhead.'

A fleeting smile crossed his face. 'Idiot. I would have said that my favourites were Catherine Zeta-Jones and Velma from *Scooby-Doo* if I'd known you were a brunette. I just wanted to get your attention.' He continued softly, almost as if he was talking to himself. 'There was something about you when I first saw you sitting at the bar by yourself. You were trying to act tough but you seemed sad and . . . I don't know, vulnerable, I guess. Maybe I just recognised that lost look because I'd got used to seeing it on my own face every time I looked in the mirror.'

Hero took a deep breath. 'I did turn up that day,' she finally said. 'At the Met, I mean. And I saw you. But you didn't see me.' She swallowed hard. 'I'm not exactly the type that stands out in a crowd. And I just – I couldn't. You were expecting Lola. I didn't want to disappoint you, by being me.'

He gave her a look so filled with tender understanding that she wanted to fling herself into his arms right then and there. But she held back as he continued his story.

'So when I was ready, I moved back to Sydney and I started Serendipity with Jake. I'd now lost two incredible women. It seemed important to make people appreciate the time that they have together. And then I found you again and I was determined that this time I wasn't going to lose you. But you seemed equally determined to fight me the whole way.'

'I had a boyfriend named Elliott once,' Hero said quietly. 'He was a lot like you. Funny and romantic and charming. Everyone loved him. *I* loved him. I thought he was the one. And then I found him in bed – in *our* bed – with another girl.' She stopped, realising that this was the first time she had spoken about Elliott in years. Strangely, it no longer hurt to talk about him. 'I was scared to trust you. I didn't want to go through that again. It just seemed . . . easier to be with someone like Pelham.'

There was silence for a long moment. Then Hero realised that there wasn't much point in resisting her instincts any longer. Without further ado she made her way over to the couch and sat down beside Oscar. Taking his face in her hands, she looked at him with an expression that was more eloquent than any words she could ever utter. And then she kissed him.

Perhaps ten minutes later, after a very satisfactory reconciliation, Hero raised eyes filled with genuine remorse and shame. 'Oscar, I am so sorry about that article. I'll get the magazine to print a retraction. I'll even print one in all the newspapers, if you want.'

To her dismay, Oscar, who had been restored to his usual self by this most unexpected turn of events, shook his head. 'A retraction?' he said scornfully. 'Two lines in eight-point print buried at the bottom of the business pages? No one reads retractions and you know it. Nuh-uh, Hero. There's no way around it. You're going to have to marry me.'

'*Marry you?*'

'Of course,' he said patiently, as though explaining how two plus two equals four to a very dim child. 'You've jeopardised my company's reputation and Jake and I would be well within our rights to launch litigation against you and the magazine. The only way to make appropriate reparation is for you to marry me. Then the general public will know that your story was completely without foundation and that you were complicit in our romance all along. And,' he added shrewdly, 'considering that your boss, Sasha, rang Jake to apologise, I think you ought to marry me to appease her, too. Our wedding would make a great follow-up article for the magazine.'

'You're blackmailing me?' Hero said, dumbfounded. 'You're actually *blackmailing* me into marrying you?'

'I wouldn't call it blackmail exactly,' Oscar said, tightening his grip on her waist, just to be safe. 'You could think of it more as a conciliatory gesture, to atone for your impetuous behaviour.'

'*My* impetuous behaviour?' Hero demanded, practically apoplectic. '*Of all the* . . . when you've done nothing for the last six months but run around behaving like a perfect lunatic! You haven't suffered any consequences for your actions, but I do *one* crazy thing and I have to pay for it for the rest of my life?'

Oscar considered this statement and decided it was just. 'Yep. That pretty much sums it up. So what do you say?'

'No,' Hero said firmly. 'No way.' Oscar's eyes were still filled with hope, but there was an anxiety behind them that she couldn't bear to see. 'I'll write another bloody article exposing you for a complete fraud if you don't propose a bit more romantically. I mean, where's the writing in the sky? The hot-air balloon? The marching band?'

The tension vanished from his gaze, replaced by the laughter that she knew so well and loved.

'Which bit's not romantic?' he enquired. 'Because if it's the fact you're wearing ugg boots and the dress you intended wearing when you married another man, I must point out that's not my fault. If you're talking about the blackmail, on the other hand, I accept full responsibility.'

Hero's eyes had started to sparkle. 'I knew you were a fraud all along,' she said, with mock severity. She watched curiously as Oscar suddenly clicked his fingers, then disappeared into the bedroom. 'What are you doing?' she called after him.

'Looking for something,' he yelled back. 'Ah! Here it is.' He emerged triumphantly, dropped onto one knee and took her left hand in his.

'Hero, will you marry me?'

'Sure,' Hero replied, still not taking him seriously.

Oscar's voice changed. 'Hero, I mean it.'

She looked at him uncertainly. 'You *are* joking, aren't you?'

A feeling of dread started to creep into Oscar's stomach but he fought to keep his voice light. 'Why would I joke about something like this?'

'But . . . but I'm on the rebound! And you're asking me now? Like – like this?' Her wave took in her wedding dress and ugg boots.

Oscar took a deep breath, and in stupefied silence Hero watched as he gently pushed the ring on to her third finger.

'I love you, Hero Hathaway. And I'm asking you to marry me.' Remembering his mother's advice, he hastily added, 'Those ugg boots look very warm, by the way.'

Hero gasped as she looked at the ring. 'That's *my* ring, the one I lost in New York!'

'You left it behind in my apartment,' Oscar confessed. 'Now, *that* I was intending to return when I saw you at the Met. I'll buy you a proper engagement ring tomorrow, of course, but don't you think it's a good omen that this one still fits?'

'Are you sure you didn't steal it?' she asked suspiciously.

'I'm asking you to marry me and you're asking whether I'm a thief! Honestly, of all the unromantic —'

'You stole my postcard,' she pointed out. 'But I guess you couldn't have taken the ring right off my finger without me knowing.'

'Well, I'm glad that's cleared up. Can you answer my question now, please? My knee is starting to hurt.'

'But – but – it's crazy!' she objected. 'Shouldn't we just date for a while? I mean, look at me, I'm wearing a wedding dress!'

With her hand safely clasped between his, Oscar's uncertainty had started to evaporate. 'We probably should date for a bit,' he agreed. 'But we can do that while we're engaged. And the fact that you're wearing a wedding dress is exactly why you have to marry me. I couldn't bear it if I lost you again and I ended up with someone boring and predictable. Someone who never tried to seduce me while wearing a Pussycat outfit complete with a wig made out of pubic hair. Or who stopped to change out of a wedding dress before coming over to apologise. In fact, I really think I'd be quite shocked if you ever showed up at my flat in normal street clothes.'

Seeing that she was listening intently, he pulled her down onto his knee. Hero clasped her hands around his neck.

'You're *not* joking,' she said uncertainly.

He smiled, but in his eyes she saw an expression of longing mixed with hope.

Hero took a deep breath. 'Well . . . okay then.'

And although it hadn't been the most traditional of proposals or acceptances, the kiss that followed was definitely deserving of a close-up and full-blown orchestral score.

31

The wedding

Clarence made his way along the church aisle and stopped beside a half-empty pew.

'May I?' he asked, indicating the vacant seat.

Geoffrey smiled. 'Of course. This is the bride's side.'

Clarence settled next to Geoffrey. 'Actually I don't know either of them very well,' he confessed. 'I was quite surprised to be invited at all.'

'Are you here by yourself?'

Clarence nodded. 'I broke up with my boyfriend a few months ago. He became utterly impossible when the winter frosts set in. Spent night after night wrapping the rose bushes in hessian sacking while I shivered in bed by myself.' Clarence cleared his throat and then said, with a slight blush, 'May I say what a lovely skirt that is?'

'This old thing? It's the underskirt from a mid-nineties Collette Dinnigan piece. I just took off the lace overlay and teamed it with a nineteenth-century bodice.' Geoffrey lowered his voice and added,

'I can't believe how many woman aren't wearing hats here today. Personally, I think anyone who wears a fascinator as a substitute for a hat at a formal occasion ought to just give up and run around in war paint and a grass skirt.'

'I couldn't agree more,' Clarence said, enchanted. He held out his hand. 'My name's Clarence.'

'Geoffrey.'

'Er, if it's not too personal a question, Geoffrey, may I ask your views on rhododendrons?'

'Rhododendrons? They're all right, I suppose, but for my money you can't go past a nice agapanthus.'

'Agapanthus? They grow in just about any conditions,' Clarence said, a spark kindling in his eye.

'Are you a gardener?'

'Heavens, no. I own and run a bed-and-breakfast in the Hunter Valley. The bride and groom stayed there one weekend.'

'The Hunter Valley?' Geoffrey repeated thoughtfully. 'But – that's in the country, isn't it?'

Clarence laughed. 'Of course it is.'

Geoffrey's gaze swept over Clarence's neat attire, taking in the tweed jacket, the pressed trousers and polished gleam of well-worn R.M. Williams boots. 'Bless you, William Baker,' he said under his breath, offering up a swift prayer of gratitude to his own personal deity. 'That fortune teller was worth every cent.'

At this promising juncture, the string quartet struck up. From his place beside the altar, Oscar smiled.

There was a sigh from the congregation as the bride made her way slowly up the aisle. When she reached her destination and destiny, her bridesmaid put back her veil.

Beth smiled as Jake gently took her hand and their marriage ceremony began.

✦

'All that time.' Oscar collapsed into a seat, his best man's duties finished. The reception was in full swing and he had discarded his jacket and loosened his tie. 'All that time and I had no idea Jake and Beth had something going.'

Hero smiled at him. 'Well, you had a lot on your mind,' she said fairly. 'With all the plotting and planning you were doing, it's not surprising that you didn't see what was going on right under your nose.'

'It just goes to show, doesn't it?'

'What?'

'How wrong your ideas were, about love and destiny, and there being no such thing as fate.'

'Jake and Beth getting married doesn't prove my theories wrong.'

'Of course it does. If Jake and I hadn't started Serendipity, he'd never have met Beth. They're the classic office romance. And look at us, the star-crossed lovers who met by purest chance and finally came together after numerous ordeals. And then there's Toby and Sunday.'

'Oh yes,' Hero said sarcastically. 'Gorilla impregnates classical historian. That old chestnut.'

'Face it, Hero,' Oscar said lazily, pulling her on to his lap, 'when it comes to love, there is such a thing as a timeless story.'

Before they could take full advantage of technically still being on their honeymoon, they were interrupted by an outraged, *'Well, I never!'*

Hero looked up into the incredulous gaze of Madame Callous.

'Hello,' she said cheerfully. 'I'm so pleased that you could come.'

'You're still pretending to be straight, are you?' Madame Callous demanded. 'It'll end in tears, mark my words.'

'Madame Callous, this is Oscar,' Hero said, completely unperturbed.

Oscar pushed Hero off his lap and stood up. 'Her husband,' he added, shaking Madame Callous's hand.

Madame Callous noticeably unbent, succumbing to the charm of Oscar's smile. 'Each to their own, I say,' she said graciously. 'I suppose it's fine, as long as you know what you've got yourself in to.'

Oscar looked at Hero quizzically but forbore from further queries. 'Jake was adamant that you should be here,' he said to Madame Callous. 'He says that he and Beth owe their happiness to you.'

'Who are Jake and Beth?' Madame Callous enquired politely.

'The bride and groom.'

'Oh. Well, that's very kind of them to say so.'

'Oscar gave Jake your sex signs book, after he found it on the footpath,' Hero explained.

'What was my book doing on the footpath?'

'Sunday threw it out the window. Anyway, Jake read the whole thing and that's when he realised that his sex sign was "voyeur".'

'He's a voyeur?' Madame Callous said, startled. 'Then how on earth did he end up married to that gorgeous creature?'

'He decided that he didn't want to go through life being a voyeur and sitting on the sidelines, waiting for things to happen. So he threw away his binoculars, so to speak, and finally asked Beth out. They were engaged a month later.'

Sunday, who had wandered up halfway through this conversation, asked Madame Callous in a puzzled tone, 'Why did you come to the wedding when you don't know either of them?'

'You wouldn't believe some of the things I get invited to,' Madame Callous said grandly. 'Anyway, I like to be open to all opportunities.'

'Oh, like your sign,' Sunday said. '"Open for Business".'

Everyone looked confused, while Madame Callous inwardly cursed Sunday for ruining her best joke. She turned her attention back to Hero. 'When did you end up getting married?'

'Not long ago. But that was a different fiancé I had when I was in your shop.'

'It was? Then how is it you're married to this one?'

Hero's expression grew dreamy. 'Well, we'd had a fight because I'd tried to ruin his professional reputation, you see. I was wearing a wedding dress and then he said something nice about my ugg boots and how I was the only girl he knew who would ever wear a wig made out of pubic hair. And then he blackmailed me, so of course I just had to say yes.'

'*He blackmailed you?*'

Hero nodded happily. 'It was perfect. I wouldn't have had it any other way.'

Madame Callous looked bemusedly from Hero to Oscar and then back again, but before she could respond, Hero's mother came bustling up, resplendent in a purple silk gown and matching turban.

'Sunday, darling, you look beautiful.'

'Thanks, Mrs Hathaway.'

'How's your charity work going?'

'My charity work?'

'Yes. The mountain gorillas.'

Sunday's brow cleared. 'Oh. That. It's going very well, thank you. We've saved loads of them. Heaps. Mrs Hathaway, will you excuse me? I need to check on Ben.' Sunday slipped away.

'I still can't believe they actually called their son Bennifer,' Hero's mother said, shaking her head.

Hero grinned at her. 'That's a bit rich coming from someone who named her son Hamlet. Anyway, his name isn't Bennifer. Toby was responsible for filling out the birth certificate and he put down Benjamin.'

'Was Sunday okay when she found out?' Oscar asked, putting his arm around Hero and drawing her closer.

She snuggled into him. 'I'm not sure that she knows yet. But Ben's middle name is Hyacinth, so I don't think she'll mind.'

'She wanted to name her baby Bennifer Hyacinth?' Madame Callous said, completely flabbergasted.

Hero nodded cheerfully as the band struck up. From the stage, Toby grinned at Oscar and Hero and deftly swung his microphone.

Oscar held out a hand to Hero in invitation. 'They're playing our song,' he said softly.

Hero answered his smile and took his hand. They made their way to the centre of the dancefloor as Toby launched into 'For Once In My Life'.

Madame Callous drained her cocktail and looked around for another. Geoffrey gave her a cheerful grin as their gazes connected.

'I love a good wedding, don't you?' he said chattily. 'Oscar and Hero's wedding was lovely.' He sighed with pleasure. 'Thank heavens she didn't end up marrying the one with the poker up his bum.'

'The one with the poker up his bum?' Madame Callous enquired, relieved to find herself in familiar conversational territory.

Geoffrey nodded sagely. 'He ran off with their wedding planner. Can you believe it?'

Madame Callous felt a wave of compassion for Hero. 'The poor girl. Although I must say she doesn't look very heartbroken,' she added, as Oscar caught Hero up in a passionate embrace.

'Well, she can't complain too much,' Geoffrey said fairly. 'After all, she did it too.'

'She did what too?'

'Ran off with their wedding planner.'

There was a silence while Madame Callous attempted to process this. 'They both ran off with their wedding planner?'

Geoffrey nodded. 'I believe it happens quite a lot.' And with that he tottered off in the direction of the bar, where Clarence was waiting for him.

Out on the dancefloor, Beth and Jake had eyes for no one but each other. Hero's mother was teaching Jean how to belly dance, while Hero's father was dancing with Sunday and Ben. And oblivious to all around them, Oscar was soundly kissing Hero.

Madame Callous collapsed into a chair and waved her feather-trimmed fan furiously back and forth. 'Romantic heterosexuals,' she said loudly, for the benefit of anyone who might be listening. 'They're freaks, I'm telling you. Every last one of them is an absolute freak.'